The Girl
with the
Broken Heart

You'll want to read these inspiring titles by

LURLENE McDANIEL

ANGELS IN PINK
Kathleen's Story • Raina's Story • Holly's Story

ONE LAST WISH NOVELS
Mourning Song • A Time to Die • Mother, Help Me Live
Someone Dies, Someone Lives • Sixteen and Dying • Let Him Live
The Legacy: Making Wishes Come True • Please Don't Die
She Died Too Young • All the Days of Her Life
A Season for Goodbye • Reach for Tomorrow

OTHER OMNIBUS EDITIONS
Keep Me in Your Heart: Three Novels
True Love: Three Novels
The End of Forever • Always and Forever • The Angels Trilogy
As Long As We Both Shall Live • Journey of Hope
One Last Wish: Three Novels

OTHER FICTION
Somebody's Baby • Losing Gabriel • The Year of Luminous Love
The Year of Chasing Dreams
Wishes and Dreams (a Year of Luminous Love digital original short story)
Red Heart Tattoo • Reaching Through Time • Heart to Heart
Breathless • Hit and Run • Prey • Briana's Gift • Letting Go of Lisa
The Time Capsule • Garden of Angels • A Rose for Melinda
Telling Christina Goodbye • How Do I Love Thee: Three Stories
To Live Again • Angel of Mercy • Angel of Hope
Starry, Starry Night: Three Holiday Stories
The Girl Death Left Behind • Angels Watching Over Me • Lifted Up by Angels
For Better, For Worse, Forever • Until Angels Close My Eyes
Till Death Do Us Part • I'll Be Seeing You • Saving Jessica
Don't Die, My Love • Too Young to Die
Goodbye Doesn't Mean Forever • Somewhere Between Life and Death
Time to Let Go • Now I Lay Me Down to Sleep
When Happily Ever After Ends • Baby Alicia Is Dying

From every ending comes a new beginning. . . .

The Girl
with the
Broken Heart

LURLENE McDANIEL

DELACORTE PRESS

Visit us on the Web! GetUnderlined.com

Educators and librarians, for a variety of teaching tools, visit us at RHTeachersLibrarians.com

Library of Congress Cataloging-in-Publication Data
Names: McDaniel, Lurlene, author.
Title: The girl with the broken heart / Lurlene McDaniel.
Description: New York : Delacorte Press, [2018] | Summary: To escape her father's overprotectiveness, twenty-year-old Kenzie Caine spends the summer working at a horse farm rehabilitating Tennessee walking horses, where a good deed results in a violent end to the summer and the revelation of her attractive assistant's secrets.
Identifiers: LCCN 2017037593 (print) | LCCN 2017050687 (ebook) |
ISBN 978-1-5247-1950-0 (ebook) | ISBN 978-1-5247-1948-7 (hardcover)
Subjects: | CYAC: Heart—Diseases—Fiction. | Animal rescue—Fiction. | Animals—Treatment—Fiction. | Tennessee walking horse—Fiction. | Horses—Fiction. | Summer employment—Fiction. | Love—Fiction.
Classification: LCC PZ7.M4784172 (ebook) | LCC PZ7.M4784172 Go 2018 (print) | DDC [Fic]—dc23

The text of this book is set in 11-point Goudy Old Style.
Interior design by Trish Parcell

Printed in the United States of America
10 9 8 7 6 5 4 3 2 1
First Edition

This book is dedicated to the Rescuers . . .
those who help and protect all God's creatures.

Hast thou given the horse strength?
Hast thou clothed his neck with thunder?
—JOB 39:19, KING JAMES BIBLE

A bruised reed he shall not break,
and the smoking flax shall he not quench:
he shall bring forth judgement unto truth.
—ISAIAH 42:3, KING JAMES BIBLE

One

Ciana Mercer thrust open the front door of the beautiful bungalow, set far back from the main house on her Bellmeade property, and moved aside. "Come on in, Kenzie!"

Kenzie Caine, still reeling from the stress of her sophomore-year final exams back at Vanderbilt University, stepped in to see gleaming dark hardwood floors, colorful area rugs, cream-colored walls, and what looked like brand-new furniture. "It's beautiful! I never expected something like this. Maybe a small room, or a spot in your bunkhouse, but never an entire *house!*"

"The bunkhouse?" Ciana laughed. "That's where we put the men we hire for summer work, not proper accommodations for you, Kenzie. I've already revved up the AC and evicted the dust bunnies, so let me show you around." Ciana guided her through two bedrooms, two bathrooms, and a small but well-equipped kitchen, while opening blinds to allow late-morning sunlight to flood each room on the tour. Kenzie followed, a bundle of nerves about facing the summer months ahead of her.

This was really happening. She would be in charge of bringing three Tennessee walking horses to good health before summer's end *and* putting them up for adoption. Her first solo job. "I can't wait to get busy." She was nervous, and hoped it didn't show.

"Glad you're here, but I'm surprised. I assumed you'd go home for a few days before starting."

Home. The very word tasted bitter to Kenzie. She'd officially completed her sophomore year that morning, packed her SUV, and driven the fifty miles to Bellmeade to *avoid* going home. The sunny memories of her childhood on her family's horse farm in the rolling hills of Nashville were now smeared like mud across her mind.

In the kitchen, Ciana tapped the refrigerator door. "You'll need to go grocery shopping, but I made a pitcher of lemonade for you. My grandmother's recipe—delicious."

After a year of cafeteria food at Vanderbilt, a batch of homemade lemonade made her mouth water. "You make me feel very welcome, Mrs. Mercer."

"Please, none of that! I'm just Ciana."

Kenzie thought Ciana Beauchamp Mercer, with her cinnamon-colored eyes and hair, was beautiful. Her family name was legend in Windemere, and her friendly, welcoming smile helped ease Kenzie's jitters. "Got it . . . Ciana it is."

Ciana walked to a set of sliding glass doors, pushed

aside vertical blinds, and opened a slider. "Oh, and here's the back porch." They stepped into a screened-in room with an arrangement of wicker lounge furniture. "Beyond the patio is a pathway. Just follow the flagstones to those woods and pick up the footpath. It'll lead you straight to the stable where you'll be working." As she talked, Ciana pointed across an expanse of green manicured lawn toward a tree line. "Next to the stable is the pasture for your horses. You have three. They came in last week. We'll walk over in a minute for a look-see."

"Why waste time lounging around? I want to get started."

"Rescue horse work isn't the typical summer job, you know. Your helper won't be here until Friday, but until he shows, I'll be working with you."

Tension knotted Kenzie's stomach. Dr. Kaye, the veterinarian she'd worked for the previous summer and throughout her sophomore year, had taught Kenzie well, but being fully in charge of rehabbing abused and neglected horses was daunting. She'd never been a boss before either. "I don't want to put you out."

Ciana waved off Kenzie's comment. "No problem. With the horses getting four feedings a day, trust me, you'll need my help. Our vet's already checked the horses over and vaccinated them. Dr. Perry left his evaluation report in the stable's tack room for you. He'll come again next week, answer any concerns you might have."

Kenzie felt the heavy responsibility of such a job, but also the thrill of it. Ciana said, "Did you know Kaye and I were in the Windemere horse color guard brigade together?

The guard performed precision drills before every rodeo event. I wore a lot of spangles and sparkles." Ciana laughed at the memory. "But even back then, she was keen on becoming an equine vet.

"When Kaye told me she was moving to North Carolina and asked if Jon and I had space for rescue work, we hesitated. But when she said she had the perfect person to handle it, we agreed to give it a trial run this summer. She gave us money for your work. Money for feed and vet bills, and for you and a helper. How could we say no?" Ciana swept her hand through the air. "Kaye spoke highly of you, Kenzie. She told me you possessed 'extraordinary dedication and compassion.' Kaye called you a natural healer."

The endorsement was flattering but only added to Kenzie's jitters. "I'm very grateful to all of you, but I'd do the work for free, you know." She had loved the work so much that she'd changed her major to animal husbandry and had kept her plans to herself until the previous October, when Caroline turned fourteen. Instead of attending the family party at the house, Kenzie had met her sister at a mall for lunch and a day of shopping. The memory returned in a vivid burst.

Over salads, sweet tea, and cupcakes, Kenzie said, "I have a new direction, Caro, and I want you to be the first to know. I'm going to become a veterinarian."

"Really?" Caroline wrinkled her nose. "Horses are smelly."

"Not to me, little sister. I love the big smelly beasts. I'm changing my major."

Caroline recoiled in disbelief. "What will Mom and Dad say about you wanting to be a vet? It's hard work, Kenz . . . and your heart—"

Kenzie cut her off. *"My heart isn't a problem, so don't think about it. This is what I want."*

Caroline rolled her eyes, dragged her finger through the dark frosting on her cupcake. *"You can't stay mad at Daddy forever. He misses you . . . We all do."* She sucked the frosting off her finger. *"Will you at least come home for Christmas? Even if it's just for a few days?"*

"Dr. Kaye says I can work over the holidays if I want, so I might." Caroline looked crestfallen, and Kenzie hastily added, *"I'll think about it. I promise."*

But Kenzie hadn't gone home for the holidays. She had stayed away until February, when her family's world splintered apart, and she was forced home for the most difficult week of her life.

"Doing rescue work for free. Spoken like a true horse lover," Ciana said with a laugh, pulling Kenzie into the present.

When Kaye had told Kenzie she'd sold her Nashville practice and was moving, Kenzie believed her rescue horse work was over and she'd be forced to go home. But now her mentor had given her a golden opportunity. "How about some of that lemonade?"

"Let me get it," Ciana said. "You sit." Before Kenzie could protest being waited on, Ciana disappeared inside, reappearing minutes later with frosty glasses filled with pale yellow liquid. "The weatherman's predicting a very hot summer." She handed a glass to Kenzie, took a chair. "Jon

5

handles mustangs and quarter horses, but I know about the controversy boiling around Tennessee walking horses and the Big Lick. People call it a 'thing of beauty.'"

"It's an unnatural gait caused by *soring*. And it *isn't* a thing of beauty." Kenzie regretted that she hadn't always thought that way. Always a tomboy, she used to tag along to watch her father, Avery, ride his magnificent walking horse, Blaze, in competitions. And along with adoring onlookers, Kenzie had clapped and cheered at the amazing height the great black stallion would raise his front legs performing the Big Lick. Blaze and Avery won not only numerous trophies and prizes, but also national fame for the Caine horse farm. Kenzie was sixteen before she fully understood how soring—with its medieval-like gear, obnoxious chemicals, and training methods—hurt, even crippled a horse. The exaggerated high step was a horse's attempt to escape the pain in his front legs and hooves. When Kenzie was growing up, her father had assured her, "Everybody sores a little to win, honey. No harm done." He had lied to her. And she had believed him.

"Kaye said you rode in competitions too."

"Princess Ronan and I only competed in flat-shod events that show off a walking horse's three *natural* gaits. We brought home our share of ribbons and honors. Believe me, there's no excuse for the Big Lick." Kenzie raised her glass, took a sip. "This is yummy, not too sweet, not too tart. Just perfect."

"Glad you like it. Soon as we finish, we'll walk down to the stables and I'll show you around. When we return, I'll help you unload your car and move in."

The car pulled onto the shoulder of the rural country road. The young man got out and raised the hood. He knew that passing drivers would likely think that the car had engine trouble. As he walked away, he smiled to himself, knowing that others would think its driver had gone for help. And that's exactly the impression he wanted to give.

In the darkness of predawn, he navigated a roadside gully, dipped under a wire fence, and jogged across the back fields of the Bellmeade property. He reached a fenced pasture, climbed over, skirted a stable, where he heard horses rustling in the stalls. He had no idea when the animals would be let out to pasture, but he knew someone would show up to do it. He had to be in place before that happened.

As the morning sky lightened, he ducked into a wooded area, discovered a worn footpath path, a cut-through to the stable behind him. He walked the path to where the woods ended at an expanse of lawn and the backside of a tidy house with a screened porch. He already knew that this was where Kenzie Caine would be living all summer.

He receded into clusters of blooming forsythia and redbud, and lifting a pair of binoculars from beneath his hooded sweatshirt, he settled in for what would be an all-day wait. Once night fell, he could leave Bellmeade undetected. A long day, but no problem. Surveillance took patience. And he was a very patient person.

Two

Kenzie and Ciana followed the path through the trees, toward the back part of Bellmeade, passing bushes in bloom, colorful wildflowers, and overhead trees dressed in new leaves of bright spring green. The May morning had warmed, sending up scents of fresh earth and new growth.

"Here we are," Ciana said, exiting the woods. "These woods isolate this stable and pasture from the main working area of the ranch, because we didn't want the noises to be too distracting for your horses. But before we go inside, let me show you what's around the corner." She led Kenzie around the tree line. "A few years back, we were hit by a tornado. Jon's been rebuilding and adding on ever since."

The rebuild stretched over acres of land with a barn, two smaller stables, four corrals—one holding horses milling around, stirring up dirt—training pens, a mile-long oval exercise track, and generous-sized pastures for grazing. Kenzie's family's horse farm was large, but Bellmeade was more diverse. "Impressive."

"The horses in the corral are mustangs Jon brought in from Wyoming. By September, he and his men will have the horses trained for ranch work and on the auction block." Kenzie had heard that Jon's horses brought top dollar.

Ciana waved at the men in the corral, then circled back to Kenzie's work area. Hers was a pass-through stable—open at both ends—wide enough for a horse and rider. It had six stalls, each with inside and outside locking doors, allowing horses easy access to pasture or cover in bad weather. Walking to the fenced pasture, Kenzie eyed a round pen—sometimes necessary when retraining an abused horse once it was healthy. Together, she and Ciana watched her three horses grazing—two looked gaunt and malnourished. The third, a dark brown gelding she estimated to be at least seventeen hands high, grazed alone on the other side of the pasture.

"Welcome," came a man's voice from behind her. "You must be Kenzie. I'm Jon Mercer." She turned to see a handsome man with sun-leathered skin, a Texas-sized smile, and startlingly green eyes.

Ciana circled her arms around Jon's neck and kissed him. "Hi, cowboy."

Kenzie shook Jon's hand. "Can't stay long," he said, "but wanted to say hello and tell you a little about the horses you'll be working with. The Appaloosa is an older mare found abandoned in a field. Never did find her owner.

We've named her Mamie, after a teacher I once had. As you can see, she's grossly underweight, but she's quite docile. The small bay is Sparkle, another neglected mare but younger, with some open sores, probably from an encounter with a barbwire fence. Previous owner didn't want her anymore, so we took her. Our vet's prescribed a salve you'll need to spread on her cuts. All three need serious hoof conditioning."

Both mares looked pitiful. Their winter coats hung in clumps, their manes and tails were tangles of snarled coarse hair, and both were underweight, with ribs showing. "I'll take care of them," Kenzie promised, tamping down her anger at the horses' condition. Her gaze gravitated to the gelding. "He looks to be in better health. What's his problem?"

"He's been sored and has chemical burns on his forelegs. His previous owner said the horse turned mean and gave him to an animal shelter. We brought him here."

"Who would treat a beautiful horse that way?" Ciana asked, shaking her head.

My father and his trainer, Kenzie thought.

"Hasn't soring been illegal since the seventies?" Ciana asked Kenzie.

"A toothless law. Trust me, soring is still being done, and many horse people turn a blind eye to it." As had her father, Avery, who had fired his longtime trainer, Bill Hixson—but not until *after* Avery had won the World Grand Champion title riding Blaze in Shelbyville that year. Bill's firing and charges of animal cruelty came after an exposé video was

10

leaked, destroying his thirty-year career in the walking horse industry. Kenzie had headed to Vanderbilt for her freshman year amid the turmoil, and the summer job with Kaye had kept her away.

She shook off the past when Ciana, pointing to the dark bay, said, "A caveat about Blue Bayou. He doesn't like men. Jon rarely meets a horse he can't approach, but when he went close, Blue lunged at him with bared teeth."

Kenzie's eyes widened. Such aggressive behavior was rare in a tame horse.

"It took two of my workers and a blindfold to rope and tie him to a training post for his checkup and shots," Jon said. "Perry says he's healthy but ill-tempered, so be careful. He's been hurt and he's defensive."

"The good news," Ciana said, "is that Blue doesn't mind women too much. He actually took a treat from me when Jon wasn't around. That's why we thought you might have a chance of changing his behavior."

"You don't have to take on Blue," Jon said. "I can work with him, but I have a corral full of mustangs"—he thumbed over his shoulder—"so I can't give Blue top priority for a while."

"Not a problem," Kenzie said firmly. "He's mine."

A smile turned up a corner of Jon's mouth. "I didn't take you for a quitter."

Neither Ciana nor Jon had asked about her heart issues, which Kenzie appreciated. Kaye had told them about Kenzie's heart but had also assured the Mercers that she could do the job. "I won't let you down."

Jon turned at the sound of corralled horses neighing from a distance. "Look, I need to get my men back to work, but before I go, your help will be here Friday. His name's Austin Boyd and he's driving down from Virginia. You're in charge, but he's been hired to do the heavy lifting. Make sure he does."

Jon left, and Ciana said, "In the meantime, why don't we go back to the bungalow and get you settled?"

It took little time to move Kenzie's belongings from her car into the house; she'd left most of her belongings from her dorm room in storage holds at Vanderbilt. Her clothing filled only two dresser drawers and less than half the closet space. "You travel light." Ciana shook out a long skirt and peasant blouse, hung both on the clothes bar.

"I figured all I'd need this summer were jeans, shorts, and a stack of tees." Kenzie tucked a pile of folded shirts into a drawer. "One girly outfit, a jacket, work boots, sandals, sneakers. What more is necessary? I'm guessing the horses won't care what I look like."

Ciana laughed. "True, but FYI—we throw a July Fourth barbecue, invite the whole town. Please join us. We smoke our own meat, cook up a feast. We stage it in a tent by the big barn at the front of our property. With all the ranch work moved to the back, our boarders stable their horses in the old barn. Sometimes I exercise horses for owners when they can't get out here."

"Maybe I can help with that while my horses get healthier. I enjoy riding."

"You'd be welcome. We have a nice riding trail that starts behind your pasture. When your horses are strong enough for a saddle, take them down there. Use the exercise track anytime to give a horse a good workout. Until you go back to a college dorm, treat this place like your home, and enjoy your summer."

That word *home* again. How could she tell Ciana that her reluctance to go home went far deeper than her grudge against her father and Bill? Fearful of falling to pieces in front of her new employer, Kenzie blurted, "I saw a couple of other houses when I parked."

"One is my mother's. The other is for Jon's mom, if we can ever pry her out of Texas."

Kenzie flashed again to February, saw her own mother's face twisted with inconsolable grief. She grabbed her purse off the bed. "You know, before it's time to feed the horses, I'm going to run into town and hit the grocery store, stock up on supplies to keep company with that lone pitcher of lemonade."

She left Ciana standing in the middle of the bedroom floor and rushed out the door.

The man moved farther down the tree line to better observe Kenzie, who'd come out of the stable with Ciana at dusk. The women had rolled wheelbarrows into the pasture and, in separate corners of the field, heaped piles of fresh hay onto the ground. Kenzie wore a denim jacket against the cool evening air and shin-high rubber work boots. Once the barrows were empty, the women withdrew to the outside of the fence, and the horses approached the fresh feed, two eating side by side, while the third, in the opposite corner, ate alone. The man heard the light buzz of the women's voices but was too far away to hear their conversation.

As he held up his binoculars, he saw a man, accompanied by a large white German shepherd, joining the women. Alarmed, the watcher compressed his body behind a thick tree. He hadn't factored in a dog, hoped he was far enough downwind to escape the animal's keen nose—otherwise he was in trouble. Minutes later, the three people and the dog headed away.

Close call. He held his position until night fell, then moved swiftly across the field, crossed the road to where he'd stashed his car. He was removing brush from the top of the vehicle when he felt the cell phone in his jeans pocket vibrate and dug it out. "Yes?"

"Are you in?" asked a man's voice.

"I'm in, no worries."

"And you have eyes on her?"

"Yes."

"And you can do the job?"

"I told you I could, and I will." He hung up, started the engine, pulled onto the dark road, and drove away.

Three

—·—

Ciana helped Kenzie with each of the four daily feedings of the rescue horses, beginning with the morning grain allotment inside each stall, then the sweet hay heaped outside in the pasture. Kenzie's priorities were to make the horses feel safe and see her as trustworthy, which was not easy with Blue, who was still skittish around people. She was mucking out stalls at the end of the week when Ciana walked through the doorway leading a beautiful palomino. She stepped out of the stall, shovel in hand. "Hey, this is a surprise. Did you bring us another mouth to feed?"

"Nope, announcing my retirement and going on a trail ride. Your hired hand showed up to take over my job."

Kenzie craned her neck, her heart tripping. Time to become a boss. "So, where is he?"

"I told him to park by the big barn up front and get

acquainted with Soldier, then toss his gear in the bunkhouse. I like the dog to give visitors a good sniffing to familiarize him with their scents. That way Soldier knows who's allowed on the property and who isn't. A lot of boarders come and go, but Soldier's nose never forgets them."

Kenzie leaned her shovel against a wall, went to the palomino, and scratched the horse's white blaze beneath his forelock. "Beautiful horse. Yours?"

"Sort of. Oro belongs to my friend Lani. She asked me to sell him for her, but I couldn't bring myself to do it. Jon says I take in unwanted horses like a cat lady collecting strays. Extra feed bills, for sure, but some of the horses on our property are like family. I can't let them go."

Kenzie laughed. "Does that make you a horse hoarder?"

"Guilty. There's a reason for my hoarding, though. Lani is a nurse at our Windemere children's hospital in the cancer unit. She and I have this idea we call Trailblazers—a riding program for kids with special needs and in remission. Oro's easygoing and has a calm and patient disposition, and that makes him perfect for working with children. We'll need more horses like him."

Images of her tenth birthday and her father giving her Princess Ronan floated into Kenzie's memory. *Love at first sight.* "Horses and kids are a good fit."

"I'll have Lani stop by and talk to you about the program. She's a pretty special person, and I think you'll enjoy meeting her."

Kenzie smoothed her hands along Oro's neck and mane. His sleek coat gleamed. She wanted her rescue horses to look this healthy in the few months she had with them. "You know, Tennessee walkers make excellent saddle horses for beginners."

Ciana winked. "So I've heard. If Mamie's not adopted, she might have a home at Bellmeade. Just sayin'."

The trickiest part of any rescue program could be the adoption. Certainly, horses like Blue and Sparkle were likely to find good homes, but Mamie was old, making her not as attractive to potential buyers. "I'll see what I can do with the three out there," Kenzie whispered conspiratorially.

They were laughing when a man strolled into the stable. He nodded at Ciana, removed his ball cap, and held out his hand to Kenzie. "I'm Austin Boyd. You must be Kenzie."

Austin Boyd wasn't what Kenzie had been expecting. For starters, he didn't look that much older than she was. He stood well over six feet and had thick, shaggy, sun-streaked brown hair and blue-green eyes set in a too-good-looking face, made more attractive by a lopsided boyish smile. He was broad chested, with well-muscled arms, and wore a black T-shirt that stretched taut across his chest and shoulders, along with worn jeans, and heavy-duty work boots instead of traditional cowboy boots. Austin looked more "biker" than cowboy to her. "Yes, I'm Kenzie Caine."

"Pleasure to meet you." His gaze held hers boldly. Kenzie blinked first, turned away.

"Okay, then," Ciana said. "I'll let you two get acquainted while I ride. Enjoy!" She led Oro out the opposite doorway, mounted the palomino, and cantered away.

Pleasure wasn't what Kenzie felt at finding herself alone

with Austin Boyd. With a rush, she realized he reminded her of someone else, someone she hated.

"Everything okay?" Austin asked, glancing around the stable she'd spent days organizing. "I'm told you're the boss, so where do I start?"

Kenzie shifted her weight foot to foot, unnerved partly by her emotional reaction to Austin. "For now, just get acquainted with the place; then I'll take you to meet our horses." She grabbed her shovel, still rattled by her initial impression, a sense of déjà vu and visceral reaction that had so quickly hurled her backward through time. She returned to the stall where she'd been working, began scooping up matted straw and tossing it into a wheelbarrow. He followed her, put his hand on the shovel's handle. "Let me do this."

"I can do it!"

Looking startled, he backed away, hands raised. "Sorry. I was only trying to help."

She closed her eyes, took deep breaths. "I . . . I know. I didn't mean to yell at you. I guess I was expecting someone—" She searched for words.

He grinned sheepishly. "You mean someone more like a wrangler, a been-around-the-rodeo-scene-for-a-lifetime kind of guy? I once had a boss tell me I looked more hot dog than cowboy. Sorry if I go against type."

His description of her expectation was spot-on. She'd seen Jon's men standing by the corral—sun-leathered skin, old-soul faces. Those men would have hands scarred and burned by ropes from years of working with horses and cattle. Austin's hands were large, and although the skin looked toughened, she saw no testimony to rough, hard ranch work. She chewed her bottom lip. "Honestly, you really *don't* look like Jon's other hires."

He laughed, ran a hand through the thick waves of hair. "Want me to cowboy up for you? I don't mind, if that's what you'd like."

Her knee-jerk reaction to Austin had faded, but she couldn't deny she would have preferred a helper who looked more saddle-worn. She shook her head. "The horses only care about getting fed."

"Listen, Jon hired me to help you, and that's what I'm here for. I can look the place over later. For now, put me to work."

Taking him at his word, Kenzie gestured to a utility closet at one end of the stable. "There's another shovel in there. You can start cleaning out the two other stalls and spreading fresh straw from that bale on the floor."

"On my way." He gathered the shovel and a second wheelbarrow, removed a cell phone from his shirt pocket, settled earbuds in his ears, and went to work in the stall next to hers. Watching him irritated Kenzie. She liked silence when she worked, always listening out for her horses and being mindful of their needs. A constant stream of music or podcast chatter was no way to be on guard for anything going wrong. Kenzie scooped up a shovel of refuse and heaved it into the wheelbarrow. The pile landed badly, almost tipping over the whole barrow. She stopped, gathered herself, and proceeded more slowly and with less temper. Austin Boyd would not be the reason for her slipping this summer.

Once they were finished inside the stable, Kenzie told Austin, "Come meet the horses."

They walked to the pasture fence, stood side by side under a warm sun sparkling in a crystal-clear blue sky. Kenzie gave Austin a brief rundown on the three horses, including Blue's behavior toward males. The three horses grazed, the mares together, Blue Bayou alone on the other side of the field. "He's been sored, and he doesn't trust people."

Austin looked confused. "*Sored?* Not sure what that means."

"Really?" She was caught off guard. "I'm surprised you came to work with Tennessee walkers and don't know about soring."

"I owned a horse from the time I was a kid until I went off to college. I know how to care for a horse."

Kenzie was again dismayed. Not only did this Austin not look like what she'd expected, but it was also possible he had no serious experience working with horses. Owning a horse while growing up was hardly a recommendation, to her way of thinking. "What *do* you know?"

"I know these mares look malnourished, and we need to get their body weight back to normal. The Appaloosa looks pretty old. The other mare seems lethargic. And the gelding looks unfriendly."

This evaluation left Kenzie marginally impressed. "Well, just remember, horses are herd animals with a pecking order, and that old mare is the boss of this little herd. She and the younger mare rank above the gelding, so he's having to keep his distance. And because the females are ignoring him, and because men have abused him, Blue's very insecure. It's my job to gain his trust, make him feel safe enough to be ridden again."

"Don't you mean *our* job to make him feel safe around *us?* Since I'm part of your team, shouldn't Blue learn to accept me too?"

His questions held a challenge she hadn't expected. She wasn't thinking of them as a team, not like she and Kaye had been. They had been able to read each other's minds as they worked together. Kenzie wasn't sure she wanted such a connection with Austin. "Okay . . . so, what do you know about the Tennessee walking breed? Or about rescuing abused horses?"

"Apparently not as much about either as I should." His gaze was unwavering. In the open sunlight, under the bright sky, the man's eyes looked deep blue. Inside the stable, their color had been more green. *Chameleon eyes.*

She crossed her arms as if to protect herself. "Did you just take this job to fritter away an otherwise dull summer? I need to know, because these horses must learn to trust humans again for food and care. They'll need to be ridden, and hopefully, if we do our jobs right, adopted. They'll need their stalls mucked, their pasture area cleaned up daily. You ready to do that?"

"I've picked up manure in a pasture before, if that's what you're asking. I'll do it every day. Guaranteed. And for the record, this job is *not* a summer vacation, believe me. I'm here to work and help you. I won't slack." His voice was steady but held an undercurrent that let her know she'd crossed a line with him.

"Good to know." Kenzie tamped down her temper, reminded herself that Austin Boyd had done nothing except show up, and from the start she'd been rude to him. Why? Because he'd briefly reminded her of somebody she loathed? Because he didn't know about soring? Austin came from Virginia, so the Tennessee walking horse breed was likely foreign to him.

She ticked off the daily feeding schedule for the underweight mares, gave him a list of daily and weekly chores she wanted to accomplish, and ended with her goal to have all three ready for adoption before she returned to college in late August.

Austin listened intently, his gaze never leaving her face. "And Blue? Why doesn't he like men in particular?"

"Because he's been sored." Austin gave a shrug, and it irritated her all over again. "He's been trained to perform the Big Lick. Among other Big Lick abuses, Blue's forelegs have been smeared with caustic chemicals, then wrapped in plastic to 'cook' into his flesh, and he's been left with very painful acid burns. Even from this distance, you can see the places where his hair is permanently gone on the front of his forelegs."

Austin stared at the big horse, saw the gaps in hair growth and patches of scarred skin. Kenzie said, "Go online, watch a few videos about soring. They're eye-opening. Eventually, we'll put him in there for retraining." Kenzie pointed toward the small round pen behind them. "That's where the real work begins. But fair warning: Be careful. He could hurt you."

"I'll watch my step."

She thought she heard a double meaning in his comment, that he'd be careful around her too. "Let's get the hay into the pasture." She pushed off from the fence, headed toward the stable.

Austin fell into step beside her. "At least Blue seems to have fared better than the mares in the nutrition department."

"It's Blue's spirit that's wounded," Kenzie said. "No amount of nutrition can fix that."

Four

—·—

At 6:45 the next morning, Kenzie was dressed and pulling
on her boots when her doorbell rang. *Who in the world . . . ?*
With one boot on, she hobbled to her front door and
peered through the peephole. She was surprised to see Austin under the porch light. He grinned when he caught her
eyeing him and held up two bags from a fast-food place. She
sighed, but remembering how she'd behaved toward him
the day before, she opened the door.

"Morning!" he said. "I brought breakfast."

"You shouldn't have."

"And I wanted to apologize for getting off on the wrong
foot with you yesterday." He glanced down at her feet. "I'd
like a reboot."

She shook her head, smothered a smile. "That was an
awful pun."

He waggled his eyebrows, shook the bags. "Please? We

might have to nuke 'em to warm them up. A long ride from the drive-through window in town."

She realized that he had to have gotten up very early for the twenty-five-minute drive into Windemere to buy the food and another twenty-five back. She opened the door wider and stepped aside. "Come on in. I'll make us coffee."

"Nice place," he said, following her into the kitchen, where she turned on a light and got busy. Minutes later the aroma of hot coffee saturated the air, plates were set on the café-style table, and the packages and cartons of breakfast were unpacked and warmed. "I didn't know what you might like, so I went with high protein. Biscuit, egg, cheese, and a sausage patty. I bought a double serving of hash browns if you want to share."

She didn't admit that his choices were exactly what she'd have bought for herself. "Sounds fine."

Minutes later they sat eating and sipping black coffee at the café table, where their knees kept touching. Kenzie pushed her chair farther away. "Why go to all this trouble? We're supposed to meet at seven in the stable. We could have talked then."

Austin popped a hash-brown nugget in his mouth. "I just thought it would be nice if we got better acquainted over coffee and food . . . you know, get to know a little bit more about each other without any work distractions."

His request wasn't unreasonable, and she *was* hungry. "All right . . . you go first." Kenzie took a bite of her biscuit.

He leaned back in his chair. "Okay. I was born on a cold winter day—"

"Not that far back."

An infectious grin crinkled the corners of his eyes, green in the overhead kitchen lighting. "I grew up in Virginia. I have a brother fifteen years older than me and a sister twelve years older. Let's just say I was my parents' twentieth-wedding-anniversary surprise. When I was six, my brother was graduating from college and my sister left for college. When I was ten, my folks grew tired of city life and bought a place out in the country, where I finished growing up. When I was eleven, Dad bought me a horse. I named him Braveheart."

Austin's fondness for his family showed on his face, and Kenzie felt memories of her childhood tug at her heart. "Sounds like royalty."

"Nah, I named him after my dad's favorite movie," he said with a chuckle. "Actually, my Braveheart was a . . . who knows? A mysterious blend of horse DNA—a pinto, brown and white, who listened patiently to all my complaints and rants about teachers and girls while I was growing up. I rode him at county fairs in barrel-racing competitions through my senior year of high school. I would have pinned a corsage to his saddle and taken him to the prom if I could have."

His description of his childhood seemed idyllic, as had been her early years. She wandered inside her more pleasant childhood memories, until she realized Austin had stopped talking. She quickly glanced over and saw an amused smile on his face. "I didn't mean to put you to sleep. But to tell the truth, my life *was* pretty boring."

She offered an embarrassed smile, noticed daylight filtering through the blinds in the living room. "Thanks for breakfast, but we'd better get moving. Those horses need to eat too." She attempted to shove her chair farther back, but he hooked the toe of his work boot around the chair's leg first.

"You were right to call me out yesterday. I wasn't as prepared for this job as I should have been. Jon hired me on the word of a mutual friend who insisted I was qualified to do the job. And I am, but that's no excuse for me not to be better informed. I took your suggestion, went online and saw some pretty ugly undercover videos about soring. I also researched the Tennessee walker and horse rescue work. I read about how people like you are making a difference in the lives of these horses. I'm happy to be part of your team."

"The videos are graphic, and most of the horses I've worked with have been neglected, which is abuse, but different from soring. I know training methods to undo some of that kind of harm, but it takes time and patience."

"Elevated shoe stacks nailed improperly to a horse's hooves, heavy bands and ball chains wrapped around the tops of hooves, and the chemicals. Yeah, I saw all that in the videos. Inhumane, cruel." Austin rested his elbow on the chair's back. "Kenzie, I want this job, but if you want me gone, let's tell Jon today. I shouldn't hang around if you don't think we'll be able to work together. Horses are intuitive. They'll be able to pick up on tension between us, and that's not a good thing."

He caught her completely by surprise. Was that how

she'd come across to him yesterday? As someone unable to work with him? Perhaps he *needed* the job! Who was she to reject him based on an ill-conceived first impression?

"No." She shook her head for emphasis. "I don't want you to leave. Truly, there's no reason we can't work together. I apologize for the way I acted yesterday. . . . Don't know what got into me." She smiled contritely. "We'll start over today, okay? A reboot?" She held up her sock-covered foot.

"Fair enough," he said, breaking open a heart-melting grin.

As she put on her boots, he poured himself another cup of coffee. "And while we walk, you can tell me *your* story."

"My story's pretty boring."

"I don't need to know your history, Kenzie." His tone was gentle. "I want you to tell me about your heart condition."

They walked side by side down the flagstone path, Kenzie keeping to the stones, Austin to the dewy grass, sipping his coffee.

"How do you know about my heart?" Kenzie asked.

"Jon told me during our phone interview. He thought I should know before I accepted the job." Austin glanced over at her. "Don't *you* think I should know?"

"I would have told you," she said defensively. "My health won't interfere with my job, so don't worry that you'll be stuck with most of the workload."

"I'm sure you're capable of handling the work. Jon said you've done it before, so my being overworked isn't a concern. I told Jon I was on board, and now I'm telling you the same thing." They were into the woods now, where the air was cooler and sunlight hadn't yet penetrated. "Just so you know," he said with an exaggerated drawl, "I was a Boy Scout growing up, so I have first-aid training."

Incredulous, Kenzie stared at him. He winked, and she saw a twinkle in his eye. "A Boy Scout, huh?"

"You got something against Boy Scouts, lady?"

"Just the cocky ones."

He laughed.

"So, no regrets about driving all the way from Virginia to do horse rescue work?"

His tone turned serious as he said, "No regrets for me, but if we're going to be a team, I'd like to hear the particulars about your health from *you*. I already blew it by not knowing enough about the horses I'm expected to work with. I don't want to make the same mistake with my only teammate."

She slowed, knowing he had a point. She mentally sorted through what she absolutely needed to tell him. "I take medication, and I see my doctor regularly. He runs tests once a year, gives me the results, and sends me on my way. I'm holding steady. I'm strong and can easily deal with the horses. In fact, daily exercise is good for me."

Austin stopped on the path. "How did this happen?"

She turned to face him, flicked imaginary biscuit crumbs from the front of her shirt. "It isn't a birth defect. When

I was four, I got sick . . . fever, rash, swollen lymph nodes, symptoms a lot of kids get. Eventually, they diagnosed me with Kawasaki disease."

"Never heard of it."

"Neither had my parents. It's an autoimmune disorder. Bottom line is that in a small percentage of kids, the illness causes inflammation of blood vessels, especially in the arteries around the heart. I was one of that small percentage. Unlucky me. But for now, I assure you that I can wrestle bales of hay and do hard physical work without keeling over."

Birds chirped from trees, and a squirrel leapt from one branch to another, rustling leaves and filling the silence between them. Finally, Austin asked, "And that's it? That's all you have to tell me?"

"What else do you think you need to know?"

"Symptoms? Any signs I should look for if you're feeling bad?"

"If I feel bad, I'll tell you."

She took off, but he easily caught up with her. "Hey, wait up, I still have more questions."

Irritated, she stopped, then told herself that maybe he had a point. If they were working and she had an episode of heart palpitations, or irregular breathing and galloping pulse, she would have to deal with it. She faced him. "If my heart rhythm goes out of whack, I get light-headed and dizzy. But I can feel it coming on, and when I do, I sit, do breathing exercises, and wait until the episode passes. Then I go back to work. It's no biggie."

Blood vessels constricted by stress, a rare occurrence,

could also be problematic, but she saw no reason to mention that now. She hardly knew this man, and he already had more information about her health than anyone except her parents and Vanderbilt University Medical Center. "Are we finished talking about this? We should have been at the stable twenty minutes ago." They resumed walking. "Hard work won't hurt me, and I'll tell you *if* or *when* I feel something going wrong. But you have a say-so too. If my health is more of a problem than you want to handle, you have *my* permission to quit."

"Why would you think I'd quit?"

"When I was a freshman, I had a roommate change dorm rooms because she was afraid I'd have a heart attack in front of her. My doctor had insisted I tell her about my health issues. The girl freaked out, said she couldn't handle that kind of pressure."

"*Could* you have a heart attack?"

She waved him off. "Maybe someday, but certainly not this summer. I had a checkup in April and my doctor said all's well. And just to be clear, I detest having somebody hover over me like I'm going to explode at any minute. That's what makes it nice to work with horses. They like to keep their personal space to themselves."

"Get too close and they kick or bite the horse that's crowding them, right?"

"You *do* know horses." Her comment was clipped, unfriendly.

He ducked in front of her. "I know people, too, Kenzie, and I've come to help, not hamper, your work."

Her heart thumped, the rhythm totally unrelated to her health. She broke eye contact, stepped up her pace, not slowing until she broke into the open sunlight at the side of the stable, where she took a deep breath, feeling like a swimmer underwater a few seconds too long.

Five

Kenzie had posted a work schedule on the tack room door—daily and weekly tasks that she and Austin needed to perform to keep the rescue horses on a track to recovery. She took charge of the bothersome paperwork, but from day one, she insisted Austin give Blue his morning grain allotment. The first time Austin approached the stall's half door, Blue flattened his ears and backed into a corner. Kenzie told him, "I want you feeding him every day. It lets Blue know where his food comes from and who's giving it to him. Creates consistency and trust. Lower his feed bucket in with a rope until he gets used to you and lets you walk it in."

By week's end, Blue allowed Austin to enter the stall with the feed bucket, although the horse still hugged the stall's corners until Austin walked out. "When do we start working with him and changing his behavior?"

"I've been thinking about snapping a lead rope on his halter and taking him into the round pen." She gestured toward the outside enclosure earmarked for training.

"I've never used a pen to train. Looks small."

"Too large a space and a horse can avoid a trainer. Too small and the horse might feel threatened."

"I don't want you getting hurt."

"Oh, he won't hurt me. *You're* the one who'll be working him. By the end of summer, you and Blue will be best buddies."

"Braveheart *liked* me, and so far, Blue's not a fan."

She smiled. "Don't worry. The technique is simple, and horse tamers and trainers use it all the time. You'll go into the pen with Blue, sit on an upside-down bucket, and ignore him."

"That's it?"

"For a while. All you do is sit there with a pocketful of treats and snub him. Horses hate to be ignored. You'll move the bucket from place to place inside the pen every day. Sooner or later, Blue will decide to come over and check you out. Then you'll reward him with a treat. Eventually, you'll stand, pet him, talk to him, and start grooming him. A curry comb will feel good to him."

"Then what?"

"Once Blue's comfortable with you, you'll bring in a saddle. It might make him nervous, but he knows its purpose. When he's calm, put it on him, but don't mount him. Be kind, but firm, and once he understands you're not going to hurt him, put your foot in the stirrup. If he balks, back

34

off. Try again the next day. Once he knows you're the boss and you begin to ride him, he'll quickly become a true Tennessee walking horse. The gaits are genetically programmed, and Blue's a natural." She flashed a smile.

"You make it sound simple."

"It isn't, but I'm confident you'll win him over."

"Well, if I'm gonna be sitting on a bucket all afternoon in the sun, I better grab a hat."

Another smile. "Before you do, I want us to give the Gray Lady a bath. Long overdue."

"She does look a little scruffy."

Kenzie slipped a halter on Mamie, attached a lead rope, walked her outside, and tied the rope to a hitching post. "First, a good grooming." Kenzie swept a curry comb down Mamie's flank, brushing off hunks of old winter coat, working carefully over the horse's still-visible ribs. While Kenzie brushed, Austin ran his fingers, then a comb through the mare's knotted mane and tail. Once satisfied with their basic grooming, Kenzie squirted a stream of heavy-duty horse shampoo into a bucket, and Austin filled it with fresh water from a nearby hose. After wetting down the horse, the two of them stood on opposite sides of Mamie and gently scrubbed off layers of dirt and grime with large, soft sponges.

They moved in unison, from her forelegs to her underbelly and across her back, where Austin broke Kenzie's concentration with, "So . . . Ciana tells me you'll be a junior at Vanderbilt in the fall. What's your major?"

"I want to be a veterinarian. I'll do my undergrad work

at Vandy, transfer to University of Tennessee in Knoxville for my master's. Equine-only practice."

Kenzie moved to Mamie's withers and began shampooing the horse's mane. The sun beat down, the air growing warmer and mingling the scents of grassy earth, soap, and clean horse hide. It was a smell she wished she could dab on like perfume. "How about you? In college? Graduated?" She had guessed they were about the same age when he'd first arrived, but now she wasn't sure. His self-confidence, the way he interacted with her, pegged him as older. If only he'd come with a paper résumé.

"In the hunt for a law degree. Prosecution side—you know, jailing the bad guys and getting justice for victims."

She wanted to tell him that the law offered little justice but didn't want to get into the nitty-gritty of *how* she knew. "So you're in law school?"

"Not yet. Just thinking about it. University of Virginia has a good program."

Despite Kenzie's rejection of her father, Avery still paid for tuition, fees, and textbooks. He had cut off funds for extra expenses, one of the reasons she'd taken the job with Kaye. During her freshman year, her mother slipped Kenzie a loaded debit card, although Kenzie had insisted, "I don't want anything from my father, not even his money." But her mother countered with, "Don't be foolish. You can't spend pride and stubbornness." All true, but she'd used the card sparingly, and put it in a drawer once she began earning weekly paychecks.

"Might take a while to get a pay-as-you-go law degree," Kenzie observed to Austin.

"Haven't you heard? Anything worth having is worth the struggle to get it." He ducked his head beneath Mamie's neck and flashed his signature grin. Their gazes tangled. Her pulse accelerated. He picked up the hose. "Stand back and I'll rinse her off."

Kenzie stepped aside and Austin fanned water over Mamie's freshly scrubbed body. After the rinsing, Kenzie picked up two curved plastic body scrapers and handed one to Austin, and together they removed excess water from Mamie's coat. Austin walked over to turn off the hose, and Kenzie stepped back to admire the clean horse. Seconds later, she felt a cold splash of water against her back. She yelped and spun.

"Oops," Austin said, without an ounce of remorse and with pure mischief in his blue-green eyes.

She threw the soapy sponge in her hand and scored a direct hit to his forehead. "Oops," she echoed smugly.

"Ah-ah, now you're in trouble, lady." He hit her again with a stream of water, soaking her from the neck down.

She shivered when the cold water plastered her shirt to her skin. She picked up the bucket and flung what remained of the soapy bathwater at him, scoring a partial hit. He dropped the hose to duck the bucket she also tossed.

"Missiles? You're throwing missiles at me? I'm unarmed!"

"You should have thought of that before you started!" Laughing, Kenzie darted to the dropped hose, grabbed it, and, jutting her thumb into the stream, forced an arc of water at him. He tried to dodge it, slipped in the mud, and got soaked. He flung a handful of mud at her.

She ducked, picked up a wad, and fired it at him, then added another blast of water from the hose.

He raised his hands. "Truce! You win! I surrender!"

Kenzie offered a self-satisfied smile. "As you should. Now why don't you put the *clean* horse back in the pasture, and I'll forget to file a harassment complaint with your boss."

"Yeah, she's tough," he said, rising to his feet, wiping mud off his jeans. "And I'm really sorry I took her on." His grin was anything but contrite.

She was wet but triumphant, and hadn't laughed that hard since . . . *Before Valentine's Day.* She sobered quickly. Playtime was over. "Please put Mamie in the pasture. I'll rinse the sponges." She dropped the soggy blobs onto a nearby cement pad, hosed them down, and stomped on them until the water ran clean and all the laughter and fun of the water fight had vanished.

Austin found Kenzie sitting on a bale of straw nestled in shadows, wrestling to remove the tight band at the end of her soaked plaited hair and fighting to hold back tears. Gently, he asked, "Can I help?"

"I can get it." She pulled the braid over her shoulder, squinted, and struggled with the wadded elastic scrunchie. "The water made it tighter," she explained as her fingers fumbled. The knot held fast.

He stepped behind the bale. "Let me."

"It's hopeless! I'll have to use scissors." She hated that

her voice quavered with unshed tears from a sadness that had sneaked up and grabbed her by the throat.

"Hey, who just spent an hour taking knots and snarls out of a horse's mane and tail? I've got this."

She dropped her hands. He lifted the braid, inspected it. "When I came inside, you looked upset. I didn't hurt you out there, did I? Because I didn't mean—"

"No!" she said vehemently. "I'm just . . . just frustrated with this stupid hairband."

"I don't want to pull your hair, so scream if I do."

He was working to get a smile, or a snappy comeback, but she wanted none of it and kept silent. She felt his gentle tugging, heard him mutter as he held up the weight of the braid with one hand and worked with his other. Somehow his big hands discovered the secret of the band's Gordian knot, and minutes later, she heard, "Aha! Mission accomplished." He dropped the offending band over her shoulder onto her lap and threaded his fingers to unravel the tight twist of the braid, flattening and smoothing until her hair hung in loose blond waves down her back.

The way he stroked her hair, this stranger's hands, weaving, touching, moving with soft surety through her thick locks . . . She closed her eyes. *Practiced hands.* Her eyes shot open, and she scooted off the bale of hay. "Sorry I doubted your abilities. Thanks for the help."

When she turned, his gaze grabbed hers. "Your hair is beautiful. Do you ever wear it down?"

She felt as if the stable had shrunk and the air become too thick to breathe. His eyes were mesmerizing, like a booby trap that would snap back and hurt her. She turned away, breaking the sight-thread holding her to him. "I . . . I can't. My hair's baby-fine, straight as a board, and gets in the way of my work. I'm thinking about cutting it." That was a lie, but she said it anyway.

"Pity," he said softly.

She needed distance between them. A lot of distance. She walked outside.

Austin followed and, keeping his tone light, said, "Well, I don't know about you, but I'd like to get into some dry clothes before we tackle another feeding. Unless we're going to bathe another horse today. No use changing if we are."

"No, not today. We'll bathe Sparkle tomorrow. Why don't you fill the wheelbarrows with hay for the mares while I go to the house and make us sandwiches? After we eat, you can start Blue's training."

He winked, and she darted off, shaking out her damp hair, recalling with a delicious shiver the feel of his fingers lacing through the strands.

Six

"Hi, are you Kenzie?"

Kenzie was readying buckets of grain for the mares' late-afternoon special feeding and turned to face a woman with brown eyes, brown hair, and a sunny smile. She was on foot and dressed in hospital scrubs.

"I'm Alana Kennedy—Lani. Ciana sent me to meet you."

"Yes. You're Oro's owner, and a nurse?"

"True, but my job has turned me more into Oro's occasional rider these days. My life's been so busy this past year I don't have much time for my old friend. Not like I used to, anyway. Feel free to ride him whenever. Do you have time for a chat?"

"Sure. Let me grab a couple of folding chairs from the tack room." Kenzie dragged two metal chairs into the larger stable area, offered one to Lani, and took the other.

41

Lani closed her eyes, inhaled. "I miss the smell of horses and hay and saddle leather." Her eyes popped open. "After a day of smelling antiseptics, disinfectants, and chemo meds, this place is nose candy for this girl."

A kindred spirit. "Just last week, I was wishing I could bottle the aroma of horse shampoo and clean horsehide and use it as perfume!"

"I'd buy it!" Lani said.

"We'll make each and bottle it!" Kenzie said, raising her hands. "We'll call them Hay Luscious and . . ." Kenzie searched for another name.

Lani straightened. "I know! Horse Scents." Again they laughed at their silliness. "Ciana told me I'd like you, and she's right. I've been trying to get out here for days, but my job kept getting in the way."

"And Ciana told me you work with children who have cancer. It must be difficult."

"I love the work. There are bad days, but there are good ones too. We sent an eleven-year-old home today in a second remission from leukemia. When David left, he had nineteen balloons tied to the arm of his wheelchair—one for every day he'd been in treatment. His dad brought him one each day for being brave."

Kenzie thought back to what her father had once meant to her. *No more.*

"Anyway," Lani said, "I came to talk to you about the Trailblazers program Ciana and I want to launch for kids like David and his nine-year-old sister, Cami. She was born with Down syndrome. I believe these two kids are a perfect fit for the program. I went through 'horse therapy' when I was thirteen, when my aunt Arie died. I was miserably sad. My daddy bought me Oro, and over time this dear palomino healed broken places inside me. So I know getting close to a horse can help children, just like you help these horses. Two broken things come together—win-win."

"Sounds ambitious. And like more work for you."

"I believe in kids and horses, and how they help each other. How old were you when you began taking care of a horse?"

"I was ten. She was a Tennessee walker." Because of her self-imposed exile, she hadn't ridden Princess Ronan since . . . ? She backed away mentally. *Too long.*

"Well, then you know how easily a child can fall in love with a horse. Learning to care for a horse teaches life lessons, and as a bonus, kids gain self-esteem."

"I *do* know, but horses also need feed, vaccinations, and vet care . . . expensive things."

Lani waved Kenzie's words aside. "Money for the program will come, and Ciana has already told me I can work from here. Look, why don't you come by the hospital and we'll talk, and I'll introduce you to some of the children I think will benefit from Trailblazers."

Kenzie's early memories of hospital stays, tests, and doctor visits were unpleasant. These days, she found the yearly experience less fearful, but tedious, even as an outpatient. "I really don't like hospitals."

Lani nodded. "Most people don't, but—" Just then Lani's phone sang out from the purse she'd plopped beside her chair. She held up a finger to pause their discussion, reached in, and, seeing the readout, answered. "Well, hello, good-lookin'."

Kenzie heard only Lani's side of a brief conversation, but the tone of intimacy was unmistakable. Lani promised the caller she would be home soon and signed off, her eyes glowing. She dropped the phone back in her purse. "My fiancé, Dawson Berke."

Kenzie eyed the glittering diamond on Lani's left hand. "Your ring's beautiful." Lani held it out as Kenzie admired it. "When's the wedding?"

"July, the third Saturday. We would have preferred sooner, but every church and venue was filled for June, and—"

"Who are you?" came the sharp bark of Austin's voice from the doorway. "What's your business here?"

Kenzie whipped around, saw him looming at the east end doorway, his body in shadows, the brim of his hat pulled low. Friendly, affable Austin suddenly looked dark and ominous.

"Oh! I—I'm Lani," she responded, startled.

He crossed the space, stood behind Kenzie's chair, hands gripping the metal. Kenzie jumped up, faced him, anger rising like a wall inside her. "Aren't you supposed to be with Blue?"

"Finished. He's back in the pasture." His steely gaze never left Lani.

Not intimidated, Lani held out her hand and offered a warm smile. "I'm a friend of Jon and Ciana's. And you are . . . ?"

"Austin Boyd." He relaxed, came around Kenzie's chair.

"Sorry, didn't mean to come on so strong. It's just that we don't get many visitors back here."

"Not a problem." Lani's smile was forgiving as she stood. "I have to run, but, Kenzie, please consider stopping by the hospital to talk again. I'm sure you'll have some ideas for Trailblazers. Ciana said you're smart and kind. I'd love your input."

Flustered, Kenzie said, "Not sure *how* I can help . . ."

"That's what we'll figure out together." Lani tossed the straps of her purse over her shoulder, held up her phone. "I'll send you a link to our hospital website and our social media, and you can look at our children's cancer pages, check out the work we do."

"I . . . I don't do social media." Kenzie's confession made both Lani and Austin stare at her.

"O-kay . . . ," Lani said. "I'll text you my schedule for next week, and we'll set up a time for you to visit."

"My phone's old-school. Not smart. I'm not really a big texter either." Kenzie squared her chin, knowing she sounded like a freak of nature. Who didn't text? "I don't like distractions when I work or study," she explained hastily. "But I have a laptop and an email address I'll give you."

Lani snapped her fingers. "I have a better idea! Dawson and I are having a pool party with friends on Memorial Day. Why don't you two come? I'd love for you to meet Dawson. He's amazing, but I *am* prejudiced."

"Oh, I don't think—" Kenzie began.

"Why not? It's a holiday, and we could use some R and R," Austin blurted, polishing his words with his heart-melting smile.

"Not a holiday for our horses. They still need to be fed four times a day."

"According to your schedule and the vet, we can back the mares off to three feedings a day," he added before she could protest. "Plus, I can get the horses covered by a couple of Jon's men living in the bunkhouse with me. They'll check on them for us while we're at the pool."

"We're starting at eleven in the morning, and there'll be burgers. Dawson's a grill genius," Lani chimed in. "Drop in anytime, stay as late as you can. Come on. It'll be fun. And we can talk poolside about Trailblazers. Much nicer than sitting in the hospital."

Kenzie disliked being pressured, but Lani's enthusiasm was infectious. "I guess we could stop by."

Austin said, "I *do* have a smartphone, so I'll give you my number and you can text me details." He fished his cell from his shirt pocket.

After trading phone information with Austin, Lani flashed Kenzie a smile and, with a wave, hurried away.

Once Lani was out of earshot, Kenzie ripped into Austin. "Why did you think it was all right to make plans for *me?*"

"Us," he corrected her. "She invited *us.* I thought we were a team. That's the impression you've given me. We work together. Why not go to a pool party together?" His expression softened. "Have I slacked off on this job for one minute?"

A rhetorical question. She knew he hadn't. "I . . . I don't like being around strangers."

"You know me and you know Lani. Two down right there."

"What about Blue? You're supposed to work him every day."

"Blue's taking food from my hand. He literally followed me around the pen today begging for a treat—'Thank you very much, Austin.'" He tipped his head in self-congratulation.

His update surprised her, because he hadn't been working with Blue for long. "That's . . . that's progress. Thank you very much, Austin," she echoed.

Austin touched the brim of his hat, accepting her compliment with only a grin. "When I walked in, you and Lani looked like longtime best friends."

"And you *yelled* at us. Scared us both."

"Yeah, sorry about that. Course, that was before I knew about the pool party."

The man could be maddening and confusing, but also disarming. Kenzie capitulated. "All right, we'll go as a team . . . but just for a little while, so that Lani and I can talk."

"I'll let her know," Austin said, tapping his phone.

Resigned, Kenzie stepped aside. She *had* liked Lani—would like her even if they didn't have a love of horses in common. Stepping out of her "boss" role with Austin was what had spooked her, knowing that she was drawn to him far more than she wanted or needed to be. "And ask her what we can bring to the party. Now let's get back to work."

Austin paced outside under the eaves of the bunkhouse while the other hired men slept. He, too, should have been in bed after the long day he'd put in, but he couldn't take a chance of being overheard. He felt the burner cell buried in his jean's pocket vibrate—the prearranged phone call. Only two numbers were programmed into the throwaway phone. He glanced at the screen before answering: *Caller 1.* "Yes, I'm here."

"How's it going?" the man on the phone asked.

"Working hard."

"Has she accepted you?"

"More or less. When we're not working, she keeps to herself. Prefers being alone."

The caller at the other end of the line huffed impatiently. "What are you doing about that? Remember our arrangement. She needs to trust you."

"These things take time. I can't steamroll her into liking me."

"It's imperative—"

Austin cut him off. "I know how to do my job. You said you'd let me handle things my way."

"And *you* don't forget who's signing your checks."

Austin tamped down his temper. "Is that all?"

Disgruntled silence. Finally, the man growled, "For now. I'll call again in a week. You call *me* if there's a problem."

Austin disconnected, slid the cell into his pocket. He felt Soldier sniffing his pant leg and crouched, scratching the big white shepherd behind the ears. "Hey, old boy." Befriending the dog had been a priority for him. Dogs were pack animals, and while Jon would always be the alpha of Soldier's pack, Austin wanted to be a trusted member.

Soldier nosed Austin's shirt pocket. "I didn't forget you," Austin said, and reached into the pocket for the napkin wrapped around a few pieces of meat he'd saved from his steak dinner. He shook the meat onto the grass. Soldier nosed the meat, gobbled it, and gave Austin a hopeful look. Austin chuckled, stood. "Next time." He headed for the barn at the front of the property, and Soldier fell into step at his side. Together, they walked the perimeter of Bellmeade in the moonlight.

Seven

— ∙ —

"Big place," Austin said as he drove along the perimeter road of Lani's apartment complex. He'd already passed two other pools on the property. He tossed his cell to Kenzie riding shotgun next to him. "Right or left at the fork up ahead?"

She looked at the phone's map. "Left. And the pool for Dawson's building will be on the right." Kenzie stared out the windshield, nervous, knowing she'd have been much happier staying at the stable with her horses. She reminded herself she'd agreed to come and told herself to suck it up.

Minutes later, Austin pulled into a parking space across from a pool, a banner laced through iron slats of a fence: BERKE PRIVATE PARTY. Balloons tied to the tops of the railing danced in the warm breeze. He turned off the engine.

They went through the gate carrying their towels and

cooler, and Lani, wearing a colorful tropical print cover-up, hurried over and took Kenzie's hand. "So glad to see you two! Come, meet Dawson."

She beckoned to a man in the water and he swam to the pool's side and hauled himself onto the cement deck. Lani said, "Honey, this is Kenzie and Austin, the couple from Bellmeade working with the rescue horses I told you about."

The couple? Kenzie started to object to Lani's intro-duction, but Austin stepped forward and held out his hand. "Good to meet you."

Dawson looped one arm around Lani, shook with Aus-tin, grinned at Kenzie. Dawson's black hair was slicked back from his high forehead. His eyes were the color of dark chocolate, his jaw square, his body tall and lean-muscled. Kenzie decided to simply smile and ignore Lani's assump-tion.

Looking over Kenzie's sleeveless aqua-blue top and jean shorts, Lani asked, "Did you bring a suit? You can change upstairs in the apartment if you want."

"I left my swimsuit in storage at Vandy. Never thought I'd go swimming this summer working on a horse farm."

"Maybe I could lend you—"

"No, no. I'd rather sit and watch everyone else swim."

"Maybe there's a hose nearby," Austin mumbled in her ear. She shot him a scowl. "I *did* wear a suit," he said to Dawson, stripping off his shorts and T-shirt. He was power-fully built, well muscled across his chest and upper arms, with flat abs and a tapered waist. Kenzie hadn't seen him bare-chested and tried not to stare.

51

"Good, because we're about to play some water polo. You can be on my team." Dawson called out to others, and soon they had mixed couple sides of seven each in the water. Goalies were assigned, and small orange cones placed at each end of the pool on the concrete above the water to serve as goalie nets. "Make 'em count, people."

The teams hit the water, and Lani and Kenzie found chairs at a patio table shaded by a bright yellow umbrella. Others who weren't playing lay stretched out on loungers in the sun or gathered around patio tables drinking sodas and beer. "You can sit with your friends," Kenzie told Lani. "I don't mind just watching the game."

"I see *plenty* of the others; most of them are nurses who work with me. A lot of the people here will be attendants in our wedding."

Kenzie's eyes widened. "Wow, big group."

"It's going to be a big wedding. I grew up in Windemere, and both Dawson and I work here, so everybody knows us. The list of guests keeps growing." Lani offered a shrug and a grin.

Kenzie had never collected many friends. In the private high school she had attended, she'd kept to herself, her aloofness caused in part by her health issues, but also because she simply felt more comfortable with horses than with people.

The scent of coconut suntan oil and lotions mingled with the smell of chlorine from the splashing water, reminding Kenzie of summer days spent by her family's pool. A voice called from inside her head, *"Kenz! Watch me dive!"* The sound was so real, Kenzie glanced to the far end of the pool, saw only orange cones, and caught her breath. "How did you and Dawson meet?"

"High school. He was a transfer student in his senior year, and totally ticked off about his dad moving him to Windemere. I was a junior, so at the time I could only worship him from afar."

"But you ended up with him."

Lani's gaze followed Dawson in the water, the look of love clearly stamped on her face. "Yes, I did."

Kenzie gave Lani a questioning stare, inviting her to tell more, but Lani only smiled. "A long story for another day."

Kenzie changed the subject. "Okay, then how can I contribute to your Trailblazer program?"

"A horse." Lani's smile lit up her brown eyes. "Ciana told me you have a rescue mare she thinks might be perfect for a child. An older mare."

"Mamie." Kenzie nodded enthusiastically. "Yes, she's very docile and sweet tempered, loves attention. And special treats."

"How about if I bring David and Cami and their parents out to Bellmeade to meet Mamie?"

"Oh, she's not ready to be ridden yet. Not even by a child. Not until she reaches her proper body weight. We're still working with her."

"Understood. I only want to bring the kids to see how they take to the horse. If they do, I'll begin teaching them the basics of horse etiquette with Oro, the other inductee into my program. Once Mamie's ready, David and Cami can begin Trailblazers together."

Kenzie carefully considered the request and saw no

reason why the children shouldn't meet Mamie. "That'll be all right."

"How about this coming Saturday?"

"Can you spare the time? Isn't there a ton of stuff to do before your wedding?"

Lani rolled her eyes. "As if I'm in charge of my wedding! My sister, Melody, and our mom are in control. I'm just going along for the ride."

"You have a sister?"

Lani grinned. "Mel's a force of nature. Our folks live in Alaska. Mom's a teacher. She and Dad will be staying with Melody, and I'm letting Sis and Mom handle all the wedding details. I just plan to nod and agree."

"And you're all right with that? I can't imagine not having control of things that are important to me, like the horses. I like handling every detail of their care. I especially want a say in who adopts them."

"Actually, I'm grateful for their help." Lani's mood turned pensive. "A few years back I learned a hard lesson: Most of us are *not* in control of our lives. We might *think* we have control, but in the end, we have very little. We just have to roll with whatever comes along, good and bad."

Kenzie understood what Lani was saying. Her own medical issues had taught her as much. Control of one's life was illusory, a lesson she'd learned all over again on Valentine's Day.

"Doesn't mean we should give up, though, does it?" Lani's face brightened. "For me, the good news is that I know Mom and Mel love me, and so details about flowers, caterers, menus, and venues have very little importance to me. All that matters is that at the end of the day, Dawson and I are married. I love him with all my heart."

Love, marriage, a lifetime commitment. Not part of Kenzie's game plan. "For me it's college and, one day, my own veterinary practice."

"However, just to be clear, I *did* choose my own wedding dress." Amusement danced in Lani's brown eyes.

Kenzie could only imagine how beautiful she'd look, and felt a tug on her heart for brides who would never be, weddings that would never happen.

Just then a whoop rose from the pool, and Dawson shouted, "Winners and still champions, Team Berke!"

Kenzie and Lani clapped as the players climbed out of the pool, shook off the water, and grabbed towels. Dawson and Austin padded over to their table, where Dawson bent down and kissed Lani on the mouth. "Cold lips," she said with an exaggerated shiver.

"Warm heart," he countered with a wink.

Austin wrapped a towel around his waist and settled into the chair nearest Kenzie's. The shade of the umbrella had shifted, and water droplets on his shoulders caught sunlight, adding sparkle to his tanned, taut skin. His blue-green eyes found hers, his expression unreadable. She looked away.

"Good game, Boyd. Thanks."

"Anytime."

Dawson headed toward the poolside grill, and Lani followed. They laughed and stole kisses as he flipped burgers.

Austin's gaze flicked around the pool area, at the guests,

the parking lot, and the balconies of the apartments over-looking the pool. Kenzie wondered if he thought any of the bikini-clad women were attractive or if he had someone special in Virginia waiting for him. *None of your business,* she told herself. "Lani wants to use Mamie in her Trailblazers program once the horse is strong enough, and Ciana's already expressed interest in keeping the horse at Bellmeade. Lani's asked to bring the kids out to meet Mamie on Saturday. What do you think?"

"I think it's a good idea. And thank you for asking my opinion."

"Well, as you keep reminding me, we *are* a team."

The soft buzz of conversation from the pool deck, an occasional laugh, the smoky scent of grilling burgers, pitch-perfect weather, and Austin's solid presence gave Kenzie a sense of well-being she'd hadn't felt in months. If only she could put the feeling in a box, store it, take it out to ward off memories of what she could not change. *No control.*

She took a deep breath. "We should probably leave after we eat."

He rolled his shoulders. "The horses are covered a hundred percent. The guys will handle everything, so we don't have to leave too early. That is, *if* we're having a good time. I know I am. How about you?"

She felt a flare of anxiety, remembered Lani's words about rolling with whatever comes along. "What about Blue? You know how he is around strange men."

"Are you saying all men are strange?"

"Well, now that you mention it . . ."

He grinned, and she matched it with a smile of her own. "All the guys have to do is feed him. We'll put Blue in his stall when we get back. Don't worry. Kick back. It's okay to have a good time."

She saw his grin deepen and something bloom in his eyes that made her heart beat faster. "Then I say let's go eat."

He stood and offered his hand, and she took it. His palm was calloused from work. She felt the strength of him leaching through her skin, and she curled into the calming, pleasant feeling.

Austin was by her side all evening, meeting people whose names Kenzie would never remember, hearing funny stories from Dawson's fellow construction workers and shoptalk from nurses. A cake was brought out and everyone clapped. A surprised Lani asked, "What's this?"

The engaged couple's names were written in green icing and twined together like vines across a blanket of thick, snow-white frosting. Dawson kissed Lani to more applause and the clicks of phones snapping photos. Music poured through speakers, and as the sun sank, underwater lights lit the cool water. Swimmers returned to the pool, but Austin remained by Kenzie's side, and together they lingered as night oozed across the sky. As the party wound down, Austin leaned into her and said, "We'd better go. I didn't ask the guys to cover the morning feeding."

She startled, realizing she'd been lost in the magic of the evening. On the ride along the dark country back roads to

Bellmeade, she listened to Austin's thumbs drumming on the steering wheel, keeping rhythm to songs from the radio. He tapped the buttons frequently to keep the music flowing. Kenzie hummed under her breath, until he hit a station conducting a sports interview and she heard the unmistakable drawl of a voice that shattered her sense of well-being.

"So with five full-ride scholarship offers, it was hard to choose. But today I signed with Alabama."

Austin aimlessly punched to another station and another riff of music. "I like this song. How about you?"

She didn't answer, and he gave her a curious sidelong look. He seemed surprised to see not the mellow, smiling Kenzie who'd gotten into the car with him, but another version instead—Kenzie sitting ramrod straight, hands balled into fists in her lap, and acting nothing like the girl who'd left the pool party with him.

Eight

As soon as Austin pulled into the parking area at Bellmeade's front barn, Kenzie hopped out of the car. "Wait," he called. "I'll walk you home."

"No need," she tossed over her shoulder, leaving before he shut off the engine.

He scrambled from the car, watched her figure recede across the dark lawn, saw Soldier standing alert, his attention pivoting between Kenzie and Austin. "Go!" he said to the dog, and the shepherd ran, caught up with Kenzie, and matched her pace to the bungalow.

Austin grabbed Kenzie's empty cooler from the backseat and stood on the bunkhouse porch until he saw the internal lights glow just as Soldier trotted up to him. "She tell you good night? Because she didn't tell *me* good night." The dog's tail wagged. Austin flipped open the cooler, took out a single cooked burger he'd pilfered from the pool party, broke it, and dropped the pieces onto the lawn. "I didn't forget you, buddy."

Later, Austin settled into bed, fingers locked behind his head, sorting through Kenzie's strange behavior. What had happened to set her off? She'd been reluctant about going to the party, but after the water polo game and her conversation with Lani, she'd seemed to enjoy herself. They had eaten burgers together beneath the yellow umbrella, and she'd later held his hand while Lani dragged them around to meet bridesmaids, groomsmen, and attendants. He'd instinctively known that she was "crowd shy" and that her hand in his was nothing personal, simply a way for her to be social around strangers. He hadn't minded. His palm held the memory of her small hand clasped in his. That afternoon, he'd thought she was beginning to trust him. He *needed* her to trust him.

When had things gone wrong? He closed his eyes, replayed scenes in his head. All was well until the drive home. She'd seemed content, even tossed him smiles and eye rolls whenever he sang along with a familiar song. He had changed stations frequently, and with one exception of some guy talking sports, had kept the music flowing during the ride. Austin struggled to recapture the words of the male voice and failed. He'd quickly changed the station, and seconds later, when he'd glanced at her, he'd seen that she'd gone rigid in the seat. What had been the trigger? He couldn't recall the list of songs they'd heard, but perhaps one held a bad memory. . . . A breakup song?

He rubbed his eyes, still stinging from the chlorine. Or

was the sting from Kenzie? He poked his phone, saw that it was after midnight, and knew that six-thirty would come quickly. He needed some sleep. Maybe during the morning feeding he could wheedle an explanation from her. They were a team; she had said so. He'd never had this much trouble getting close to a woman before. Kenzie Caine was a whole new ball game. He had to figure her out before he could finish the job he'd agreed to do.

The delectable scents of frying bacon and fresh coffee, not his phone alarm, woke Austin before six the next morning. Groggily he got up, showered, shaved, dressed, and went into the main area of the bunkhouse. The large living space held sofas and comfortable chairs, along with a large-screen TV. At the far end of the room was an industrial-sized open kitchen and a large farmhouse-style table. Delores, the cook, stood over the stove, stirring a giant cast-iron skillet of scrambled eggs.

"Morning," Austin said, pouring himself a mug of black coffee.

"Mornin' to you, too, Mr. Austin." Delores beamed him a smile. She always put a "Mr." in front of the men's names, even though he'd told her it wasn't necessary.

Jon had three full-time hires working with him: a local guy from Murfreesboro, another from Wyoming, and Miguel, Delores's husband. Miguel and Delores were an older couple, from a ranch in Texas where Jon had grown up. Rumor had it that the pair came up every spring and summer to work at Bellmeade and returned to Texas when Tennessee's colder weather settled in.

"Tortillas or biscuits with your eggs? I made fresh salsa too."

"How about all three?"

Delores laughed. "Of course."

He settled at the table with his coffee and thumbed through morning messages on his phone, mostly junk mail. The other men staggered in sleepy-eyed, poured themselves coffee, and sat down just as Delores set heaping bowls of hot food on the table. A stack of plates and utensils were clustered in the table's center. "No tofu?" Austin joked, making Delores giggle like a schoolgirl.

"Can you find some cream puffs for Pretty Boy here?" Scooter, from Wyoming, drawled.

"Maybe some of that fancy English marmalade too," added Clyde, the local guy. "Man's got a hard day ahead."

Austin gave a good-natured shrug and dug into eggs and bacon. The two older men had nicknamed Austin "Pretty Boy" their first week at Bellmeade, openly resenting him because he kept to himself, always refusing to join them on their visits to town to blow off steam. He also knew they considered his job of helping Kenzie "soft" and "easy," while they wrestled with ornery wild mustangs alongside Jon Mercer.

"You shouldn't tease," Delores clucked, winking at Austin. "Mr. Austin works hard, same as you."

Miguel hooked his arm around his wife's ample waist and gave her a hug. She patted his shoulder and began pouring another round of coffee into empty cups.

62

"Pretty Boy with Pretty Girl. Hard job, all right," Clyde said, a hint of sourness in his voice.

Ignoring the men's jabs, Austin said, "Thanks for helping with our horses yesterday." Working with the beautiful blonde day in and day out might look cushy to these two, but they had no idea what it was like to deal with her mercurial temperament.

"The big gelding's a mean cuss," Scooter said. "We couldn't get near him. Had to leave him in the pasture all night."

Austin tensed. He'd forgotten about telling Kenzie they'd check on the horses after returning from the party. He hadn't, and hoped she hadn't gone to the stable alone in the dark. "Not a problem," he said, heaping a second helping of scrambled eggs onto a warm tortilla and rolling it up. "Gotta run. See you for dinner."

"Can't wait!" Clyde called as Austin tore out the front door.

Hoping to beat Kenzie to the stable, Austin jogged all the way, but when he arrived, she was already filling the grain bins in each stall, where all three horses were waiting to be fed. He quickly realized that the bunkhouse crew might not be charmers, but they knew enough about horses to have left Blue's outside stall door open so that the gelding could come inside at will. "Hey, good morning. You should have waited for me."

She barely glanced at him. "Woke up early, thought I'd get started."

63

"You sleep all right?"

"Of course." Her smile was tight, and dark shadows under her eyes belied her answer.

Austin quickly scooped a serving of grain into Blue's bucket from a plastic hinge-lidded container. The big horse was used to Austin by now, and began to eat instead of backing away. "I'll get the hay ready," he told Kenzie. Without a word, she nodded, dismissing him, her braid bobbing.

He used a pitchfork to heap the loose hay into a wheelbarrow. After a few moments he looked over his shoulder and saw Kenzie sitting on a bale of straw, her face in her hands.

He lowered the wheelbarrow, came closer. "What's up?"

She raised her head, scooted off the bale. "Nothing. I thought I'd groom the mares after they eat and exercise Oro on the trail for Lani."

"Why don't I ride along with you? I can take one of the boarder's horses—Ciana has an exercise rotation schedule on the barn wall. I don't mind pitching in. Less work for you."

"It isn't a chore for me, and you should work with Blue."

Her got her message—she didn't want him around. He tried again. "What happened to the 'teamwork' concept? Did it occur to you that I might *like* to ride the trails with you?"

"I . . . I guess I didn't . . . I don't know . . ." She refused to make eye contact.

He stepped in front of her. "Look at me, please." She did and he saw that her eyes were bloodshot, swollen, and damp. "Kenzie, what happened to you between yesterday at the pool and coming home last night? You ran off as soon as we got here. This morning you've hardly spoken. You've been crying. Did I do something wrong?"

"The world doesn't revolve around *you*," she snapped.

Good, he thought. Fire from Kenzie was better than ice. "It doesn't? Why, I could have sworn yesterday when we held hands that you liked having me close to you. So much so that if I'd walked you to your door last night like I wanted, I might have gotten a kiss."

She recoiled. "Kiss *you*? You conceited jerk! What makes you think for one minute that I'd ever want to kiss you? A kiss means something, and you mean nothing to me! *Nothing.*" Glaring, she crossed her arms. "You're not even my type. You'll *never* be my type!"

Boiling anger might make her spew out whatever was eating her alive, and he wanted to know, *had* to know, if he was going to continue to work with her. He offered himself as a target, edging closer, purposely crowding her. "Since you seem to know so much about me, please tell me what it is about me and my 'type' that you dislike. I'm curious."

She shoved his chest hard, but he stood immovable. "Your *type*." She fairly spat the words. "I *know* who you are. You're all glib and charming, all smiles and compliments! You think every girl who sees you will fall at your feet. I'll bet women lap up your lies and flattery. Bet they hang all over you, give you whatever you ask them for." She drove a finger into his chest. "I'll bet you played football in high school and made a girl believe you loved her and talked her into doing things she would *never* have done in her right mind!"

Austin stood silent, a sick sensation in his stomach. He

began to understand that Kenzie wasn't seeing him standing in front of her and that her vivid description was of someone else. Softly, he asked, "What did the girl do?"

"Why, she did whatever he asked because she *loved* him." Sarcasm dripped from her voice. "And when he asked her to . . . to send pictures of her naked body to him, she did . . . because he said he *loved* her. And how did he reward her love? He posted the photos on social media and the g-gossips and Internet trolls, total strangers who didn't even *know* her, had never even *met* her"—she gulped a breath of air—"they shamed her! Made f-fun of her, and when the poor g-girl couldn't take it anymore, she went home . . . and she . . . she—" Kenzie's voice cracked. She furiously swiped her wet cheeks.

Austin's muscles tightened, wanting to find this guy and pound him to a pulp. "Please tell me what the girl did."

Kenzie's blue eyes looked haunted. "The girl went home in February . . . and . . . and on Valentine's Day . . . she hanged herself."

He exhaled slowly, rocked by her words, at a loss for what to say. Only platitudes came to mind, hollow words, wholly inadequate to give solace. "Kenzie . . . I—I'm really sorry. I mean . . . that's a terrible way to lose a friend."

Through clenched teeth, she hissed, "S-she wasn't m-my friend! She was my *sister*!"

Her words slammed his midsection like a fist. She shoved him again, and this time he let her push him out of her way.

Kenzie bolted from the stable. Austin made no move to stop her.

Nine

The power of Kenzie's story, the horror of it, bit hard. He wished he could even the score with the hateful people who had driven Kenzie's sister to kill herself. But Kenzie was also a victim. Reading hateful posts about someone she loved had left deep wounds. No wonder she shunned social media. He rolled his shoulders to loosen tension. His rational mind reminded him he had a job to do—he couldn't get involved. Yet he had spent weeks with Kenzie and hated seeing her in such crushing pain. Perhaps he'd grown soft, allowed his personal feelings to tip the balance between personal and professional. He knew better! It was perfectly all right to care *generically*, broadly, the way a person would because *of* a situation, but not because he had feelings for the person *in* the situation. *Back off*, he told himself.

And yet he couldn't walk away. Not only was he locked

in place at Bellmeade by circumstances out of his control, but he now had to find a way to make a fresh start with Kenzie. A way to say he felt sorry for what had happened without tumbling further into emotions that would keep him from doing the job he'd been sent to do. He needed a plan—at least for today. She had wanted to groom the rescue horses, but that could wait. An idea began to percolate, and he jogged to the bunkhouse, went inside, and found Delores in the kitchen doing prep work for lunch.

"Mr. Austin! Is everything all right?"

"Yes, I'm fine. I . . . um . . . I need a favor." She waited while he parsed his thoughts. "Will you make a couple of sandwiches? No, more than that . . . a picnic lunch? Nothing fancy, just make enough for two."

Her eyes twinkled. "But of course. It would be my pleasure."

"Thanks. I'll be back in fifteen."

"All will be ready."

He hurried to the big barn and, once inside, was relieved to see that Ciana hadn't turned the horses out to pasture yet. Unlike the stables in the back, the older barn had no outside doors, so someone had to lead the horses to pasture. Oro was just finishing his grain, and the next stall housed Dark Matter, a chestnut gelding Austin had exercised before in his spare time. Austin grabbed gear from the tack room and quickly saddled both horses, led them to the bunkhouse, tied them to a porch railing, and ducked inside.

Delores beamed him a knowing smile and handed him a bulging double-sided saddlebag. "Two sandwiches on my homemade bread, some fruit, two bottles of water, and some chocolates."

"Chocolates?"

"I assumed you are not planning to go riding with Mr. Clyde or Mr. Scooter." She offered a saucy wink.

"You assumed correctly. Thank you, Delores. Miguel is a lucky man to have you."

"I tell him so every day. Now go."

Outside, he untied the horses, mounted Dark Matter, and cozied the saddlebag over the horse's withers. Leading Oro, he rode to the rescue work stable. He tied the horses to the hitching rail, muttered, "Here goes," and strolled inside. Knowing she wouldn't desert the horses in her care, he found Kenzie right where he expected her—sitting on a metal chair, surrounded by bridles and halters she was cleaning with saddle soap. She ignored him, scrubbing the same spot on a leather bridle with a vengeance until it looked as if she'd rub a hole through it.

She also had changed clothes, smoothed out the dark places beneath her eyes with makeup. He walked closer, took a stance in front of her chair. She continued to snub him. "Soccer," he said.

The unexpected word made her look up. "What?"

"I played soccer in high school, not football, and I mostly rode the bench because I wasn't very good. No girls fell at my feet. I broke no hearts. I did have a girlfriend, though, and that's all she was, a girl who was also my friend. She had a horse and we were in 4-H together. We rode in barrel riding competitions at the county fair from time to time.

We kissed once just to try it out and broke out laughing. No chemistry. No magic. We graduated together and moved on. I haven't seen her for years. We're not even Facebook friends."

As he spoke, color and heat crept up Kenzie's neck, spread across her face. She loosened her death grip on the bridle and rested it in her lap. Fearful she'd crack and begin to cry again, she inspected the bridle. She spoke, her voice watery. "I . . . I didn't . . . shouldn't have said the things I said to you. I made dumb assumptions, and I—I'm sorry. You did nothing wrong yesterday or last night. And I had a very good time at the party. Please believe that." She thought of how many times she'd had to apologize to him for behaving rudely. He must have thought she was crazy.

Austin crouched in front of her chair and gently removed the bridle from her lap. Without it, she felt defenseless. "Kenzie, what you've gone through is life-shattering. February, you said? That was only a few months ago. This kind of pain can't be laid down in a few months." He resisted the urge to take her hand in his. Not a good idea on too many levels. "Look, I . . . um . . . I'm no counselor. I don't know how to tell you anything more than I'm sorry about what you've been through. I had no idea how bad you've been hurting all along. If I'd known . . ." He searched for something else to tell her and gave up.

"No merit badges for grief counseling?" She offered a tiny smile.

Relieved to see it, he smiled too. "None."

"Talking about what happened to Caroline—that was

her name—isn't easy. It made the news when . . . when it happened." Another stain on her family. "I barely made it through the last couple of months of classes. Working with horses, then knowing I was coming here for the summer, well, that helped to keep me going. I guess stuff was building up inside me, and . . . and I'm sorry for falling apart and attacking you. That wasn't fair. I guess neither one of us knows much about the other, do we?"

"True." He warned himself away from asking a barrage of questions. "A wise man once wrote that there's a time to mourn and a time to dance. You deserve to mourn." He shifted his weight. "However, right this minute, I've got two saddled horses outside waiting for riders. What do you say? Want to take them for a spin?"

The idea of a good long ride appealed more than she could express. "Y-you have them ready?"

"And lunch to go." He stood, held out his hand. "Team-work."

Gratitude *to* him, *for* him, brought her to the verge of tears. She stood, took his hand, and said, "I think both are super great ideas."

The riding trail Jon and Ciana had laid out for exercising horses meandered along Bellmeade's generous property lines, skirting fences around fields of growing alfalfa grass, cutting through a generous thicket of woods, and ending at a turn-around with a picnic table, benches, and a fenced grazing area where trail horses could graze. A leisurely ride up and back could take forty-five to fifty minutes. Taking time to picnic could stretch the ride much longer. Today, Austin was in no hurry.

Although most of the trail was wide enough for horses to walk side by side, he let Kenzie take the lead, content to follow and watch her well-practiced seat in the saddle. He admired the straightness of her back and the way her braid hung between her shoulder blades, moving with Oro's gait and catching sunlight. She seemed content with a slower pace too.

The fresh air, the warmth of the sun, the sound of Oro's hooves, and the sway of his walk soothed and settled Kenzie. The ride gave her time to clear her head and calm herself. The adrenaline rush from her earlier outburst had made her heart pound erratically. Not a good thing. She took deep, measured breaths to steady the beats. She'd held the hurt of losing Caroline inside herself for months, and telling Austin, saying the words *She hanged herself,* had been painful but cathartic. The memory was as fresh as the day a counselor, sent from the admin building, had come into her psychology class at Vanderbilt, walked her into an empty room, and as gently as possible delivered the news. Not all of it, just that her sister had died and that her father had sent a car to bring Kenzie home. Once home, she learned the rest of the story. Caroline had committed suicide, had chosen death over life.

Kenzie shook her head to dislodge the lingering shadows. *No more today.* She wanted to be in the present, the here and now. Austin had gone to some trouble to give her a pleasant experience, and she wanted to soak in it. And she wanted him nearer. Over her shoulder, she called, "The trail's wide enough for both of us, you know."

He nudged Dark Matter with his heels, and the horse stepped up and fell in beside Oro. They rode in amiable silence with the plodding sound of hooves and the occasional squeak of saddle leather making trail music. Minutes later, they were in the woods with leaf patterns falling over them.

In the shaded light, Austin's eyes looked jade green. She was getting used to how his eyes changed colors; the familiar definition of his muscular arms, browned by the sun; the sound of his voice when he said her name. She was getting used to *him*, this man. She shifted her gaze forward, wary of such an attraction. *Not. Possible.*

When they broke into the clearing and dismounted, Austin tossed the saddlebag on the old wooden table and released the horses into the field. As he unpacked their lunches and spread the goodies on the table, Kenzie grabbed a water bottle. "Quite a feast you whipped up."

"Full disclosure: Delores made the goodies. But I saddled the horses," he added, making Kenzie smile.

"Oooh, chocolate!" She reached for a piece of the wrapped candy, and Austin playfully scooped it aside.

"That's dessert."

"The perfect place to start." She defiantly snatched a piece and popped it into her mouth.

A bluebird hopped onto the end of the table from a tree. Kenzie tossed a bread crust away from the table and the bird swooped to follow it. "I . . . I want to apologize. I shouldn't have dumped on you this morning the way I did."

"If you ever want to talk—"

"No. I . . . I really don't want to talk about it, about that day . . . when . . . it happened. Maybe sometime, but not today." She unwrapped her sandwich and began to eat.

"Not a problem," he said, irritated at himself for asking. A *rookie mistake*. He was already blurring the line between professional and personal interest with this trail ride and picnic. He needed to tread carefully for both of their sakes.

They ate, finishing the food in silence, until Kenzie said, "Thank you."

"For what?"

"For this picnic. For being *you*."

He scrambled to his feet and started gathering the debris from their lunch and stuffing it into the saddlebag. "We better get moving. It's past time for another feeding."

Taken aback by his haste, his brusqueness, Kenzie wordlessly watched him gather their horses. This morning, he'd sought her out after her outburst. He had been kind and sympathetic, taken her on a trail ride and a picnic—all above and beyond his job description. She mounted Oro and urged him into a trot, all the while thinking that Austin Boyd was a total puzzle, as curious and strange as his changing eyes.

Austin was asleep when the vibration from the burner phone under his pillow woke him. He groggily pulled it out, sat up. The readout announced *Caller 2*. He punched the talk button. "Yes?"

"How're you doing?" The man's voice was scarred by years of smoking.

"Things are all right, but . . ." Austin left the sentence hanging.

"But what?"

Austin saw the gray light of morning peeking through the room's window curtain, meaning it was almost time to get up anyway. "I'm ready to leave this place."

"Are you serious? Seems to me you've got it pretty cushy, *and* you're being paid to stay put for three months, so lie low and stay the course."

Easy for you to say. Austin wanted to push back, but how did he confess that his feelings for Kenzie were becoming a problem? Being with her every day, talking, joking, touching, and learning of her deep sorrow, was threatening his ability to remain detached.

"It's necessary, and you know why." The man's raspy tone went kinder. "And remember, you *agreed* to remain in place before you left the city. So just *do* it. And call me if there's something I need to know."

Austin punched off, mulled his lack of options in the dark. The tightrope he walked had grown tauter, trapping him between what he had sworn to do, and what he wanted to do.

Ten

"Here they come," Kenzie said to Austin. They stood outside the stable watching Lani and a family of four walking toward them: Mom, Dad, and kids David and Cami. Oro and Mamie were bareback, wearing halters and lead lines looped around the hitching post.

Lani waved. "Hey! I've got two excited kids here."

"The little girl looks excited, the boy not so much." Austin spoke into Kenzie's ear from the corner of his mouth.

"Horses are big animals and kids are small. Seeing a horse up close can be intimidating, so smile and look enthusiastic." Kenzie was nervous, hoping Mamie wouldn't act up with strangers. Today was important to her. She wanted to help jump-start the Trailblazer program for Lani and Ciana.

At the sound of Lani's voice, Oro's ears pricked forward and he turned his neck toward the newcomers. Mamie flipped one ear toward the approaching people but otherwise showed no interest. The little girl shouted "Horsey!" then broke free of her mother's handhold and ran full speed toward the horses with arms wide open.

"Cami!" her mother yelled. "Stop!"

Austin stepped forward and scooped up the child. "Whoa, little one! Where you going so fast?"

Kenzie's heart wedged in her throat as the child gave Austin a brilliant smile and a hug. "Cami ride horsey!"

Just then, the mother caught up, looking frantic. "Sorry! She's so quick!"

"I got her." He carried Cami closer and let the child lean in and hug Mamie's neck. "No riding today, but you can pet her."

"Cami *love* horsey." The child planted a wet smear of a kiss on Mamie's sleek well-groomed neck.

Lani hurried over, shaking her head. "I should have seen that coming. All Cami talked about in the car was hugging the horsey."

Relieved that Mamie had remained calm during the commotion, Kenzie gave the Gray Lady a treat. "If this didn't spook her, she'll likely be perfect for Trailblazers."

After rounds of introductions, Austin eased Cami into her mother's arms. Both parents chattered enthusiastically, and slowly, David, the eleven-year-old, began to warm to the animals. He stroked Oro, whose coat gleamed golden in the sunlight. "Shiny," Cami said, and combed her fingers through Oro's thick white mane.

"Why don't I show you folks around?" Austin offered.

The group tagged after him and entered the stable, leaving Kenzie and Lani at the hitching post.

"How did he figure I wanted to talk to you alone?" Lani asked, amused.

"He reads minds," Kenzie said, thinking of the many times over the past weeks of their working together when he'd walked into the stable and instantly picked up on her mood. "Probably got a merit badge in it," she added drily.

Although she wasn't privy to the inside joke, Lani laughed. "Well, he was spot-on today. I wanted a few minutes of privacy to give you this." She pulled a thick ivory envelope from her purse with Kenzie's and Austin's names calligraphed in black ink. "A wedding invitation. Dawson and I want both of you to come. Please."

"Oh, you don't have to—"

"I know I don't *have* to, but I *want* to. This is going to be the best day of my life, and I want to share every minute of it surrounded by people I care about. Casual dressy for the ceremony, a big reception at a fabulous venue, great food, cake, and a special DJ! Believe me, my mother and sister have made sure Daddy spares no expense."

Kenzie snickered. "I'd like to come, but I shouldn't speak for Austin." Ever since she'd told Austin about Caroline, she'd felt lighter, more at ease. But although Austin had been kind to her, recently he'd been less talkative, less playful. She read his behavior as creating distance.

"I want *both* of you to come, so ask him as soon as we leave and have him text me. Ciana and Jon and everyone from the pool party will be there. It's not like you won't know anybody. Besides, it's going to be a fabulous wedding!" Lani's brown eyes sparkled.

"I'll talk to him."

"Do you think Mamie will be ready for riding by the end of July?" Lani shifted the subject. "If so, I'd like to begin working with Cami and David when Dawson and I return from our honeymoon. We'll be gone two heavenly weeks."

"It all depends on her body weight and how she takes to a saddle and rider. I'll talk to the vet next time he visits."

When the group left, Austin untied the palomino, telling Kenzie, "I'll walk Oro to the big barn, leave Mamie with you. I think the meet-and-greet went well." Kenzie stood with arms crossed, chewing her bottom lip, the envelope sticking up from her hand. He pointed. "I see my name on that envelope you're holding."

"It's an invite to Lani and Dawson's July wedding."

"Do you want to go?"

She recalled how he'd jumped all over Lani's invitation to the pool party. Not so fast this time. "Yes. I . . . um . . . I've never been to a wedding before."

"I guess the bigger question is, do you want me to come along?"

She studied both their names, so beautifully scripted on the outer envelope, and knew that she'd rather have him with her than go alone. "Yes, but only if you want to."

He felt his balance on the tightrope sway as he struggled with how to best answer. A wedding was certainly no good way to keep distance between them, but when she looked up, her amazing blue eyes melted his resolve. "Then let's do it."

Kenzie rarely opened her laptop, but a glance at the calendar hanging on her kitchen wall one evening reminded her that she needed to boot it up. June 17 was fast approaching. She sighed and set the laptop on the kitchen table. When the machine booted, she pushed the tab to bring up her email account. The screen quickly filled with a plethora of messages, mostly junk, but the ones she'd expected to see—five all together—had been sent over the last two weeks. All from her father. She opened the one sent that morning, punctuated by an *urgent* tag.

Kenzie . . . Please stop ignoring me! You know what's coming up next week. You MUST come home. Please. I can't stress enough how necessary it is for you to be present for this one single day. Your mother isn't doing well, and NEEDS to see her daughter. I know you hate me, but stop punishing her for my sins. Please come home. I'm not asking for me, but for her.

Dad

Tears welled in Kenzie's eyes. She kept seeing Pamela Caine on the cold February day of Caroline's funeral, crumpled and sobbing in her husband's arms. Kenzie had held in her own grief, refusing to break apart at the graveside. She had been driven back to Vanderbilt that night by a friend of her mother's, where she'd thrown herself into classes. Her father had asked for privacy from the media about Caroline, but the request had been ignored, and Kenzie spent days dodging such stupid reporter questions as *How do you feel about the social media aspects of your sister's death?*

Cloistered in her dorm room, she'd called her mother's cell phone and discovered it had been shut down. Likewise, her email account. Avery had erected a protective shield around his wife so that callers would have to go through him with questions. Kenzie was relieved that her mother had a safety net, but it had cut her off, too, and at the time, she didn't want to go through her father to reach her mother. Forcing herself to concentrate on her college classes helped shutter her mind from what had happened, and when the job at Bellmeade was offered, she'd jumped on it. But now she had no recourse except to go home for the one day her father asked of her.

Kenzie felt the dam break as hot tears slowly rolled down her cheeks. She missed her mother terribly, felt guilty because locking Avery out of her life had meant locking out her mother too. And now there was no Caro serving as intermediary. Kenzie buried her face in her hands and wept.

Austin knew something was troubling Kenzie. He could read her moods easily these days, but he also knew that he had to wait for her to open up, because, like Blue, she had to come to him. They were outside under a hot sunlight, bathing Blue—something the big horse liked; plus, Austin's weeks of working in the round pen were paying off. Blue was a whole lot calmer. While Austin had saddled Blue, he had yet to ride the big horse.

Water trickled from the hose on the ground, and Austin

81

kept the soapy sponge moving over Blue's flank. *No playfulness today*, Austin told himself. *Just get the job done.*

Kenzie stepped around the hind end of the big horse. Austin glanced at her but kept silent. She took a shallow breath, said, "I need a favor."

"Sure. What do you need me to do?"

"I want you to come someplace with me on June seventeenth."

"That's day after tomorrow."

She nodded.

"Not a bridal shower, I hope."

The faint edge of her smile showed. "No. I want you to come home with me to Nashville, to the house where I grew up."

An internal alarm went off. "What's up?"

"It's my mother's birthday. Mine too. My father is begging me to come, and . . . and I told him I would. For Mom."

"Wait! You and your mother have birthdays on the same day?"

"Yes. Our birthdays used to be a huge celebration, big parties with family and friends, but now . . . after Caroline . . ." He watched Kenzie's blue eyes shimmer. "I know I have to go see her, be with her on our birthday, and I don't want to go by myself."

"I don't know, Kenzie. . . . It doesn't seem like somewhere I belong. I'm a stranger, and it's a family thing."

"Just me, Mom, and my father. No one else is invited. And I don't want to face the whole day with only the three of us staring at each other. I don't know what I'm walking into. He says Mom's in a bad way. Please, come with me?"

"I'm your shield? Seriously?"

She nodded. "If you don't mind. Dad and I've had problems for a couple of years. About his horses and a trainer," she added quickly, unsure of what Austin might have heard. After all, he was from Virginia, and news of the feud likely hadn't been national news. "I'll tell you all about it anytime you want to listen. So, you will come with me?"

He picked up the hose, ran a stream of water over Blue's withers, flank, and hindquarters. He hesitated, fluctuating between holding back and not wanting to disappoint her.

"I've got your back, Kenzie, but you should tell your dad that I'm coming along. Not everybody likes unexpected company showing up."

Austin took the passenger's seat in Kenzie's high-end SUV, and she got behind the wheel. "Nice ride."

"My high school graduation gift," she said, putting the car in gear and heading down the Bellmeade driveway. The day had turned gray and cloudy, and the air was heavy with the smell of ozone. Rain was coming. On the drive along the winding back roads through low rolling hills toward her family's horse farm, Kenzie explained about the break between herself and her father. Austin saw by the way she gripped the steering wheel that she was dreading the visit. So was he.

When she finished her story, he summed it up. "So you've stayed away from home for almost two years knowing that your father was willing to let this trainer sore his horses in order to win the top prize in Shelbyville. When he fired the trainer, things turned ugly. Is that about right?"

She nodded. "Once Bill's training methods became public knowledge in that news documentary, my father was forced to fire him. Bill blamed the leak on my dad, and when he started making threats against our family, their feud hit the front-page news. Dad had to take out a restraining order." Kenzie paused, taking a breath. "People took sides. Some horse breeders sided with my father, who saw no harm in 'proper' soring, as if there is such a thing, but animal rights people believed Bill and Dad were devils. Bill swore he only did what Dad wanted doing, and Dad swore he didn't know about Bill's abusive methods. I believe both are lying."

"I would think your father would have taken most of the hits, since it was his and the trainer's feud, but were *you* threatened?"

"Believe me, the whole family was guilty by association. The Internet was on fire with hate toward all of us. I mostly ignored the meanness at the time, but after Caroline, I dumped every type of social media you can think of." Kenzie slowed the car.

From his passenger window, Austin saw picturesque white fences stretching along acres of rich green pastureland. She braked and turned into an entranceway between the fencing. Tires crunched on gravel that smoothed into concrete. Atop the crest of a hill he saw a colonial-style white-brick mansion trimmed with black shutters, and a black front door. His jaw dropped. "Home?"

Kenzie parked and turned off the engine. "Home."

Eleven

Austin exited the car, staring up at the mammoth house. "When you told me you grew up on a horse farm, I was thinking more Old McDonald's."

"E-I-E-I-O. This is it."

"And all this land is your family's?" He gestured to a checkerboard of green pastures fenced in white, where horses and foals grazed. In the distance, he saw rooflines of several stables.

"Dad breeds Tennessee walkers. It's a business." She remembered standing beside her father watching the new foals frolic and hearing him claim, "All champions." She had been so proud of him as a child. "Come on, let's get this over with."

They walked to the oversized shiny black front door, decorated with a large wreath of summer flowers. She pushed the bell, and Austin heard it chime musically from somewhere inside. "No key?"

"I left it behind in February."

"You didn't mention I'd be coming with you, did you?" He experienced a sinking sensation.

"Didn't want an argument." Kenzie took hold of Austin's hand just as Avery Caine swung open the door in front of them.

Avery's gaze took her in like a thirsty desert crawler. "Happy birthday, honey-girl." He opened his arms.

She ignored his overture. "Hello, Dad. Where's Mom?"

Avery was a big and handsome man, slimmer and older-looking than when she'd last seen him in February. His hair was steel gray, his eyes the same blue shade as hers. When he saw Austin, his eyes widened, then narrowed. "What's this?"

"Not a what, a who," Kenzie said. "Meet Austin Boyd, the man who helps me with the rescue horses at Bellmeade." Kenzie shoved her and Austin's way past Avery and into the cavernous foyer.

Austin stole a quick glance around. Twin elegant staircases covered with ivory carpet curved upward on either side of the foyer to a landing where the cloudy gray sky showed through a massive round window. A glittering chandelier of cut crystal hung dramatically from a high ceiling painted a pale rose.

"Pleased to meet you, sir." Austin held out his hand.

Avery reluctantly shook hands, his expression as cold as the marble floor of the foyer. "This is a family event. No one else has been invited."

"Austin's my guest. Please treat him like one," Kenzie insisted. "It's my birthday too, you know."

"I can wait in the car," Austin offered.

"No, you won't." Her eyes challenged Avery's as she spoke. "We stay together. Now can we please see Mom?"

"She's in the sunroom." Avery turned on his heel and Kenzie followed, fighting to steady her thudding heart. Coming here was much more stressful than she'd expected. Happy childhood memories faded into the darkness of February, blurring into a grief-edged montage: The coldness of the day she'd arrived home, the sounds of weeping, sobbing, and questions from police detectives that faded into footfalls of mortuary attendants across Persian rugs as Caroline's body left the house on a wheeled cart. Later, the cloying smell of countless floral arrangements and sounds of classical music melting into darkened corners of a house without light.

Becoming dizzy, Kenzie clutched Austin's arm. He looped his arm around her waist, steadied her. Avery never glanced back, but stopping at the house's spacious sunroom, he told Austin, "Please, family only."

Austin slipped Kenzie's arm over her father's and stepped away. Because Kenzie's knees felt weak, she made no objection. Her mother sat in the heirloom slipper chair of her great-grandmother, its fabric faded by time. Avery walked Kenzie over and stooped. "Darlin', Kenzie's home."

Pamela Caine was impeccably dressed in white linen slacks, white silk blouse, and simple white sandals. Her hair and makeup were beautifully done, but Kenzie clearly saw that since February, her mother—always trim and fit—had lost too much weight. Pamela's smile was soft and welcoming, but seemed somehow disconnected and muddled, her eyes unfocused. *Drugs?* The thought was startling.

Kenzie kissed her mother's cheeks, knelt, and took her hand. "Happy birthday, Mom."

"It's been so long! Why didn't you come home sooner?" Her mother's eyes teared and Kenzie felt a knot in her throat. "Let me look at you. Oh my! You look so pretty."

From her scant wardrobe selections, Kenzie had chosen to wear her long skirt and peasant blouse. "You look pretty, too, Mom."

"Happy birthday, dear Kenzie. I've missed you so."

The weight of sadness in the words twisted Kenzie's insides. "Missed you too, Mama."

Pamela brightened. "Avery has set up our party outdoors, on the veranda."

Kenzie glanced at the double doors leading to the tile-covered terrace that stretched across the back of the house, a completely furnished space with an outdoor kitchen, fireplace, and large-screen television. *All the creature comforts.* "Then let's go have a party." She stood and held out her hand, but her mother reached for her father's.

Kenzie stepped away, took a few deep breaths in an effort to calm her heartbeat, which has gone erratic. "Mom, I brought a friend with me."

"I . . . I thought it'd be, well . . . just the three of us?" Pamela looked confused, hesitant, somewhat fearful.

Avery leaned in to his wife, patted her hand hooked

through his arm. "A man she works with. It'll be all right, honey."

Once out on the terrace, and after introductions, Pamela settled and turned into the familiar gracious hostess Kenzie had known growing up. "Lovely to meet you, Austin, and for such a festive occasion." Pamela gazed tenderly at Kenzie. "Twenty-one today. How the time flies."

Her mother's eyes grew misty once more, and Kenzie knew that Pamela's thoughts had turned to Caroline, the daughter who wasn't present and never would be again. "Mom, why don't you show Austin the koi pond before rain comes? I bragged to him about how you named every fish in it."

Austin cut his eyes toward her but recovered quickly and held out his arm. "If you don't mind, I'd really like to see it."

Pamela took his arm. "Of course, it would be my pleasure. Just across the lawn at the far side of the flowerbed. Koi ponds are very peaceful."

Kenzie watched them walk away, and when they were out of earshot, spun toward her father. "What is she taking? She's not herself at all. How much weight has she lost? She's way too thin."

"Slow down. She's under a doctor's care, sees a therapist twice a week. The pills are for depression. If you kept in better touch, you'd know all this." Avery's comeback was quick and bit her because it was true. "You never came home after your semester ended. She looked for you and I had to make excuses about your new *job*." He said the word contemptuously. "And when you *do* show up, you're dragging some poor chump who works with you."

Kenzie's chin quivered. "It's too hard being here."

"Well, it's pretty hard living here too. Place is like a mausoleum without—" His voice caught. "She won't even go inside Caroline's room. Looks just the same as it always did. Like she might come home any minute."

"You go inside?"

He gave a brusque nod. "Sometimes, late at night after your mother's asleep. She sleeps a lot," he added wistfully. "I sit on the bed and stare at all Caro's messiness. She never picked up a thing, as you know. Stuff just lies where she dropped it." He paused, gathering himself. "But I feel better when I'm inside her space. Her room smells all powdery and sweet . . . like she always did. I look at that big ballerina painting hanging on the wall and the old photos taped to her mirror of kids I don't even know. It's like she just stepped out for a minute."

Kenzie's vision blurred with tears. "Are pictures of *him* still there?"

"I removed every trace of that vermin." Avery's jaw clenched. "I'd kill him with my bare hands if I thought it could bring her back."

A warm breeze pushed the scent of impending rain through the terrace. "He took a scholarship to Alabama," Kenzie said.

"I heard." Avery's eyes turned rock hard. "If there'd been any way I could have held him accountable . . ." He let the words of deep regret trail into silence.

"He covered his tracks well, and knowing and proving are two different things." Kenzie's heart twisted with unfulfilled revenge. "We did all we could, Daddy."

Avery caressed Kenzie with his gaze. "Nice to hear you call me 'Daddy' again."

She stiffened, remembering that she was angry about him soring horses. The wound wasn't as deep and fresh as it had been before Caroline's death, but it still felt tender. "I'll keep in better touch with Mom, and I'll come home before I return to Vandy in August."

"We're back," Austin called as he and Pamela stepped onto the terrace, arm in arm. "Beautiful fish."

Avery rushed to take his wife's arm. "How about us having a party?"

Pamela smiled, and Kenzie could see that the time her mother spent with Austin had lifted her spirits. Austin *did* have a way about him that made a person want to lean on him, trust him.

The four of them went to a table where all the trappings of a party were laid out on a festive polka-dot tablecloth— sandwiches on a sterling silver platter and covered with a glass dome, a silver carafe of coffee, china teacups, crystal goblets circling a pitcher of sweet tea. Small glass plates and sterling silver flatware rounded out the ensemble.

The table's centerpiece was a bejeweled candelabra displaying two tiers of decorated cupcakes with fluffy pink frosting. The top tier held a cluster of gift bags. Kenzie reached into the pocket of her skirt and brought out a small box and put it with the other gifts. In it was a gold charm she'd bought at Christmas for her mother's bracelet. Looking at the gift was a painful reminder of her choice not to visit then, as well as the regret and heartache in the months that followed.

"Very nice," Kenzie said, knowing that Avery would have had the party catered. She also saw that the table setting pleased her mother, a lover of old-Southern elegance.

Conversation flowed around Kenzie's work with the rescue horses, and when it lagged, Austin offered a tidbit, an observation, a funny story. Somehow having him filling up the fourth chair at the table made the party bearable, and again Kenzie was thankful that he'd come with her. When presents were opened, Pamela admired the gold charm, said she'd have it put on her bracelet "right away." Avery locked a glittering diamond bracelet around her wrist.

Kenzie opened her gift bag and discovered a gold necklace with a diamond horseshoe pendant and the number 21 in chips of blue sapphires across the U-shape.

"You like it?" Avery asked.

Her father would have certainly had it specially made for her. "Pretty fancy for a girl mucking stalls," she said, slipping it around her neck, fingers fumbling with the clasp.

"Let me." Austin jumped up. His fingers felt warm on the nape of her neck and goose bumps skittered up her back. "There," he said, standing back.

She fingered the pendant. "Thank you. It's beautiful."

"Perfectly lovely," said Pamela, and turning to Avery, added, "I believe I'd like to go up to our room now. I'm tired, and so I beg you all to excuse me."

Kenzie saw the strain of the day clearly on her mother's face. Everybody stood and Kenzie wrapped her arms around her mother, swallowed the thickness in her throat. She wanted her mother again, that vibrant woman she'd known growing up. "I love you, Mama."

"And I love you," Pamela whispered in Kenzie's ear. "And I miss you very much."

"I promise to call and come visit you more often."

Her mother's hand slipped from hers. Avery, holding his wife close, told Kenzie and Austin, "I'll sit with her for a while upstairs. You don't have to rush off. Stay as long as you can." The words were more of a plea than an invitation.

In the quiet aftermath of her parents' departure, Kenzie felt numb, as if the grayness of the sky had migrated inside her. "There's not much to do around here, so we can leave."

Sensing that she was torn between staying and going, Austin pointed to the farthest end of the sloping lawn beyond the terrace at a building that resembled a miniaturized duplicate of the main house. "Is that a pool house back there? I wouldn't mind if you showed me around this place. It's different from Bellmeade, and I'd like the two-dollar tour," he added with a grin.

"Our horses—"

"Will be fine for a few more hours." He and Kenzie had put them into their stalls before heading out for the day because of the sweltering weather. "They're safe, and I'm in no hurry."

Kenzie quickly realized that neither was she.

Twelve

Kenzie set off across the green lawn and Austin fell into step beside her. The building's front door opened into a large three-sided room filled with patio furniture arranged for conversation around a fire pit. A changing room stood at one end, along with stacks of baskets filled with pool floats and water games. The missing back wall allowed access to a paver-style deck surrounding a pool lined with bright Moroccan tiles. Low and high diving boards and a water slide hung over the blue water's deep end.

"Impressive," he said, walking to the pool's edge. "Looks like pool heaven for kids."

"We loved the pool. Mom sat under that umbrella in a lounger." Kenzie gestured to a table with a folded green canvas umbrella that she could tell hadn't yet been opened for the summer. "This is where Caro learned to dive. She was good too. Tried out for the community swim team in seventh grade and made it."

"And you?"

"I was never much of a swimmer, but I cheered for her at meets." As Kenzie glanced around, she saw that the area looked shipshape and well kept, ready for a family who would not come again. So many summer days spent poolside, now left desolate and devoid of happy children.

"There was no community pool in the boonies where I lived, but we had a creek nearby." Austin pulled her into the present. "That's where me and a bunch of rowdy friends swam. Braveheart loved the water. It came as high as his underbelly in places, and we conquered many a water dragon"—he paused for dramatic effect—"dragonfly," he finished with a grin. "Sometimes when the guys rode their horses over, we'd pack food, take long rides, build campfires, and spend the night. Have you ever slept under the stars in a sleeping bag?"

"Never. We camped out in the pool house."

"Wow, you really roughed it," he mused, glancing over his shoulder at the luxurious room. She jabbed him in the arm. He hooked his thumbs on the back pockets of his khakis. "By the way, I enjoyed the birthday party. And for the record, and at the risk of you shoving me in the pool, your dad didn't come across as an ogre. He seemed happy to see you, and it looked like you just showing up made his day. Just sayin'."

"My father and his trainer abused horses. I can't forgive him for that." Yet even as she said the words, the old hurt and anger was not as raw and ragged as it had once been. In the familiar surroundings of her family home, and with her and Avery's brief conversation about Caroline, her ire had cooled, and her perspective subtly shifted. Her father's concern for her mother was etched in the lines of his face, and Kenzie clearly saw that he grasped Pamela's fragility. On this day, Kenzie and her father had been more comrades than adversaries.

Austin bent, plucked a yellow dandelion poking between two pavers, and offered it to Kenzie with a grin. "I liked your mom too. She treated me like a welcome guest instead of an interloper. I'm glad I had a chance to meet her."

Kenzie toyed with the flower. "Our family was always the focus of Mom's life. She doted on us. She went to every one of Caroline's ballet classes and swim events, and came to every riding competition of mine and Dad's. When I was growing up, she and I rode together and had long girl talks. Her horse, Buttercup, was a gift from Dad." Kenzie's voice filled with nostalgia. "Why, I'll bet Mom hasn't ridden ever since—" Kenzie stopped abruptly, heading off dark memories.

Covering the awkward moment, Austin said, "Why don't we continue the tour?"

"The stables are on the far side of that pasture, and we shouldn't leave without you seeing Blaze, the grand champion. We'll cut across the side lawn and climb over the fence rail." She pointed and they started across the lawn just as the skies opened. "This way!" she shouted, changing course.

Together they ran toward a freestanding white gazebo positioned a short distance from the main house and arrived breathless and laughing. "We should have seen that coming!"

The octagon-shaped gazebo had half walls lined with hinged boxes for seating and a plank floor. "Nice," he said, making a circle to take in the view of the edge of the main house's terrace, the pool area, and a swath of flower gardens.

"Daddy had it built for Caro and me. Told us it was our dollhouse where could play on rainy days." She began to lift hinged tops and pull out floor cushions and old blankets, handing them to Austin. "We used to pretend it was a castle and we were prisoners, and a prince was coming to rescue us."

Together she and Austin spread old quilts and mounds of pillows on the floor. They sat and he asked, "Any princes ever show up?"

"Not once." She smiled and lay down, resting her head on a pink pillow. "But we played with dolls and ate a lot of lunches out here waiting for them." Summer rain pattered on the roof, and soon the space grew cozy. "Look up," she said.

He stretched out beside her and on the gazebo's ceiling saw four painted unicorns, their magical horns sparkling with glitter paint. He laughed. "Unicorns? Seriously? You lived on a horse farm with *real* horses."

"I preferred the real horses, but Caro wanted unicorns, so Dad commissioned the artwork. She loved fairy tales and Disney movies, and was also four years younger than me, so she held on to the dream of Prince Charming a whole lot longer." Kenzie stopped abruptly, as childhood images of Caroline tumbled through her head.

Her sister's wild frizz of strawberry-blond hair, wide blue eyes, and plump cheeks, her favorite doll tucked under her arm in a headlock.

"But why won't you play dolls with me, Kenz?"

"Because I don't like dolls anymore. I'm too old for dolls, and so are you. You're acting like a baby!"

"I should have been kinder to her." Kenzie whispered the words, forgetting that for Austin, her confession would make little sense. She cleared her throat and offered a self-conscious shrug.

Sensing she needed a diversion, Austin said, "So tell me, how did you make the leap from unicorns into the harsh world of reality?"

"You really want to know?" He waited for her to say something flippant. "My first wake-up call came when I was twelve and my doctors told us that my heart and blood vessels were damaged and scarred from Kawasaki disease. That's when I stopped believing in princes and unicorns."

Hearing the serious tone in her voice, he rose up on his elbow. "But you told me you take medicine for your heart."

"Medicine slows the process, but it doesn't fix the problem. Plus, even at twelve, I didn't want anyone to think of me as ill or impaired. I didn't feel like I was broken. Why act like it? I decided I'd be strong and fearless. I became an anything-you-can-do-I-can-do-better kind of person. Having a crappy heart condition wasn't going to slow me down. So far, it hasn't."

"Was your dad your role model? He seems like a take-charge kind of guy."

"Back then he was, but when I was eighteen, part two of my reality check slapped me in the face. I discovered the truth about him and how he mistreated horses."

"Technically, his trainer mistreated his horses."

Kenzie gave him a withering glance.

"I know it's none of my business, but it's obvious your dad cares about you, and yet you steer clear of him. Two years now?"

She held Austin's blue-green eyes, the blue gone in the murky daylight as if by magic. "You think me unforgiving, don't you?"

"I'm just commenting. I know how much you love horses, but still . . ." He let the sentence hang, knowing by speaking out he'd taken a risk.

"You're right—it's none of your business." She said the words softly, then added, "But please, I want you to understand something: I *love* my father. He's given me the best life possible, and I'm grateful. So, yes, I love him. I just don't like him very much."

Rain pattered on the roof, soft as teardrops. Austin switched gears. "So tell me, how was your sister different from you, the girl who loved horses?"

"Caroline was tiny, pretty, and girly, much more like Mom. They liked doing the same things together—shopping, arts and crafts, that kind of stuff." Kenzie wrinkled her nose. "I liked the horses, the feel of wind on my face when I rode, the control I had over a thousand-pound animal to make him change gaits and turn on a dime with a squeeze of my knees and a tug of the reins. I want to keep that feeling of power for as long as I'm able."

He felt an uptick in his pulse. What was she so afraid of? What *wasn't* she telling him? "You work as hard as any man I've ever known," he offered. "Plus, you're better-looking."

Her blue eyes, fringed by long lashes, pulled at him. From the beginning, he'd found her intriguing, physically beautiful, emotionally wary, and cloaked in a thick shield of self-protection. But today she'd pulled back the curtain on her psyche, and Austin was struck by a wave of tenderness. She hadn't braided her hair, and the damp strands fanned out on the pillow in feathery waves. His gaze drifted along her high cheekbones, the curve of her jaw, the dimple in her chin, then stopped cold on the horseshoe pendant nestled in the hollow of her throat. Instantly, he realized he'd let down his guard. Despite all his self-lectures, he'd almost slipped up. Kenzie Caine was off-limits in every way.

He jumped up. "Looks like the rain shower's over." His tone was gruff, curt. "It's getting late, and as much as I'd like to see your father's prize stallion, I think we'd better get back." He stood and began picking up the pillows and quilts and stuffing them into the seat boxes.

Disoriented, she scrambled up beside him. Without warning, his tender expression had transformed and been replaced with steely indifference, like a mask set firmly in place. "Let me help," she said as the hinged lids banged shut.

"I've got this," he insisted without glancing at her.

She backed off, leaving him to finish the job.

By the time they arrived at Bellmeade and were with the horses, Austin had returned to his affable, wisecracking self. Kenzie, however, remained baffled. Lying beside him, on pillows and quilts that smelled of laundry soap and lavender from her childhood, surrounded by the soft sounds of falling rain, she had shared memories effortlessly, something she would not have done even days before. And when he'd leaned over her, listening to her every word and looking into her eyes, she'd felt a fluttering sensation in her heart, an acceleration in her pulse unrelated to any medical strictures levied on her heart issues. *This* heartbeat had come with another stirring. *Desire.*

When his gaze had lingered on her eyes, her lips, her cheeks and throat, she'd thought he would dip his mouth to hers, kiss her. And her thudding heart had told her that was what she wanted too. She'd waited, breathless with anticipation, but instead he had pulled away, begun cleaning up, and the fire inside her swiftly died. During the drive home, she'd felt foolish, like a schoolgirl with a silly crush, but now that they were working side by side, they had returned to their familiar roles—Austin talkative and helpful, Kenzie focused and dedicated.

They fed the horses in their stalls, and with the rain now over, Kenzie said, "They've been cooped up all day. Let's snap on lead lines and take them for a walk."

They led the three horses around the pasture in an easy amble, Kenzie with Mamie, Austin putting himself between

Sparkle and Blue and following silently. The rain had rinsed the air, leaving it clean, clear, and scented with wet grass. Above them, the sky was streaked with pinks and reds that promised a sunny tomorrow.

"I guess we should call it a day," Kenzie said as they locked down the horses for the night. She'd been on an emotional roller coaster since sunrise, and revisiting the past, facing her father for the first time since Caroline's funeral, and worrying over her mother had been draining. The cravings she'd experienced in the gazebo for Austin had also confused and disoriented her. She'd long shied away from dating relationships, and certainly didn't need or want a summer fling. "Thanks for coming with me today."

"Anytime." She headed toward her bungalow. "I'll walk with you. It's dark."

"No need. I know my way, even in the dark."

"Happy birthday," he called after her.

She gave a wave of her hand and kept moving, never once looking behind her. Never once seeing that she was followed.

Thirteen

Preparations for the Fourth of July party at Bellmeade began on July 1. Barbeque smokers and grills were rolled out and set up on the cement parking pad alongside the old barn. A large yellow tent was erected in the center of the front yard near the main house. Inside the canvas enclosure, chairs and tables were assembled, and a fleet of fans stood like sentries along the canvas walls to cool guests. For days, the smell of smoked pork, beef, and chicken hung in the summer air. On the morning of the Fourth, caterers appeared with kettles of side dishes to set on serving tables draped in red checkered tablecloths.

By noon, guests began arriving and parking along both sides of the frontage road, then either walking up the long tree-lined walk or riding in a golf cart provided at the front of the driveway. Kenzie watched a parade of people through the front window of her bungalow. She recalled large parties her parents had given when she was growing up, but never on this scale.

She'd come in from the back after she and Austin had completed morning duties with the rescue horses and had showered and changed into navy blue shorts and red top, the shirttails tied in a knot at her waist. She ditched her boots for red sandals, dabbed on makeup, and tied her blond hair in a ponytail with a bright white ribbon. She spritzed on a whiff of honeysuckle fragrance and headed toward the tent.

Ciana, standing outside the tent greeting people, offered Kenzie a sunny smile. "You look lovely! So glad you decided to come."

"Would have been hard to *not* come," Kenzie said with a laugh. "Looks as if half the county is showing up."

"People look forward to this, and everyone needs relief from the heat. We were going to have some fireworks after dark, but with the grass and trees so dry, we decided against it." Ciana glanced skyward, then back at Kenzie. "Today's going to be another scorcher. Weatherman says high nineties."

"The pasture grass is more brown than green these days. Thanks for the extra hay. We were running low."

The light rain on her birthday had not quelled Tennessee's ongoing drought, and trees and grass were dry tinder. Horses were expected to graze all summer, cutting down on feed bills, but with the drought, every horse at Bellmeade needed additional hay.

"You're welcome. Buying hay is our best option to keep the horses healthy. So, how are your horses coming along? Last time I saw them, they were looking good."

"Mamie's almost ready for Lani's Trailblazers program, and Austin's working exclusively with Blue. He says Blue only tolerates him, but I think they both like each other more than they let on."

Ciana laughed. "Good to hear. How about Sparkle?"

"She's been doing well, but she's been off her feed the past couple of days. Seems restless today, roaming the pasture, pawing the ground." Ciana looked thoughtful, making Kenzie's heart kick up a beat. "You think something could be wrong?"

Austin was nursing a beer, observing Kenzie and Ciana from a distance. While he couldn't hear what they were saying, when he saw a look of concern cross Kenzie's face, he went over to the two women. "Big happy crowd. What's up with you two?"

"I was telling Ciana about Sparkle, how she isn't eating."

"Yeah, she hardly touched her grain this morning."

Ciana's forehead furrowed. "Let me grab Jon and we'll go take a look at her."

Kenzie mentally revisited the morning with Sparkle. Caring for the three horses had become such a routine that she'd not given Sparkle's morning behavior enough scrutiny. What had she missed? Ciana returned with Jon and the four of them went to the rescue pasture, arriving in time to see Sparkle rolling on the pasture ground, feet kicking the air.

"Colic!" Jon and Ciana said in unison.

"I'll call Perry." Jon whipped out his cell phone.

Dread knifed through Kenzie. When she'd worked with Kaye, the vet had discussed the serious problem with Kenzie, but this was the first time she'd ever seen a horse suffering from it.

Austin saw Kenzie's face go pale. "Are you all right?"

"She acted restless all yesterday . . . one of the first signs. I missed it. Did you notice?"

He shook his head. "Sorry, no. But I never had that problem with my horse."

"I should have caught this, or at least suspected that something was wrong."

Ciana shook her head. "Don't take any heat for this, Kenzie. The early signs are easy to miss." Ciana was being kind, but Kenzie felt guilty. She was in charge. This shouldn't have happened.

Jon pocketed his phone. "Doc's on a lake fishing, so he's over an hour away, but there are some things we can do until he gets here. Bring her in," he said to Austin. "Tie her in the round pen to minimize head movement and we'll start pouring mineral oil down her throat. Then we'll walk her, and that will help distract her from the pain in her gut."

"We'll take care of her," Austin said. "You have a lot of people expecting to see you at your party."

Jon slapped his forehead. "Oh yeah, forgot about that."

Ciana looped her arm through Jon's. "He's right, Jon.

Let them handle this. As soon as Doc gets here, I'll send him back. Come on, cowboy."

Jon grimaced but agreed. "There's a gallon of mineral oil on a shelf inside the stable for the mustangs. Get all you can down Sparkle, making sure she swallows as much as possible. She won't like it, but it'll help. It'll be messy too," he added, glancing at Kenzie's pretty outfit.

"I have a change of clothes in the tack room. You two go be with your guests."

"If you need help before Perry arrives, come get me," Jon called as Ciana dragged him away.

The summer sun beat down, and heat radiated up from the hard-packed red dirt as Sparkle pawed the earth and ducked her head to try nipping her belly, another symptom of colic pain. Austin put his hands on Kenzie's shoulders and turned her to face him. In the bright sunlight, his eyes looked blue, ringed with a hint of green. "It's going to be okay, Kenz. We'll do this together. She's going to recover. Why don't you put her in the pen while I get the mineral oil?"

Worried, holding her bottom lip between her teeth, she saw that Austin had also dressed for the party. "You should change your clothes."

"I have old clothes stashed in the tack room. You go ahead and change while I'm gone."

"Sounds like a plan. Now go."

He saluted. "Yes, ma'am."

Jon hadn't lied when he said getting a gallon of mineral oil down a horse would be messy. Sparkle didn't take one bit to being force-fed the viscous liquid and fought against every swallow. Austin poured the oil in increments into the horse's mouth and pushed Sparkle's head upward while Kenzie massaged her long neck to force the liquid down, all the while talking and trying to soothe the anxious animal. By the time they were finished, all three of them were coated with an oily film. At about that time, Dr. Perry showed up.

He looked at them and chuckled. "Whooie! I see you've already done the hard part. Let me check her out." They calmed the horse while he checked her gums for the symptomatic bluish tinge and ran his hands along Sparkle's swollen, distended belly. He took the mare's temperature and listened to her heartbeat and gut sounds with a stethoscope. With the exam complete, Perry said, "I think you caught the problem early. A good thing. I've seen horses die from severe colic."

Kenzie, still angry at herself for missing Sparkle's symptoms, was relieved by Perry's words. "Sorry you had to come out on your holiday."

"No problem. Fish weren't biting anyway."

"Now what?" Austin asked.

"That mineral oil may take a while to do the job, so keep checking on her. In fact, I suggest one of you plan on spending the night with her. Walk her every few hours, but when she's tired, put her in the stall so she can lie down if she wants. I'll recheck her in the morning." He gave Kenzie a big grin. "For what it's worth, I saw the other two out in the pasture, and I remember what they looked like the first time I examined them." He settled his hat on his head. "You've done a good job with these horses. You should be proud to put them up for adoption."

When the vet was gone, Austin told Kenzie, "Look, I don't mind staying the night with her. Clean up and put on that pretty outfit again. Go to the party."

"Me? Sparkle is *my* responsibility and I messed up. I can't go *party*. But you should go have a good time. Honestly, I don't mind spending the night with her."

"Whaaat? And let you take all the credit when she poops? Not happening! But since you won't leave, we'll *both* stay all night."

Kenzie shook her head. "You're being stubborn." She added a smile, because it was now only midafternoon, making for a long wait with a sick horse before the coming sunrise. "And I appreciate your offer, thank you."

"So you're on board with us spending the night together?"

"My pulse is racing with anticipation," she deadpanned. They laughed together.

"Teamwork." He took the rope attached to Sparkle's halter. "I'll walk her first."

"And why don't I grab us some food from the feast in the tent while you do."

"You sure you want to go there looking like that?"

She looked down at her work clothes smeared with oil and dust stirred up in the round pen. Even her braid felt slick and dirty. She groaned, "Good point. Neither of us look our best to be seen by the whole town. Why don't I call Ciana and ask if someone will bring us some food?"

"Good thinking." He moved Sparkle from the pen toward the pasture, yelling out, "And ask for ribs. Lots of ribs. With hot sauce."

Kenzie went inside the stable and made the call. After talking to Ciana, she found an old towel and wiped off the oil residue, mulling over how much she had come to depend on Austin. He certainly shouldered the bulk of the physical labor, which she appreciated, but he had also tempted her away from the grief that had held her hostage for so long. Day by day, inch by inch, he'd chipped away at her shields— protective shields she'd set in place long before ever losing Caroline. Necessary shields. Kenzie believed she had two hearts. One she couldn't control. Another she could.

She watched Austin lead Sparkle around the pasture, the pace slow and steady. Kenzie had worked closely with this man for almost two months, and during that time he'd found a place within her second heart. He had a killer smile, eyes that changed colors, and a streak of kindness a mile wide. But when the horses were healthy and adoptable, when this summer was over, Austin would leave on his journey toward law school, and she would return to Vanderbilt to chase her own dream. She and Austin Boyd were on different paths, with separate life plans and destinies. They would go their separate ways. Until that happened, all she needed to do was fence off her second heart, guard it, and not let him in.

Fourteen

"Food's on its way," Kenzie called to Austin from outside the door of Sparkle's stall. "Why don't you bring her in for a rest?"

From the far side of the pasture, Austin gave her a thumbs-up and headed toward the stable, leading Sparkle, her head drooping, eyes half closed. While he'd been outside in the sweltering heat, Kenzie had spread fresh straw inside the stall to make the horse more comfortable. At the hitching post, Austin looped the rope and Kenzie wiped Sparkle's damp flank with a towel. "Poor thing. She's really hurting."

"I'm sure the oil will do the trick by morning, and she'll feel a whole lot better."

"I know!" Kenzie snapped her fingers. "We can give her a sponge bath from a bucket of water. It could help her feel better." Drought conditions restricted the use of water, so the horses hadn't been bathed with a hose in a while, but a bucket bath was doable.

Just then, one of Jon's men, Clyde, rounded the corner towing a wheeled ice chest and calling out, "Room service."

"Party crasher," Austin joked. Clyde let his gaze roam over Kenzie's body, and Austin immediately stepped in front of her and took the handle of the chest. "I got this. Thanks."

"Just wonderin' why you're getting special treatment from the boss."

"Sick horse," Kenzie said, emerging from around Austin's back, her arms crossed, her gaze cool. "Colic."

Clyde let out a whooping laugh that startled Sparkle enough to jerk against the rope. "A fine way to spend the Fourth! Party's hoppin' and band's tunin' up for dancin'."

Austin settled the horse and shot Clyde a stony glare. "And thank you for your concern about our sick horse. Now why don't you go have another drink before this horse lets go and you step in it."

Kenzie gave Austin a smile that said "Good one!"

Clyde glowered, stepped away from Sparkle's hindquarters. "No need to be unsociable."

"No need for you to hang around," Austin said.

Clyde gave a curt nod and stalked off, grousing under his breath.

"I don't think he likes you very much," Kenzie said in a singsong voice.

"Feeling's mutual. He might be a good wrangler, but he's pretty much a jerk. Best to stay clear of him."

Kenzie shrugged, then turned toward the horse. "Let's put Sparkle in her stall before we eat. She may want to lie down. We can give her a sponge bath afterward."

"Good suggestion. Especially the eating part."

He shut Sparkle in her stall while Kenzie busied herself setting up a card table and two folding chairs. She opened the ice chest and burst out laughing. "Ciana brought the party to us. Enough food to feed a small army, and decorations too."

Kenzie spread a red-checked cloth over the table and set a bright blue plastic vase stuffed with sparklers and American flags in the table's center. She set the table for two with plastic ware, plates, and napkins and unloaded multiple containers. Minutes later their plates were heaped with a Southern food festival of pulled pork and chicken, spare ribs, baked beans, slaw, green beans, and fresh corn bread.

"This will be a July Fourth long remembered," Austin said as they ate. "Not exactly the kind of fireworks I expected."

"Are you whining?"

"Me? Whine? Never. Just making small talk."

"No, it sounds like whining to me." Kenzie offered a smug smile and leaned back in her chair. "Careful, there are brownies down in that cooler, and I'm boss around here."

"Are you threatening to withhold dessert from me, a loyal employee?"

"No, just making small talk."

Austin pushed aside his plate, holding a pile of bones, crossed his arms. "Am I gonna have to file a report with HR? Pretty sure the department will take my side."

Sparkle snorted in discomfort, cutting off the banter. Austin pushed back his chair. "I'll walk her again before dessert."

"No, it's my turn." Kenzie went to the stall, urged the horse to her feet, and led her outside to the pasture where Blue and Mamie stood, heads down, swishing away flies with their tails. Heat poured down from the sun and up from the ground. *Too hot for man or beast,* Kenzie thought as she walked. The food she'd eaten lay like a lead weight in her stomach. She felt woozy and light-headed, her heart racing. Taking in gulps of air, she stumbled to the stable, managed to get Sparkle inside, and got herself out of the stall on wobbly knees.

Austin, putting away food containers, said, "That was a short walk." He looked up, saw she was in trouble. Rushing to her side, he gripped her elbows. "Whoa! You feeling all right? Come sit."

"A little . . . dizzy. The heat." She fought for breath.

She looked pale, felt clammy to his touch. He got her to a chair, where she felt the breeze from a fan. "I found this hiding in the utility room behind some old horse blankets." He grabbed ice from the food chest, rubbed it along the back of her neck and down her arms with one hand and filled a red plastic cup with ice and water with his other. "Drink this . . . small sips."

She sipped and then held the plastic cup against her forehead, where water droplets cooled her skin. "Thanks. I just . . . got dizzy. . . ." As the ice melted, Austin stroked wet palms across her throat and the nape of her neck, then along her arms and wrists, her pulse points. She closed her eyes, basking in the feel of cold ice, moving air, and Austin's hands. His hands. Her eyes snapped open. She moved to elude his touch. "I—I'm okay now. Truly." He crouched in front of her, a worried look on his face.

"Are you sure? Your color's better. Still dizzy?"

She took a long, slow slug of water to assuage thirst, to regain equilibrium. When she lowered the cup, she smiled to reassure him. "Honest, the ice and water did the trick. I'm fine." The concern on his face tugged on her. She glanced away. "I think we should bring the other two horses inside. Let's give all three of them sponge baths. I think it's the kindest thing we can do."

He tipped his head, considering her suggestion. Sponge baths for three horses would take time and energy. They had the time, but he was afraid she would overtax herself. "It's a good idea, but how about we wait a bit? With daylight lasting so much longer, we'll have plenty of light later to do the job. And so long as the sun's out today, I'll walk Sparkle." She started to rise, but he gently pushed her down. "I'll bring the horses in; you sit."

Her legs felt rubbery, and she didn't want to fold in front of him, so she remained in the chair. "They'll need water."

"I'll handle it." Austin rounded up the other two horses and shut them into their stalls, made sure each had buckets of fresh water, then returned to Kenzie's side. "I also have an idea. Why don't we go to your place and take quick showers? Not sure that mineral oil bath we took is doing either of us any good."

Kenzie stood under the stream of barely lukewarm water, relishing the velvet feel of it on her skin. She rinsed shampoo from her hair and languished a moment longer before turning off the stream. Feeling thoroughly clean, she stepped from behind the curtain, grabbed a towel, and wrapped it around her body. She wiped her hand across the mirror and gazed at her reflection, searching for any aftermath of her heart episode, saw none. She'd left Austin on the screen porch waiting for his turn to shower. She'd invited him into the air-conditioning, but he'd refused. "I'm too sticky and nasty to sit on your furniture. I'll wait here."

She went into her bedroom and dressed in a baggy white T-shirt and cutoff jean shorts. Toweling her hair, she emerged on the porch. "Next."

He had been thumbing his cell phone, but stood and drank her in with his eyes. "That was fast."

"Just conserving water!"

Her face glowed. Her skin, the color of pale gold, looked soft and supple, her every movement fluid, graceful as a dancer's. It was all he could do to keep from touching her. "I've been listening to music from the tent. Sounds like a real Western bash."

She cocked her ear and, recognizing the tune, hummed. "Not the day we planned, is it? Sorry we're missing the fun."

"Hey! What could be more fun than a constipated horse?"

The sun glowed low and red-orange over the tree line in the back of her yard. Their gazes locked, held a moment too long. "Better get to it," he said, breaking the connection. He scooped up the shirt and jeans meant for the party and took a wide berth around her. He paused at the door. "It'll be cooler if you wait for me inside, you know."

"But my hair will dry quicker out here." She flashed her pretty smile, sat, stretched her long legs in front of her. "The shower was a great idea, but I want to check on the horses."

"Don't go without me."

"Wouldn't think of it."

Austin stood under the water, washing off the film of oil with a bar of soap, the aroma of her shampoo assailing his senses. He kept seeing her leaving the stall weaving, her face the color of milk. For all her earlier insistence that she could work as hard as anyone, today he'd seen her fragility. As his hands had stroked and cooled her heated skin, he'd felt the erratic thumping of her blood coursing in her throat, temples, and wrists. *Worrisome.* The picture shifted to her coming onto the porch, cheeks glowing, eyes bright and sparkling. Two Kenzies—one guarded and turned inward, the other incredibly open and beautiful. *Desirable.* He switched the water from warm to cold, letting it stream over his head and body until he shivered, hoping to rinse away her image from his brain. Do. Not. Touch.

When he returned to the porch, she was replaiting her hair. "Almost done."

He watched, fascinated, as her fingers artfully intertwined three separate sections of hair into a single braid.

She picked up a scrunchie from her lap and wound it around the small hank of hair at the bottom. Her simple, graceful movements looked incredibly sexy. "There," she said, smiling and rising. "All set. Ready to go?"

"Totally ready."

On the walk through the woods tinged with blue shadows, he felt the burner phone vibrate from deep inside his jean's front pocket. His caller would have to wait; it'd likely be hours before they could connect. He slid a glance at Kenzie walking beside him. In the waning light, she looked as soft as an impressionist's painting, as vulnerable as a child. He clamped his jaw shut. What had he gotten himself into?

Fifteen

In the cooler air of evening, standing on opposite sides of the horse, Kenzie and Austin gave Sparkle a sponge bath out of water buckets. Kenzie spoke soothingly to the mare as she worked, but whenever her eyes met Austin's, he'd wink or cross his eyes, making her smile. Sometimes she'd flick water on him, and he'd duck, challenge her to try again. After finishing, Kenzie put the ailing horse in her stall, and they tackled sponging down the other two horses as well, then tucked both inside their stalls for the night.

By the time the work was finished, stars glowed in the sky. With all the horses cared for, Austin pulled the two metal chairs out onto the grassy area between the hitching post and the pasture's fence. He set the chairs side by side so that they'd have a clear view of the sky above open pasture land. "How about we attack those desserts?"

"I thought you'd never ask. Afterward, I'll do the Sparkle Walk of Hope."

Kenzie snickered at his description of their all-night task as she went inside. After rummaging in the ice chest, she returned with two plates of cake thick with buttercream frosting and brownies shot through with chocolate chips and pecans.

"You didn't tell me about the cake this afternoon."

"Surprise! Two desserts."

As they ate, stars shook out like white confetti on black velvet. Sounds of music from the party tent floated on the smallest of breezes to join the music made by tree frogs and crickets from the woods behind them. In the distance, sprays of color began to shoot into the night and send sparkling lights cascading downward. Kenzie pointed. "Fireworks! Look! I thought there was a moratorium."

"It's July Fourth. No town is going to dump their fireworks display. I heard Windemere would launch from the fairgrounds."

Kenzie kept her eyes skyward, enjoying every array. "When I was growing up, Caroline and I—" She stopped, took a breath. "Sorry, didn't mean to say that."

He waited a few beats before saying, "Feel free to talk about your sister. In my opinion, sharing good memories of good times is a good thing to do."

Kenzie watched the sky as a brilliant waterfall of colors cascaded in a downward shimmer, reviewing childhood memories—the ones to keep and the ones too painful to release from the cages where she'd stuffed them. She set down her plate. "I think you would have liked Caro. She was sweet, kind, happy, loved making friends. If we were standing in a line waiting for something, Caro chatted up the person behind us and in front of us. She couldn't help herself. She was very trusting." *Until she trusted the wrong person,* Kenzie thought. *Good memories only.* "My sweet sister led with her heart, if you know what I mean. She wanted to be liked by others; it was important to her. We were different that way. Exact opposites, I'd say."

"Well, I think *you're* kind. I've seen you with the horses, how you light up whenever Mamie nuzzles you for a treat or if Sparkle ambles over for a scratch behind the ears. They trust you. I'll bet when you let someone inside, you become a friend for life."

She cut her eyes sideways, but Austin was staring into the distance as another flash of color filled the sky. "I wasn't much of a friend to Caro when she needed me. She used to talk to me about everything. But she never told me what she was going through at school last fall. She never told me about the sexting, the photos, or the bullying. She'd even asked me to come home for Christmas, and I didn't. I should have checked up on her, kept in closer touch. Instead . . ." Kenzie's voice trickled down.

Knowing that Kenzie was caught in the quicksand of guilt, Austin could have said, *"It wasn't your fault. . . . Don't blame yourself,"* but knew such phrases were overused by people who didn't know what else to say. Kenzie wasn't asking him for absolution, so he sat still, letting the night sounds cover her silence.

Minutes later, her voice came as a whisper in the night. "We attended this huge private school complex, three separate campuses, all with stellar academic programs, and every sport, club, and arts program you can imagine. I graduated in June, and Caroline moved into the high school campus as a freshman that fall. I could have, *should* have helped her navigate the pitfalls. Many of the seniors, juniors when I knew them, were entitled, you know? They thought they were special, above everyone else."

"Yeah, every school has slots. The nerds, the jocks, the popular crowd, the wannabes, the rebels—there's nothing new under the sun."

She nodded, knowing he understood. "Our high school also had hierarchies like you described. But at the very top were the Untouchables—kids who got away with anything and everything, and teachers and administrators who glossed over their sins."

"That happens in real life too."

"They killed Caroline's spirit, you know. Those nasty posts online tore her apart. She never said a word to me about what was happening to her while it was going on, and I was too caught up in college life to notice she'd stopped communicating with me." Kenzie's tone was melancholy. "And in the end, he destroyed her."

He. Austin's thoughts flew to the first time Kenzie had poured out Caroline's story. *He said he loved her. . . . He posted the photos on social media.* Austin wanted to ask, "Who is *he*?" but held back. Knowing the identity of the mysterious guy who'd crushed Kenzie's sister wouldn't change the story's outcome. Caroline would always be gone. He blew out a breath of frustration.

Just then, the sky lit up with a flurry of fireworks, rockets launched one right after the other, bright, beautiful colors falling downward like colored rain, followed by faint sounds of popping. Kenzie stood. "Don't go yet," he said.

"Why not? Show's over." Austin heard a tremble in her voice as she turned toward the stable. "I'll take Sparkle on her walk. You can have the next shift."

He didn't try to stop her, only sat and watched as she led Sparkle around the field, Kenzie's white tee catching ambient light from the stable and giving her a ghostlike aura of floating in the dark.

In the gray light of the morning, Austin crouched beside a sleeping Kenzie. At around three a.m., sitting bolt upright, back braced on Sparkle's stable door and long legs stretched out in front of her, she'd fallen asleep. Instead of waking her, he'd found a couple of winter horse blankets in the tack room, made a pallet on the floor, gently tipped her on her side, covered her with a lightweight blanket, and eased a folded saddle blanket under her head as a pillow. For the rest of the night, he walked the horse and kept vigil over Kenzie.

Kenzie slept, curled and snuggled, and Austin couldn't take his eyes off her. Her skin was the color of pale porcelain and looked as fragile. Before she'd drifted off, he'd noticed dark circles under her eyes, and her breathing sounded labored. However, once she slept soundly, her breathing eased. Kenzie was a solitary person, a girl who'd lost trust, first in her father, then in her sister, who had shut Kenzie out of her life. He wished he could change things for Kenzie Caine, the girl with a broken heart, who had confided in him. He was finally understanding she had no one else.

He wanted to touch her, smooth her hair, which was partly undone from its plait. He wanted to bend down and kiss her awake. He pushed aside the urge and sat back on his heels, knowing that he was no Prince Charming. In the end, he, too, was going to betray her trust.

Kenzie awoke to the rich aroma of fresh brewed coffee. She blinked, momentarily confused, then glanced over and saw Austin grinning and holding a steaming mug toward her. "Good morning."

"What . . . what happened?"

"You fell asleep, and before you chew me out, I decided to let you *stay* asleep. Teammate decision." She reached for the coffee, letting the fragrance infuse into her senses before sipping the black elixir. "And FYI, about forty minutes ago, I walked Sparkle and—drumroll—success!"

"She did the deed? Really?" Kenzie's sleepy smile lit up her pretty face.

"Indeed!" He winked. "And she's feeling a whole lot better."

"That's good news. Doc should be here in a bit for a recheck."

"While we wait, you want some breakfast? We have left-over cake. I left you a piece." She wrinkled her nose, threw off the blanket. "Come on," he chided, still crouched. "Think of it as a doughnut on steroids."

She ran her tongue over her front teeth, made a face. "I want to go to the house, wash my face and brush my teeth. I'll grab some juice and a protein bar too."

"Not fair!"

"Oh, don't sulk. You can come with me."

They walked through the woods that, despite the early morning hour, foretold with clinging dampness the rising humidity. The day would be another scorcher. At the house, she freshened up, untangled her braid, and smoothed it into a ponytail. She returned to the kitchen to see Austin holding open the door of her refrigerator and poking around. "I see eggs," he told her.

"Ciana keeps me supplied from her henhouse."

"I can cook us an omelet. Beats a protein bar, don't you think?" He pulled out the refrigerator drawers. "Don't see much else, though. What the heck do you eat?"

She shrugged. "I keep forgetting to grocery shop."

"We should do that today after taking care of the horses."

"We?" She arched an eyebrow.

Tactical error. He had to stop thinking of them as a unit beyond working with the horses. They weren't. He distracted her with, "Score!" and held up a block of cheddar cheese shoved far back in a vegetable drawer. "A little moldy, but I'll cut off the bad spots and toss fresh cheddar in the eggs. Why don't you sit while I cook?"

Minutes later they were eating scrambled cheese eggs

and drinking orange juice and fresh coffee. "Tastes yummy. And you were right, it beats a protein bar." He'd been uncharacteristically quiet. She set down her fork. "Can I ask you something?" He nodded, concentrating on his plate. "A favor really, for this weekend." He looked up, his blue-green eyes unsullied by lack of sleep.

"What kind of favor?"

"There's a big walking horse competition at the fairgrounds this coming weekend. I want to go, and I'd like you to come with me. I know it's a lot to ask, when you have free time coming after our all-nighter—"

He interrupted. "I don't mind going. Might be fun."

She brightened. "It's a good-size competition, too, everything from a lead line category for kids to juried competitions in flat shod riding. And Big Lick events." He gave a questioning look. "Those events are supposed to be 'humane' in this show," she quickly explained. "Short stack shoes properly applied, ball chains weighing less than six ounces around the top of the hoof, when horses were trained to high step. Personally, I think it's a cop-out. To my mind, it's still a form of soring. I don't mind going alone, so don't feel obligated."

The look in her eyes told him she had an agenda she wasn't going to mention this morning. He sipped his black coffee. "Can't think of anything I'd rather do with my day."

Sixteen

—.—

The day's sweltering heat had not deterred the crowds from coming to the fairgrounds. Austin found a parking space amid scores of cars, trucks, and horse trailers in a dusty field, and they made the long walk to the main rodeo arena, its fence peppered with colorful pennant flags hanging listless in the heat. Giant canopies shielded outdoor bleachers and attendees from the sun, but around several smaller show rings, people held up umbrellas to ward off the relentless sun. "Place is packed," Austin said as they wove their way toward the fairground's giant barn.

"You should see Shelbyville in late August. The show lasts eleven days and draws two thousand horses and about a quarter million people."

Austin gave a low whistle. "I guess you've been to that show?"

"Not for years." Nearing the oversized barn, she stopped.

"Wait, take this. We need IDs to get inside the competitor's barn." She handed him a badge that read EXHIBITOR.

"But we don't have a horse in the competition." He stood his ground, examining the official-looking badges. "Where did you get these?"

Anxious to get moving but knowing Austin could be like a dog chasing a stick, she heaved a sigh. "I called and asked my father for them, and he was only too happy to supply us with the badges."

Austin tipped up the straw brim of his cowboy hat, studying her. "So you're talking to your dad again?"

"Only when necessary." She lifted her chin.

"How about your mother? How's she doing?"

"I'm not neglecting her, if that's what you're wondering. We talk and email, and she says she likes her new therapist. I believe her because she sounds more upbeat. She's still sad, but she's doing things with old friends again. You know, lunch, playing golf, a little shopping."

Kenzie turned, but he stepped in front of her. "Good to hear. In my opinion, you're good medicine for her."

She wore a plain blue ball cap, with a walking horse emblem on it, and had pulled her long braid through the gap at the back. She edged around him. "Back to today's business."

"And just what *is* today's business? Why do we *need* to go inside the barn?"

"Because that's where the truth lies."

They halted at the table set up in front of the barn and showed their badges. A teenage girl searched a list of names

128

on a clipboard, found theirs, and checked them off. "Have a good competition," she said cheerfully.

"Count on it." Kenzie blasted a sunny smile that quickly faded when the girl looked away.

Inside, Austin saw a hodgepodge of roomy stalls and pens built to hold broncos and bull-riding steers competing in rodeo events, but instead housed Tennessee walkers of all sizes and colors. Men and women wearing numbers pinned to the backs of their shirts congregated in clusters, many riders in Western gear, others dressed for riding English.

Kenzie strode past most of the stalls, heading toward the back end of the barn. Midway, she stopped. "Wait. Close your eyes and tell me what you smell."

Austin obliged, breathed deeply, opened one eye, and glanced down at Kenzie. "Horses and sweaty people."

"What else? The odor is subtle, but it's in the air. Try again."

He concentrated, hoping he could deliver. It took a minute, but mingled with the aromas of horses, sweat, and saddle leather came a scent like fumes from a lawn mower. He opened his eyes, saw Kenzie standing in front of him, arms crossed, her expression expectant. "Gasoline?" he ventured.

"Close. It's kerosene."

He went on alert, his gaze darting every which way. "A fire?"

She waved off his question. "No. But it means some people have rubbed kerosene on the forelegs of their horses before coming today to compete."

He stared down the corridor of full and empty stalls,

remembering what he'd seen in the videos about soring. "But you told me it's illegal."

"So's drunk driving, but people still do it."

"How do they get away with it? You said this competition had high standards. Aren't there inspectors?"

She rolled her eyes at his naiveté. "*Private* inspectors are all that the law requires these days. And not all inspectors are honest. They look the other way, or . . ." She paused, waiting for him to fill in the blank.

"Or take a bribe."

"A smaller venue competition like this one isn't as well 'inspected' as a national show." She used air quotes.

Austin inhaled again. "Apparently not." He remembered the scarring on Blue's forelegs, spots where hair would never regrow, and now, after weeks of working with the horse to undo the damage to his body and spirit, he got angry. He glanced around at the competitors' nonchalance. Surely they could smell the same things he and Kenzie did. "Do these people know what's going on here?"

"Some do. But the Big Lick events are crowd pleasers, and there are owners who believe that doing away with it at competitions means people will stop coming to shows. And that could affect the popularity of the breed. And breeders like my father will suffer economically."

"And big crowds mean big money, right?" She nodded. "Sounds like a vicious cycle."

"It is. I personally don't think the walking horse will ever fall out of favor. They're great saddle horses. But that high step is eye candy, so it's doubtful it will totally go away.

Rules are in place to make training stricter." She shook her head. "I still don't like it. We'll go up in the stands later and watch a few Big Lick events, and you can judge it for yourself."

"But that kerosene smell is a sign that not everybody's playing fair."

"I know inspectors are here. But it's common to train however you want, then try and mask your training methods days before a show."

"In other words, cheat."

"I owe you a merit badge."

He grinned just as an announcement called a class of riders to the show ring. He and Kenzie sidestepped horses and people, a short parade of beautifully groomed horses, some with manes crimped into waves and smartly styled. He kept checking to see if the passing horses were wearing stack shoes, and none were.

"The groups are divided up. Judges determine winners in each group; then those winners will return, be judged, and receive prizes."

"Long day," Austin said.

"A long two days. There are a lot of events."

Austin saw the big picture now. As he'd suspected when she'd asked him to come with her, Kenzie had a reason for being here. And he was certain that he was going to play a role in her plan. He asked the question he knew she wanted to hear. "Can you show me horses you suspect have been sored?"

"Be happy to."

The barn's entire back area was less populated. There were stalls, but also empty pens and cages used during 4-H events to hold calves, pigs, prize chickens, and other farm animals. The kerosene odor was also more potent. A few stalls held horses. "Are these the sored horses?"

"No, most belong to the workers helping with the show who chose to come on horseback rather than trailer in. You saw the parking lot. Much easier to ride in if you live close enough to the fairgrounds."

Kenzie stopped in front of a stall, crouched, and peered through the openings in the slats. Austin joined her. "What do you see?"

"A horse, a mare, lying down." The smell of kerosene was stronger. He didn't have to guess why.

"Welcome to the dark side of the mirror." Kenzie and Austin stood in a single fluid movement.

"Is she supposed to compete today?"

"I'm sure her owner *expects* her to compete."

"Can she?"

"That's why we're here—to make sure she doesn't."

"Do you know this owner?"

From behind them a voice thundered, "Who are you? And why the *hell* are you back here looking at my horse? Get out!"

Austin spun to face a short, wiry man, close to him in age. His expression was hostile, and his fists balled. Austin fisted his own hands, kept them at his sides, on the ready.

Only Kenzie stood unflappable, her back still toward the man. She slowly turned, gave him a hard, cold stare, and said, "Hello, Billy. Austin, meet Bill Hixson the Third."

"Austin Boyd." He nodded but didn't offer a handshake.

The man's eyes trained on Kenzie, widened, went hot. "If it isn't the bitch who helped destroy my grandfather."

Austin moved lightning fast to insert himself between Kenzie and the angry Billy. "Now wait a minute! You can't speak to Kenzie that way."

"What are you, her flunky?" Billy edged closer. "You're both trespassin'. Get out."

Kenzie tried to push her way around Austin, but he stood solid as a wall. "It's all right," she insisted. "I can take care of myself. I'm not afraid of him. Not now. Not back then."

As if she hadn't spoken, Austin told Billy, "Step away." Billy stood unfazed, glaring. He leaned into a boxer's stance, raised his fists.

Austin said, "Don't."

The quiet delivery of the single word seemed to make an impression. Billy measured Austin with a look, snarled, uncurled his fingers, and lowered his hands.

Kenzie attempted to step in front of Austin again, but his arm shot out, rock hard and immovable. She pushed. "Will you stop it! I have something to say to him, and you're in my way. Move!"

Austin obliged by lowering his arm, allowing her to slip in front of him while he remained solidly behind her.

"You can't show that horse, Billy. What you're doing, what you've *done*, to her is wrong."

"It's my horse. Butt out."

"She's been sored, and you didn't back off her soring soon enough. Look at her. She can't even stand up."

Billy peered over Kenzie's shoulder. "She's just lazy."

"She's hurt!" She lunged forward, but Austin's hands caught her shoulders, immobilizing her. She tried to shake him off, couldn't.

Billy went inside the stall and coaxed the horse to her feet. The mare rose and staggered a bit, but remained upright. "See," Billy flung over his shoulder. "She's just fine. Now get!"

Before Kenzie could say another word, Austin caught her around the waist. "Let's go."

Kenzie struggled briefly in his iron hold but couldn't break free. Midway up the aisle, and into foot traffic, he released her. She stalked off toward the front of the barn, Austin close behind.

Finally, she whirled on him, tears of fury brimming in her eyes. "Why did you stop me? You saw how crippled the horse was!"

"What were you going to do, Kenzie? Attack Billy? Swat him like a fly? And what should I have done? Beat the crap out of him? Is that why you brought me with you? Because you expected me to handle the guy and maybe hurt him?"

Without warning, her heart began to pound out of control. A black haze floated across her eyes; then dizziness struck, swirling, tossing her toward the dark. She shuddered a breath and reached behind her to grab hold of something solid to keep from pitching forward.

In a fluid motion, Austin pulled her into an embrace that appeared like a casual boyfriend hug but was meant to keep her from falling.

His voice, urgent with concern, sounded through the fog in her brain. "What can I do to help?"

"Get me outside."

Seventeen

He looped his arm around her waist, and holding her upright, nuzzled her shoulder against his. "Can you walk?"

"Think . . . so . . ."

"One foot in front of the other," he whispered, leading her around groups of people congregated in the barn. "We look just like two people who can't keep their hands off each other. No one is taking notice of us. Keep moving."

Her legs felt like jelly, but the strength of his arms helped her move forward. Soon they were in the daylight. Fresh air and sunlight began to revive her.

Austin saw a lone tree around the side of the barn, guided her, and lowered her so that her back was braced on the tree's trunk. He crouched in front of her. "Let me get you a bottle of water."

"No. Don't leave." She took deep breaths, waiting for

the episode to pass. "I'm okay, just got a little overstressed."
The look of concern on his face made her wince. "Don't
look so worried. It's happened before, whenever my blood
pressure goes wacko. But I'm top of it now."

Memory jerked her back in time.

*She was barely sixteen. A summer day . . . riding Princess
bareback, hearing a horse in distress from the barn where Bill
and Billy trained. Peeking inside, seeing Bill beating a terrified
horse, chains around its front forelegs. Running into her father's
den. "Daddy! Bill's hurting our horses! I saw him with my own
eyes! Stop him!"*

*Her father's face reddening. "Did you go down to the training
barn I expressly told you to stay away from?"*

*The truth slamming her. He knew. Her daddy knew! "Don't
make this about me! This is about what Bill's doing to our horses!"*

*"Now calm down, honey. You know it's not good for you to
get in a lather."*

*Her heart was doing cartwheels, the room spinning, and her
father's voice sounding as if coming through a tunnel, the room
going dark . . . waking in her daddy's arms, seeing tears in his
eyes. "Sorry, Kenz . . . so sorry, baby. I love you, honey girl. . . .
I didn't mean to upset you. Forgive me . . . please, forgive me."*

*Her heart fluttering, her eyes shut, hearing his words, knowing
he was sorry about her passing out, not sorry about Bill's "training" methods.*

On that day in his den, something had broken between
herself and her father that had never mended.

She returned to the sunlight, to Austin's worried eyes. "I
have to stop Billy."

Austin put his hand on her shoulder. "Wait. Your team-mate is calling a temporary time-out." He thought fast. "When was the last time you ate?"

She attempted to stand. "Breakfast?"

"Well, it's after three. You need to eat something."

"I don't want to eat. I want to stop Billy from riding that poor horse today."

As her color returned and her breathing normalized, "truculent Kenzie" appeared. "Come on, a short change of course is all I'm asking. Can't go into battle on empty stom-achs. Plus, I'm hungry too," he confessed good-naturedly. "I saw a line of food trucks when we were walking across the field. Let's grab a bite."

"I have to stop him now."

"No, you don't. We have time, Kenzie. Let's take care of us first. You need a plan, not another fight with Billy." He snapped his fingers, diverting her stony stare. "Hey, I saw an ice cream truck too. How about some ice cream? I mean, who doesn't like ice cream? It can fix a lot of things that go wrong."

His familiar half-smile, his persuasive blue-green eyes, softened her resolve. She *did* feel weak. He was right. She needed nourishment to finish her battle. "Okay . . . I'll go for ice cream."

"And fries? There were burger and taco trucks out there too."

She struggled upright, swatting away Austin's help. "You sure managed to see a lot just walking in from the parking lot this morning. I never saw the food trucks."

"A guy thing."

"I'm not giving up, Austin. I *will* stop Billy."

"I never doubted."

At the conclave of food trucks, he bought her two scoops of chocolate-mint ice cream in a sugar cone and himself two scoops of butter pecan. He also bought fries and a burger from another vendor. They walked into a tented area with tables and chairs set up for food truck patrons. He saw a few other people sitting and eating, but for the most part, Kenzie and Austin had the tent to themselves. They chose chairs across from each other at a square table near the back of the tent.

"This is melting faster than I can lick it." She chased drips down the cone with her tongue.

"Amateur," he joked, devouring his cone in a few bites. He started on the burger. She finished her ice cream, filched a few salty fries from his plate. "Do you want your own?"

"Of course not. Don't you know food always tastes better off someone else's plate?"

Seeing that she was once again in full control, he dropped several fries on a napkin and pushed it in front of her. After a minute of silence, he said, "So tell me more about this Billy dude."

"He showed up during the summers to 'help' his grandfather train Dad's horses." She scowled. "Billy learned everything he knows about soring from Granddaddy Bill."

"Okay, I get that you hate Billy because of soring, but during today's shouting match, you said you weren't afraid of him . . . not now, not back then. What did you mean?"

She balled her napkin, not recalling the words, but the look of keen interest on Austin's face gave her no reason to doubt she'd said them. Billy was a side note, a wart on her personal history and of little consequence, but Austin *had* stepped into the fray for her. "If you must know, Billy was grabby. Billy liked to touch without asking permission."

Austin's pulse accelerated. "Go on."

"Billy was the first guy to ever kiss me."

"And you regret kissing him? We all make mistakes."

"I didn't say I *gave* him a kiss. He *took* a kiss from me. Big difference. I was thirteen; he was eighteen. He was always staring at me whenever he came to help Bill. Really, *leering* better describes it. I avoided him, but one day I was in our family stable saddling Princess for a ride, and he came up behind me, started rubbing my shoulders, telling me he thought I was pretty. I froze. He said other stuff, too, sexy stuff things I didn't understand at the time. I was freaking out."

Austin locked his fingers together, keeping his hands steady. The idea of Billy coming on to her sickened him.

"Then he turned me around and planted a big wet sloppy kiss on my mouth. I shoved him, jumped on my horse, and took off. Billy was a creep then, and he's still a creep."

Austin nodded in agreement. "Earlier, I asked why you wanted me to come today and if you'd brought me to beat the crap out of him. Now I wish I had."

"If I'd told my father at the time it happened, he might have gotten rid of Bill then. But I was ashamed, afraid it was my fault, that I'd somehow encouraged him, but I didn't say anything. I wish I'd told Dad. It might have saved our show horses a lot of pain."

Austin's dislike for Billy grew exponentially. "Don't blame yourself for what Billy did. He was five years older than you. He knew better." Austin wanted to say a lot more, but this wasn't the time or place. Instead, he asked, "I assume you steered clear of Billy after that?"

"Trust me, I avoided him like the plague every time he showed up with Bill." She flashed Austin a smile. "But just so you know, I asked you to come with me today because I wanted your company, not because I needed help facing Billy."

"You knew he'd be here?"

"Not for sure, but I suspected it." Her eyes met his across the table and held on. Her heart went soft as rainwater, and she wished she could verbalize how he made her feel. *Safe* was as close as she could come. "Anyway, thanks for coming with me." She stood abruptly. "Speaking of the devil, we need to go to the barn."

Austin stood more slowly, shaken by the current that had passed between them and the tide of feeling swelling inside his heart. He saw again how she'd crumbled inside the barn, felt how good it had been to have her in his arms. Gruffly, he asked, "All right, what do you want to do?"

"I think I have an idea. I got it while I was eating my ice cream." She offered a mischievous smile. "You were right about ice cream fixing things."

They returned to the big barn and stopped at the table out front, where a mix of people were sitting and talking. Kenzie saw that two men wore inspector's badges. She singled them out, offering both men a polite but troubled smile. "Excuse me. . . . Can I have a few minutes of your time?"

Austin, by her side, tensed when the men gave her an appreciative once-over with their eyes. "Sure, what can I do for you, little lady?" asked the one with a beard.

"I . . . um . . . I was at the back of the barn and . . . and I saw that a horse in one of the stalls looks hurt. And I, well, to be frank, the whole area stinks of fumes."

The two men glanced at each other. "Are you reporting that you believe a horse in today's competition shouldn't be competing?" asked the other inspector.

By now she had everyone's attention at the table. "Yes. I have no doubt that the horse has an issue. I'm no expert, like the two of you, but in my opinion, the horse isn't fit to compete in *any* show ring."

"Well, that's just terrible," snapped a woman at the table. Other voices buzzed disapproval. "And it makes me mad! We advertised a clean show here, a level playing field. Why don't you check it out, Pete?"

The bearded man lurched to his feet. "Maybe we should." The second man joined him. "Where exactly in the barn is this horse?"

Kenzie described Billy's location and the two men left. The woman at the table who'd spoken up eyed Kenzie's badge. "You're Avery Caine's daughter, aren't you?"

Kenzie stiffened. "Yes, I am."

"And you're doing horse rescue work these days, aren't you?" The woman's face broke into a smile. "Let me shake your hand. My husband and I own rescue horses. They're like members of our family. And without people like you, horses like ours would have to be put down. Thank you for the work you do."

A chorus of agreement came from others at the table. Astonished, Kenzie blinked, felt a surge of pleasure. "I— I'm glad to help. Thank you." Maybe being a Caine wasn't as toxic as it was a few years ago.

As she and Austin walked away, he slung his arm around her shoulders and steered her toward the parking field. "I think your work is done here. And I'm betting that those ladies won't let those men off the hook. They'll make sure Billy's disqualified."

"We could stay, watch the Big Lick show, and know for sure."

"I don't care about the show. I want to take you to dinner, and I've heard there's a great steak house out by the expressway. Are you hungry yet? Because all you've eaten lately is ice cream."

She poked him in the ribs. "Is that all you think about? Food? Your next meal?"

And you, he thought, but said aloud, "Constantly!" And hoped she believed his fib.

Eighteen

The dinner stop made them late for feeding their horses. As they worked in semidarkness, dispersing hay and shutting down for the night, Austin kept a watchful eye on Kenzie. He was looking for any residual effects of her heart episode from the afternoon. He saw none, only her quick, practiced movements of doing the job she loved. On the Fourth, she'd been able to get on top of the episode quickly, but today, if he hadn't been near her, she likely would have collapsed. His thoughts were interrupted by the jangle of Kenzie's phone.

She pulled her cell from her jean's pocket, read the display, and answered with a cheerful, "Hello, Lani!"

"Hope it's not too late to be calling."

"Nope. What's up?"

"I need a favor . . . a huge favor from you and Austin. But I want to ask you in person, face to face. Can the two of you meet with me Monday during my lunch hour around one? We can meet in the cafeteria, which by the way is excellent, in case you're hesitant to eat hospital cafeteria food."

The words had tumbled from the phone so rapidly Kenzie almost didn't catch them all. "Wait, slow down." Austin had walked over, and Kenzie repeated Lani's request for his benefit. He offered an "okay by me" shrug.

"Sure, we can meet you."

"Oh, thank you!" Lani sounded relieved and somewhat breathless. "I'll tell you everything when we meet."

"Any thoughts on what she might want?" Austin asked after Kenzie disconnected.

Her brow puckered. "Not one. I hope she hasn't hit a snag with her Trailblazers program."

A wispy cloud scuttled off the face of a late-rising half-moon, and in its light Austin thought of them together at the restaurant, sharing a table for two, candlelight flickering, sculpting her cheekbones. *Light and shadow. Strength and fragility.* He held out his hand. "We'll hear her out soon enough. Come on, I'll walk you home."

Tonight, she didn't refuse his offer. They took the long way around, skirted the woods and strolled through Jon's work area. She liked holding his hand, thought back to their beginning, to how he'd come across as overly self-assured and asking if she wanted him to quit. So much had changed between them, and now she couldn't imagine anyone else working with her.

They approached her bungalow just as another cloud covered the moon. "Hey, your porch light's out."

She felt his hand tighten as he scanned the darkness. "Yeah, my fault. I keep forgetting to change the bulb."

"Let me change it for you while I'm here." At the front door, he reached up and discovered the bulb was simply loose. When he tightened it, they both shielded their eyes from the glare.

"Ouch!" she said. "Turn it off."

He quickly complied, and just as quickly realized he was standing too close to her in the dark. The warmth of her body, the scent of sweet hay on her clothes, strawberry fields from her hair . . . intoxicating. Every muscle in his body tightened. He longed to take her in his arms, hungered for the feel of her warm mouth on his. Yet at the same time, he knew that if he gave in to the raw, urgent need, he wouldn't be able to stop with a single hug or a simple kiss. Or from going inside the house if she invited him.

The desire Kenzie had felt the afternoon in the gazebo flared like a match. How simple it would be to close her eyes, tilt her chin, offer her lips to his. She waited on the brink of indecision, and in that nanosecond understood that if she walked into the fire of him, she wouldn't come out unchanged. Fear of such a fire flared.

She took a tiny step away, and so did he. Breathing hard, he reached above her head and again tightened the bulb. This time neither blinked under the glare. Austin backed onto the lawn, and Kenzie dug for her key, and with shaking hands, she unlocked her front door. "See you in the morning," she called, hardly able to catch her breath.

"At seven," he answered.

Inside, she headed straight for her bedroom, and without turning on a lamp, threw herself flat across the mattress, growling in frustration. She lay splayed in the dark, her heart pounding, and fisted the coverlet. She took long, deep breaths to calm herself, knowing she was in no danger of passing out. The racing of her heart was natural, ordinary, a response to a hunger long suppressed. She had felt Austin's heat as much as she'd felt her own. He had wanted her. She understood *her* reason for hesitating, but not his.

Austin jogged to the old barn and, breathing hard, stretched flat on the grass and stared at the sky, heart racing like a bullet. *Close call.* He'd almost lost himself in her. Soldier trotted up, wagging his tail. Austin reached over and scratched the dog behind the ears. "No treats tonight, buddy. But you're welcome to sit awhile." The big dog stretched out and rested his head on his front paws.

Austin knew what he must do, what he *should have* done weeks before. He ripped the burner phone out of his jeans and toggled to the second number on his two-number call list.

The man answered on the fourth ring, his voice thick with interrupted sleep. "Boyd? What's up?"

"I want out."

"Hold on. Let me go to the next room." He could picture the man shaking grogginess out of his head. "What do you mean, you want out?" This time the man's voice came through clear and sharp.

"I don't want to do this job anymore."

"Why? What's happened?"

Austin realized this part of the conversation would be more difficult. "I'm tired of hanging around this place." The excuse sounded lame as he said it.

"Tired of scooping up horse poop?"

"More complicated than that."

"How complicated? Are you in trouble?"

More than you know. "Look, what's the problem with me leaving before the girl goes back to college?"

A short silence. "I've seen photos of the girl. She's pretty, and you're with her day after day, working side by side. Nothing but horses around you. You wouldn't be the first guy who fell for the wrong person."

That the man had homed in on the truth so quickly was disheartening and embarrassing. No use denying it. "Okay, you're right. I have feelings for her, and I shouldn't."

"Are you in over your head?"

"Not yet. I'm just asking you for an early escape."

"Don't lose sight of *why* you're really there. It took time, effort, and planning to set you up at Bellmeade. You're doing three jobs at the same time. I don't doubt that the lines are getting blurred."

Austin hadn't forgotten. He had been set in place for a purpose. Pulling out would affect others. Including Kenzie. He couldn't let that happen, not after meeting Billy. He massaged his temple, reorganized his priorities and objectives, felt the tightrope he walked go taut. "You're right. I can't leave. I shouldn't have called. I just got rattled tonight."

"Then hang on for six more weeks."

"Thanks for the pep talk."

The listener chuckled. "I do what I can. I'll check back with you in a few days."

Austin clicked off, staring up at the starless sky. Soldier inched closer, and Austin smoothed the white shepherd's fur. "I'm stuck," he told the dog, knowing he simply had to stay the course and maintain self-control.

The atmosphere was strained between her and Austin the next morning. They fed the horses without much conversation, worked on separate tasks afterward, forgoing their usual camaraderie. Kenzie hadn't slept much, and Austin didn't look as if he had either. She told herself that what she'd felt on the doorstep had been a natural consequence of what happened yesterday. Austin had intervened with Billy, dealt with her sudden wooziness, *and* shared a candlelight dinner with her. The turn toward the physical had simply been an outgrowth of their long day of togetherness. Last night, she'd temporarily lost track of her personal reality. She already had a life plan in motion. Austin was a gorgeous distraction, her feelings for him a bump on the road of life. Move on.

She was brushing Mamie in the breezeway of the stable, where it was cooler, when Austin came in from the round pen. "I rode Blue in the pen just now."

Kenzie turned and gave him a thousand-watt smile. "That's terrific!" Because of the heat, training had meant shorter periods of time spent in the pen with the horse. Blue had taken a saddle but had shied when Austin had tried to mount. The stalemate between man and horse had gone on for days, but Austin hadn't given up, and today the big gelding had given in.

Kenzie's excitement was short-lived when Austin said, "I want to talk about last night." She tensed. He moved closer, stroked Mamie's muzzle. "Here's the truth. I wanted very much to kiss you, Kenzie."

"Why didn't you?" The words were out before she'd meant to speak them.

His expression softened. "Because you hesitated. I read that as your wanting me to back off, and so I did."

She well remembered the tiny clutch in the pit of her stomach. He'd sensed it. Extraordinary that he was so attuned to her. She offered a wry smile. "We'd had a great day and a candlelight dinner. I might have given the impression that I wanted you to kiss me. No harm done." She felt her skin reddening over her half-truth. Last night she'd very much wanted his kiss. "In a few weeks, we're both leaving. Hundreds of miles between us. So, walking away last night was smart for both of us. Besides, I think I have enough complications in my life already, don't you?" She placed her palm over her heart and offered a tender smile.

The gesture upended him. He grabbed a breath and stuck to the script he'd rehearsed lying alone in bed the night before. "But I don't want to walk on eggshells around you either. I want to find our balance again, that compatibility vibe we had going. Please don't lock me out."

If only I could. "I won't. We're still a team. The horses need us," she insisted with a flip of her braid.

He rolled his shoulders, shook out his arms, still not completely comfortable. Perhaps comfort would come in time. "So . . . on a high note, I went online this morning and Billy boy didn't ride yesterday. His horse was withdrawn."

"Was anything said about him soring?" Austin shook his head, and Kenzie stamped her foot. "Until these owners are called out, things won't change."

He was glad to see her flare of temper. He turned to leave. She said, "Wait! Will you give me a hand with Mamie? With both of us, the work will go faster."

His blue-green eyes remained solemn, but his smile was quick. "Of course I will."

She tossed him a brush from a nearby box, and he took his place on the opposite side of the Gray Lady. With practiced strokes, they worked as a team, sweeping off dust and dirt, regaining familiar habits, restoring normalcy and balance, out of the sun and the heat of the night before.

Nineteen

The cafeteria hummed with the music of low chatter, the tinkling of silverware, and an occasional clank of ceramic plates and plastic trays hitting tables. Kenzie and Austin, wearing VISITOR tags, couldn't locate Lani at any of the tables, so they grabbed seats along a wall banked by windows to wait. Minutes later, Lani rushed in, and Kenzie waved. Lani wove her way to their table.

"Sorry, I'm late . . . crazy day." She took a seat across from Kenzie and Austin, dropping a tote bag on the chair beside hers. She wore colorful hospital scrubs decorated with cartoon images of giraffes, elephants, zebras, and grinning lions.

"I like your outfit," Kenzie said.

"Helps us look less scary to the kids. How about we get some food before we talk? If I miss this opportunity for a

152

meal, I'm doomed to hospital vending machines all afternoon."

The line of people, most wearing blue or green scrubs, moved quickly. The food selection was bountiful, the servings generous, and in no time, Kenzie, Austin, and Lani stood at the cashier. "My treat," Lani said, handing over her hospital credit card. "I invited you." Austin protested. "And I get a discount," she added with a laugh.

Back at their table, they ate around mouthfuls of small talk about their rescue horses and Lani's busy week before her wedding, until finally, Lani shoved her tray aside and reached into her tote bag. She removed a photo and handed it to Kenzie.

The picture showed a brown-eyed girl smiling broadly. She was completely bald, had no eyebrows or eyelashes, and her skin held a yellowish cast. "Her name is Jamey Taylor. She's thirteen, almost fourteen. She has a rare form of cancer, and she's dying."

Kenzie's head jerked up from the photo. Austin slid the photo from her hand, gave it a look, and wordlessly passed it back to Lani. "Sorry to be so abrupt. Sadly, we've exhausted all her treatment options, and Jamey's parents, Jim and Martha Taylor, have decided to take her home for her final days. I'm telling you this because they gave me permission to talk to you about something very special we want to do for her."

"How can we help?" This from Austin because Kenzie had gone mute under the barrage of Lani's words.

"Two months ago, she relapsed and was admitted for additional treatment. At the time, her doctors hoped she'd respond to a new experimental therapy. Jamey was very unhappy about having to return to the hospital."

"Can't blame her for that," Austin said.

Lani nodded in acknowledgment. "In order to put a smile back on their daughter's face, her parents promised her they'd buy her a horse for Christmas. You see, Jamey's horse crazy, has begged for one for years. Because there's nothing left for us to do for her medically, she's going home on Friday."

"Does she know how sick she is?"

Lani shrugged. "No one has said the words, but I believe kids sort of know the truth no matter what they're told. Children are pretty insightful, especially teens." Lani bit down on her lower lip, gathered her emotions. Lani glanced between Kenzie and Austin. "So—and this is where you two come in—I want her to have a horse."

Kenzie asked, "How can we help?"

"I want to fulfill Jamey's last wish. I want to give Oro to Jamey, just for a little while. . . . The Taylors live in a rural area, so they have property around their house and space for my horse. And they'll pay for feed. All that's needed is someone to load up Oro and transport him, call and check on him, and bring him back to Bellmeade"—she paused, collecting herself again—"after."

Kenzie certainly understood the finality of *after*.

Lani forged ahead. "Please believe me, I'd do this myself if I could. My last day of work is Thursday, and I have no wiggle room before my wedding on Saturday. Then I'll be on my honeymoon, and I don't think this gift can wait until

Dawson and I return." Lani leaned forward in earnest. "I can't make Jamey well again, but I *can* give her a horse. I just need you two to be my helping hands. I haven't committed you, so if you'd rather not—"

"Of course we'll do it!" Kenzie said before Lani could finish her sentence. She looked to Austin, who nodded emphatically.

Lani closed her eyes. "Thank you. She'll be so excited when she sees her very own horse." She reached inside the tote once more and pulled out a folded piece of paper. "Here are her parents' phone numbers and address. I'll tell them when I see them upstairs you're on board."

"Can Jamey . . . Is she strong enough to ride?" Kenzie asked.

"It won't matter. She'll believe she has a horse. Good medicine."

"So we'll bring a saddle with us," Austin said.

"Yes, and anything else that will make Oro look like an honest-to-goodness Christmas gift." Lani looked at the oversized watch on her wrist and stood. "I've got to run."

"Wait!" Kenzie called before Lani took off. "How do we gift-wrap a horse? It's not Christmas."

Lani offered an enigmatic smile. "It is at Jamey's house."

Kenzie and Austin left the cafeteria, exited the hospital into the shimmering heat of the parking lot, and crossed to her SUV. Once in the car, she turned on the engine and the AC but didn't put the vehicle in reverse.

"What are you thinking?" Austin asked as Kenzie hesitated.

"I'm thinking that Lani's the kindest, most thoughtful human being I've ever met."

"Agreed. When do you want to call the Taylors?"

"I'll call tonight and make arrangements with them." She didn't pull out of the parking space.

"I can't help but notice that we're not moving."

"I've had Lani's wedding invite hanging on my refrigerator door since she handed it to me. I see it every day, and yet"—she shook her head—"I totally didn't notice that her wedding day is this Saturday. *This* Saturday!"

"Yeah . . . I'd lost track of the date too. So again, I ask, what now?"

She glanced into her rearview mirror. "I'm going to drop you at Bellmeade and go shopping. I haven't got a thing to wear."

Austin roared a laugh. "A woman's lament. I heard my sister and Mom say that more times than I can count."

She made a face at him, backed out of the space, and headed out of the lot. "This is serious. The skirt I wore on my birthday has grass stains around the hem."

"A crisis," he deadpanned. "Where are you going to shop?"

"Toward Nashville, familiar territory."

"Bellmeade's in the other direction. Save some time and let me come with you." She flashed him an *as if* look. "I'm serious. Maybe you can help me pick out some guy duds, because come to think of it, I don't have anything fancy enough to wear either."

"It's dressy casual."

"And so, what does dressy casual look like? Should I Google it?" He reached for his phone.

"You could probably wear the khakis you wore to my birthday party and a jacket."

"And you'll look like a million bucks and I won't. Nah . . . I want something new to wear too."

She rolled her eyes. "Never mind. We'll shop for both of us."

He offered a satisfied grin and settled into the comfort of the SUV's cream-colored leather seat.

She drove to a trendy outdoor mall where cars were relegated to large parking lots surrounding the outlying area, and shoppers walked in to a wide thoroughfare of spacious brick pathways and sidewalks. Stores, boutiques, and small bistros lined the U-shaped plaza, anchored by a movie theater with a discreet marquee at one end. Gurgling fountains, colorful landscaping, and light posts with hanging flower baskets gave the space an aura of tranquility. As they window-shopped, Austin said, "The whole place smells like crisp hundred-dollar bills, but it does seem to have something for everyone."

"It was Mom's and Caroline's favorite place to shop. They could spend hours here."

"Not yours?"

"I've never been much of a shopper." Memories of summer days of the three of them strolling the mall, of her mother and sister ducking into almost every store, while

Kenzie, if they had talked her into coming with them, grew bored and ended up sitting on benches near fountains, reading and wishing she'd stayed home with the horses.

Today, with Austin, she shelved her memories, concentrated on finding a dress suitable for a wedding. She chose a boutique with a French-sounding name, entered, and was met with a cool blast of air heavily scented with lavender. An attractive salesgirl greeted them and offered Austin a flirty smile. Kenzie crossed to a rack of dresses, flipped through the merchandise in her size, and muttered, "I don't know what I want. Everything looks the same."

Austin stepped beside her. "Not everything." He withdrew two hangers holding strappy sundresses with fitted bodices and full skirts and held them up for Kenzie. "What about these? They're pretty—at least, pretty to guy eyes like mine. Tasteful and quietly elegant," he added in a flourish of exaggerated fashion speak.

She grimaced but took the dresses and followed the sales clerk to the changing area at the back of the store. Kenzie discarded one of the dresses after one look at herself in the full-length mirror. The second dress, pale yellow, was more to her liking. The shoulder straps were wider, one shoulder plain, the other adorned with a cascade of printed flowers that fell over one breast to the fitted bodice that dropped into a low V, accenting her flat stomach. The flower motif was again scattered around the hem of the skirt. She'd never put on a dress that made her feel more girly.

With the salesgirl hovering near Austin, and Austin's elbow resting on a low shelf holding an array of costume jewelry, Kenzie emerged from behind the curtain. He immediately straightened, appraised her with his eyes, and offered a heart-stopping grin. "Nice. *Very* nice."

She spun, letting the full skirt make a wide circle, saw the hemline flowers blur together in a riot of color. Secretly, she wanted Austin to look at her, not the silly salesgirl vying for his attention. His approval mattered to her, even though she told herself it shouldn't. "You sure?"

His eyes held hers. Her pulse fluttered. "The dress is nice, but frankly, you'd look good in a potato sack."

Flustered by his reaction, she looked at the price tag hanging under one arm and flinched. "A potato sack would be a whole lot more affordable. And honestly, I can't imagine where I'll ever wear this dress again."

Austin looked amused. "To buy, or not to buy—that is the question."

"What would Shakespeare say about you twisting one of his most famous lines?"

"He'd say, 'Methinks the damsel looks mighty fine.'"

She laughed gaily, studied herself in a wall mirror, weighed her options. Nothing in her closet at Bellmeade, or in storage at college, made her feel as good as she did in this dress. If she never wore it again, it would be worth the price to attend Lani's wedding with Austin at her side.

Waiting for her to make up her mind, Austin let himself enjoy the vision of her, until he felt the familiar, and forbidden, stirrings within his body. He cleared his throat and turned his head. "Make up your mind, Kenz, because I need clothes too, and we're an hour away from Bellmeade."

"Right! Sorry." She rushed to the dressing room, quickly changed from Cinderella dress into Kenzie clothes, went to the cash register, and paid for her purchase.

Once outside in the hot sun, they crossed the plaza to a men's store, where, at lightning speed, he bought tan dress slacks, a navy-blue blazer, and a white polo shirt to wear under the blazer.

"I think you nailed dressy casual," she told him.

"I'll be the wallflower; you'll be the garden," he joked as they left the store.

They made their way to the parking lot, her walking ahead, him carrying the bags behind her. They were almost at her SUV when Austin stopped abruptly and stepped in front of her, turning himself into a human wall. "Stay back."

"Why?" She tried to get around him, but cars hemmed her in on both sides, and he wasn't budging.

"Wait!" He dropped the packages and moved forward slowly as he scanned the packed lot.

She didn't wait but crowded against his back, still trying to see around him. "Austin, what's going on?"

"Your car window's been smashed."

Twenty

Shock and disbelief rocked Kenzie. "*Smashed? How?*"

By now Austin had turned sideways and was looking at a spiderweb of cracked glass, part of it forced inward, some scattered on the ground. She sidled beside him, crunching broken pebbles of glass underfoot. She looked inside and gasped. Both seats had been slashed with long vicious wounds that left the innards oozing out of the pale creamy leather like pieces of roadkill. She kept staring at the broken window and the shredded, brutalized seats. "Who . . . Why . . . ?"

Austin put his hands on her shoulders and gently turned her to face him. "Look at me, Kenzie. Just look in my eyes." Slowly, she let her gaze drift to his. Blue eyes rimmed with green. *Chameleon eyes, serious eyes, well-informed eyes.* "Whoever did this used a special glass-break tool. He kicked in the window, unlocked the door, and slashed the seats. He was in and out in less than two minutes."

"But the car has an alarm. It must have gone off. Didn't anybody hear it?"

"I'm sure it did, but in such a large parking lot, people generally ignore them. Eventually, your alarm wound down, and by then, the guy was long gone. Kenzie, I think we should call the police."

"No! No police."

He'd already pulled his cell phone from his shirt pocket. "Kenzie, this wasn't a crime of opportunity. Look around us. The car on the right isn't even locked." She saw that all four door lock buttons were in unlocked positions. He gestured. "Look, there's stuff lying all over that car's backseat, easy pickings for a thief. In the next row, I see three vehicles with the windows down. Your car was targeted."

Despite the heat, she shivered, not wanting to accept his conclusion. "Lots of people leave their windows down."

"Your windows were closed and your car was locked. Someone likely knew this was *your* car when they attacked it. This means the cops should be involved. I'm calling 911." He held up his phone.

She folded her hand over his to prevent him from punching in the three numbers. "If I was targeted, we both know who did it—Billy Hixson. He knows I had him disqualified from the horse show, and this is his way of telling me he knows and of getting back at me."

"Even more of a reason to get the law involved." If it was Billy, the guy was far more dangerous than Austin had realized. On the day of the competition, Austin had read Billy as a jerk and a bully. This attack on Kenzie's car put a different spin on the guy. "*Thinking* you know and *proving* it are two different things. The cops might be able to verify it was Billy with a forensic analysis of something the vandal left behind."

"*Might*," she said. "I don't want the police here. I mean it, Austin."

Her blue eyes snapped like an electrical charge, and her jaw jutted. "Odds are that vandalism is a low priority for police." He waited for a better explanation; the blazing-hot sun intensified his anger. "If any media gets wind that Kenzie Caine's car was vandalized, it will be newsworthy. And trust me, my family has spent enough time in the news-cycle limelight over the past few years. I don't care about me, but the last thing my mother needs is to hear about my car being attacked. She's doing better these days. I can't take away her peace of mind."

Austin looked skyward, blew out a breath of frustration. He understood completely, but *damn*, he wanted the culprit to pay. Nor could he ignore the possibility of Kenzie being in harm's way. However, she was right about one thing: police would give vandalism damage a low priority.

"So the guy who did this—and let's say it *was* Billy enacting revenge—walks away scot-free. And you're all right with that?"

"No, but in my experience, justice is a phantom, and I've walked away from worse hurts." As she said the words, her blue eyes swam with tears, ripping at his heart. She gently removed his phone from his hand and slid it into the front pocket of his shirt. "Don't you see? The only thing that makes this vandalism relevant would be my name offering a renewed source of gossip. Something like this could land on the police-blotter blurbs that newspapers from around here print routinely. I won't take the chance."

"I assume you won't tell your father either."

"No way. He *can't* know. The only person I'm going to tell is my insurance agent." She had dropped her purse but now picked it up and fished out her cell phone. "The SUV is mine, and so is the insurance policy. I pay for it. I'll let my agent know where the car is and he'll have a loaner car brought to us."

"Will you at least look and see if anything's missing from your car? I mean, if it wasn't Billy—"

To assuage him, she carefully opened the center console, then the glove compartment. "Everything's here. No thief did this."

Austin wasn't happy with her decision, yet he accepted it. "All right. Then I suggest we go back to the mall, sit inside one of those little cafés where it's cooler, and get cold drinks. Whoever your insurer sends can meet us there." Still frustrated, he bent down, snatched up their abandoned packages, and followed her as she made the call.

Jamey Taylor's ranch-style home sat on copious acreage off a winding country road on the rural outskirts of the county. July's intense heat had turned the front lawn brown, the only greenery sprouted from a generous well-watered vegetable garden planted at the side of the house.

Kenzie had called the night before, and when Martha Taylor asked, "Can you come first thing tomorrow?" she'd agreed. That morning she and Austin quickly fed the horses and put off other chores for later. Kenzie had opted for a pickup truck as a loaner vehicle while her SUV was being repaired and had borrowed a horse trailer from Jon Mercer to make the trip with Oro.

Austin drove the narrow curvy road, parked in the driveway in front of the garage, and shut down the engine. "You ready?" She nibbled her bottom lip and remained seated. "You seem anxious."

Knowing that a child was going to die unnerved her. *Alive, one minute, gone in another. Like her sister.* "I . . . I just don't want anything to go wrong."

"Not on our watch," Austin said, and gently squeezed her hand.

Together, they checked on the golden palomino inside the trailer and walked to the Taylors' front door and rang the doorbell.

A man and woman greeted them. "I'm Martha. This here's Jim. We're so excited about you helping to make our little girl's wish come true."

"We're bringing Jamey home this afternoon," Jim added. "We wanted the horse waiting here for her as a surprise." He was a tall man with sandy-colored hair and green eyes, a wide mouth stretched wider by a smile. "Lani and the two of you are godsends."

"Come in, come in," Martha urged.

Kenzie and Austin stepped over the threshold and straight into Christmas. A corner of the room held a tree decorated with lights, ornaments, candy canes, and garlands of tinsel. Under the tree, packages lay wrapped and waiting. Above an unlit fireplace was a mantel draped with winter greenery sprayed with artificial snow, and three large red stockings, each stuffed to the brim with gifts, hung on fancy hooks. "Oh my!" Kenzie said. "Lani told me it was Christmas at Jamey's house, but this is amazing!"

"Jamey loves Christmas, and we wanted to give her this one." *Her last Christmas.* Christmas music played softly from another room, and Kenzie felt a tightening in her chest, thinking of another girl who would never see another Christmas.

Martha, all smiles, said, "Can I get you some apple cider?"

"We can't stay," Kenzie told them. "Lot of chores waiting for us at Bellmeade, plus we should get Oro out of the trailer because of the heat."

"Of course, what was I thinking? He's a gorgeous horse. Lani's showed us pictures of him on her phone."

Outside, Austin unloaded Oro. The palomino's golden coat gleamed in the sunlight, and Kenzie was glad that she and Austin had taken some extra time to brush and fluff the horse's long white mane and tail. "He is *beautiful*," Martha whispered, tears filling her eyes.

Austin handed the lead line attached to Oro's halter to Kenzie. "I'll grab the saddle gear."

They all walked to the back side of the house, where over an acre of land had been fenced with new lumber. Bright green grass blanketed the ground. "I built this enclosure for the horse," Jim said. "I set up that lean-to on the side nearest Jamey's bedroom window." He gestured at a slant-top structure enclosed on three sides, a shelter from heat that also held a watering trough and a bin for grain and hay. "Lani's told us what he'll need, and we'll take real good care of him."

The effort Jamey's parents had put into preparing for her special gift, despite knowing the horse wouldn't remain long in the field, nor Jamey in their home, brought a lump to Kenzie's throat. Losing someone quick, losing someone slow—either way the weight of sorrow was impossibly heavy. "You're going to spoil him rotten."

"The grass looks amazing," Austin said.

"We have a well on our land, so we water the pasture and the garden every evening. Just as soon as Lani mentioned loaning Jamey her horse, I sowed special fast-growing grass seed to thicken up what was already there."

"That's Jamey's room, and her bed is right under that window." Martha pointed at a window on the house's back side. "From it, she can look out and see Oro wherever he's in the field anytime she wants. You know, on the days when she might not be up to riding. Or wanting to be outside."

"But I'll be sure she gets to ride anytime she feels up to it," Jim said. "I'm a trucker, but my boss knows I won't be hauling for a while."

Seeing Kenzie standing stiff and silent, Austin guessed

where her thoughts lay. He touched her elbow and said the one thing he knew would pull her away. "We should go finish up with our horses, don't you think?"

She startled. "Oh, yes, of course." She gave the Taylors an enthusiastic smile. "You've done a wonderful job here, and I know Oro will be very content. I'll be sure and tell Lani at her wedding on Saturday."

"She invited us, but . . ." Martha didn't complete the sentence.

Kenzie and Austin told them goodbye, returned to the truck, and Austin backed the vehicle and the long horse trailer expertly out of the driveway and onto the road, where they drove the distance to Bellmeade in silence.

The wedding ceremony was set for six p.m. on Saturday at the Presbyterian church on Main Street downtown, the reception at a specialized event venue almost twenty miles from Windemere. Kenzie and Austin fed and exercised their horses, working quickly and knocking off early to shower and dress for the evening ahead. He walked her to the screened porch. "How about I ring your doorbell about five?"

"I'll be ready."

Kenzie took her time preparing for the evening ahead—a long shower with scented soap, hair washed and dried, soft makeup, including a pale lip gloss. On a whim, she left her hair down in a shimmering waterfall, fastened at the nape of her neck with a single gold clip. She stepped into the dress, examined her image in her bedroom mirror, felt transformed. Why had she gone to so much trouble? She'd never much fussed over her looks or clothing. In private school, she'd worn uniforms, and in college, tattered jeans and tees or sweatshirts, depending on the weather. On top of that, she never took time for a serious boyfriend in high school—too busy with horse shows and competitions—and at Vandy, while other girls were having date nights at frat bashes, she kept to her studies. When sorority rush week descended, she'd ignored the frenzy.

For so long, she had been drawn to logic and analysis, instead of the "touchy-feely" side of life. Caring about horses was simple. Caring for people, more complex. And yet tonight, she cared very much about what she looked like and who she would be with. "I do this for Austin," she confessed to the girl in the mirror. Kenzie's life course was already set, yet she wished to keep the memory of this night with him tucked inside her heart. She'd need it when the dark times that lay ahead came for her.

The sound of the doorbell gave her a start. "Just a minute!" She grabbed her wristlet purse and a pair of white strappy sandals with kitten heels, hopped on one foot, flung open the door, and tripped over the threshold. She pitched forward, and Austin caught her. "Whoa! Watch out." He gripped her forearms and stood her upright, and they held each other's gaze a moment too long. "You okay?"

"I wasn't throwing myself at you," she joked self-consciously. "Sorry, I lost my footing."

He couldn't stop staring at her. "Don't outshine the bride tonight."

Her cheeks warmed. "Can't happen."

In his eyes, she already did.

169

Twenty-One

The Presbyterian church on Main Street was built entirely of Tennessee River rock, stones smoothed and tinted pale gray by water and time, stacked, fitted, and mortared together in the early 1920s. The church stood on a downtown corner like a regal queen, crowned with a copper spire aged to a green patina. Inside, stone walls soared upward to dark wood beams that crisscrossed an expansive ceiling. On stone floors, rows of mahogany pews were separated by a wide center aisle, where yards of white sheeting stretched from the back of the church to the front. Stone steps, a row of candelabras with flickering taper candles, and numerous vases holding perfumed clusters of snow-white summer flowers showcased a solid marble altar and a magnificent stained-glass window set into the rock.

Finding a parking place had proven difficult, and Kenzie

and Austin rushed in, minutes late. The two slipped into a back pew just as a minister in a long dark robe stepped through an inconspicuous side door, followed by Dawson Berke and his best man. Dawson wore a formal vested tuxedo of deep charcoal gray, a black dress shirt, and a black necktie. With his jet-black hair and piercing dark eyes, he was strikingly elegant.

"Not your traditional tux," Austin whispered in Kenzie's ear.

Bridesmaids in summery dresses escorted on the arms of groomsmen came down the aisle, and once attendants were in place, a pipe organ in a balcony began playing "Pachelbel's Canon in D." Guests stood and turned to face the narthex where Lani and her father began a slow walk toward the altar. Lani was sheathed in an off-the-shoulder white gown, its bodice sparkling with small crystals and seed pearls. The dress hugged her lithe body, flared at her ankles into a flounce of satin and chiffon. Her veil, a simple layer of netting, brushed her shoulders but couldn't hide her radiant smile. A lace train trailed each measured step.

Kenzie watched, mesmerized, and as Lani passed, she saw that the bridal bouquet was a nosegay of white roses with a single red rose in its center. Kenzie wondered at that, for it seemed odd to see the vivid red burst when every other flower in the church was white.

The ceremony, the taking of the vows, and the exchange of rings came just as the last rays of a setting sun hit the stained-glass window. Guests gasped as a kaleidoscope of color splashed over Lani's white dress and Dawson's gray suit, evanescent stains that faded as daylight lost its power, and candle glow took the sun's place.

When the minister said, "You may kiss your bride," Dawson lifted the veil, gathered Lani in his arms, and sealed their marriage with a lingering kiss. As they turned toward their guests, the minister announced, "It is now my privilege to introduce you to Mr. and Mrs. Dawson Berke." Applause erupted and the smiling couple rushed back down the aisle to the joyous strains of Mendelssohn's "Wedding March." Soon after, guests poured out of the pews, but Kenzie stood immobilized, caught up in emotion, as pictures from the past flowed like water through her mind. *Little girls playing dress-up. A Prince Charming who never came. A destroyer who did.*

"Kenzie? You okay?" Austin's voice broke through her trance. She glanced around, saw that the church had emptied. Austin looked concerned. "You seemed a million miles away."

"Yes, yes! I'm fine. Let's get out of here." Embarrassed, she hustled toward the doors, with Austin jogging after her.

The ride to the reception was subdued, with Kenzie wrapped in a pensive cloak. On the way to the wedding, she'd been upbeat, talkative. Austin almost asked her if she'd rather return to Bellmeade but decided against offering her the option. The party would be lively, and perhaps the food, music, and celebration would lift her spirits.

The venue was nestled on acres of rolling land with the pavilion atop a hill, designed as an Italian villa with trellises of clinging bougainvillea vines on outer walls. By the time the two of them arrived, the main room was filled with happy chattering people lined up at tables heaped with appetizers, small plates, and coolers of cold drinks. Austin touched Kenzie's elbow. "Want something to eat?"

"Not yet." They walked into an adjoining, less crowded room with tables and folding chairs. At the front stood a rectangular table draped in white linen, ribbons, and flowers. In its center were two elaborately decorated cakes, one chocolate, the other a stately tiered tower of dazzling white frosting.

"Look at that mountain of sugar shock!"

She barely glanced at the cakes. "Can we keep moving?"

Another set of doors led to a spacious tiled patio area decorated with strings of starry twinkle lights. Groupings of tables and chairs surrounded a generous dance floor, and a DJ stood at a turntable playing an eclectic mix of dance music. Kenzie halted, skimmed the faces and groups, realized she recognized no one. She felt her chest compress. "There are so many people."

"Same people as at the church." Austin saw her uneasiness—same discomfort level with unfamiliar faces as he'd seen on the day of the pool party.

"When do you think the wedding party will get here?"

"Photographers can take a while getting their perfect shots. Don't worry. Everyone will show up as soon as they can." Austin craned his neck and, slipping his arm around her waist, said, "I see a lake down the hill. Want to check it out with me?"

"Yes . . . that's a good idea."

173

He took her hand and led her down a grassy slope toward trees strung with more twinkle lights and the sound of water lapping against reeds. Underwater lights near the shoreline shimmered as a soft evening breeze rippled the water's surface. The sloping hill, water rustling the reeds, and the hum of katydids muffled the noise from the reception. Fireflies hovered, twinkling, disappearing, reappearing. He walked her to a meditation bench and together they sat facing the lake.

Kenzie watched fireflies, waiting for her pulse to calm. Eyes forward, she said, "You must think I'm acting crazy."

"I think something upset you. The wedding?"

"No. The wedding was beautiful. I'm glad we went." She looked down at her hands in her lap. "I had a flashback. When . . . when Dawson lifted Lani's veil . . . a memory. It slammed me. I'm sorry. I didn't mean to space out on you."

"Want to talk about it? I'm a good listener."

Her birthday in the gazebo . . . sharing her memories of Caroline aloud . . . how free and weightless she had felt afterward. Then came images of Austin pulling away, shoving pillows and quilts into seat boxes. "I . . . I shouldn't dump my baggage on you about stuff that happened years ago."

"I don't mind, Kenzie. But no pressure."

She toyed with a gold hoop earring in her earlobe. "It's a funny memory, actually. And it shouldn't have brought me down like it did. I was eleven and Caroline was seven. It was summer, and we were in the gazebo, and very bored. Caro said she wanted to play dress-up. She wanted to be a bride. She had stuffed a princess dress left over from Halloween in one of the seat boxes and dragged it out."

Austin would never forget the afternoon of her birthday, the patter of the rain, the scent of her hair and skin, the gray wash of light on her exquisite face. Fear of falling had pulled him away from her that day.

"Mom cut up an old lace tablecloth and made Caro a veil that came all the way to the floor in the back and just skimmed her chin in the front. We pinned it to Caroline's wild head of hair so it wouldn't fall off."

"So what part did you play?"

"Bridesmaid. We picked flowers from the garden for her bouquet and Mom fashioned headpieces for us out of some grapevine and daisies."

"Who was the lucky groom?"

"Our dog, but he proved unfaithful. As soon as his treats were gone, he was out of there." Austin burst out laughing, and Kenzie joined him, the sound as sweet as the memory. "We marched from the middle of the lawn into the gazebo, and Caro made up marriage promises to never ever cook anything yucky for dinner or get mad for no reason, and then I lifted her veil and she kissed the air." *Caroline leaning forward, eyes scrunched closed, lips puckered.* Kenzie let the image fade into the night lit with fireflies. She turned toward Austin. "Afterward, we ate cookies and drank cherry soda. It was quite an event."

"Sounds like a happy day. I mean, cookies and cherry soda—what's better?"

"I'd forgotten about it, but today, when Dawson raised Lani's veil . . ." She paused. "My sister will never be a bride." Her voice turned whispery.

And there it was. Every single milestone in Kenzie's life

would be marked by Caroline's choice. Wreckage strewn across the landscape of a family's life, a smear that would never be scrubbed away. "Did you know the guy, the boyfriend who dumped the photos online?" The question was risky, but he asked anyway.

"His name is Dylan Lawrence." Austin waited patiently, believing she was in a mood to talk but not wanting to crowd her. After a long silence, she said, "Dylan was a junior at our school when I was a senior. Big football star. He took the team to the state championships two years in a row, helped win the title during my freshman year at Vanderbilt. He was good-looking, confident, smart . . . and controlling. He had his pick of any girl at our school."

"I know guys like that. They have an overblown sense of self-importance, like the world owes them something."

She waited a beat. "Caro was a freshman. New to the high school campus. Naïve. Longing for a boyfriend. Easy pickings for Dylan. He had a girlfriend, of course, but he still went after my sister. I know he talked her into taking those selfies and sending the photos to him. Dad and I found the file on her computer." Kenzie shook her head. "Along with a message that read 'DL . . . *Because you love me and because I love you too. Forever, Your Caro.*'" Even now, Kenzie saw the words in computer script punctuated with heart emojis.

"Did *he* spread the photos around?" In cyberspace, digitals lived forever.

"He swore he didn't. Said his girlfriend found them on his phone and went ballistic, and she and her minions pushed them out everywhere. After Caro—" Kenzie's voice cracked. She wrapped her arms around her midsection, rocked forward. "Everyone was like 'So sorry, we didn't mean any harm. We had no idea.' They built little memorials to her outside the school gym. They cried on camera for reporters. All their sympathies came too late. My sister was gone."

"Did anyone get punished?"

"Some of the girls got a few days' suspension because of their mean-girl posts. Dylan got a football scholarship."

The puzzle pieces from the night of the pool party fell into place. Kenzie had heard the announcement on Austin's car radio. No wonder she had bolted. Life really *wasn't* fair. "I've seen it happen. The guilty sometimes walk free." He couldn't tell her *how* he knew this truth, but he certainly knew it. He chose his next words carefully, haltingly. "Kenzie, it may seem that people go unpunished for what they've done in life. But often life has a way of balancing the scales. I've seen it happen firsthand."

She offered a sad smile, and he wished he could wrap his arms around her, but how could he? He had set boundaries in place, self-imposed fences. *Less than six weeks until goodbye.*

Twenty-Two

Sounds of shouts, clapping, and loud music from the hill behind them meant that the wedding party had arrived. "Want to go up or stay here?" he asked.

Her ghosts fled. She took Austin's hand and rose to face him. "I want to go celebrate. I want to have a good time. I think the wedding was amazing, and Lani was gorgeous, don't you?"

"I do." Austin, looking in her eyes, echoed the words Dawson had spoken to seal his vows, words that forever bind hearts.

Kenzie felt her heart stumble. A warning voice inside her head. *Don't fall.* Once he left Bellmeade, they wouldn't talk much again. Maybe a phone call to catch up one day, but they'd each become immersed in their separate lives, and catch-up calls would dwindle into nothingness. He was, for a few more weeks, her teammate, her friend. She backed away. "For the record, you were right. It helped to talk. Thank you for listening. Again." She tendered a smile, turned, moved a few steps in front of him.

"Wait." She stopped, heart racing. He touched her shoulder, leaned forward. "There's a firefly caught in your hair. I see its tail light."

The whisper of his breath caused goose bumps to break out over her skin. "Can you save it?"

A laugh from deep in his throat. "Most girls would have said, 'Eek! Get it off me!' "

"It's just a lightning bug. Try not to hurt it."

She offered the nape of her neck to him and he unclasped the gold barrette and let her hair fall free. Gently his thick fingers pulled aside the strands to untangle the insect's trapped wings. He relived that day in the stable when he'd unwoven her braid. Then it had been an act of kindness. Now all he wanted to do was bury his face in the silky strawberry-scented mass and kiss her neck. "Almost got him," he whispered, unsure if he was freeing the firefly or holding himself together. "There." He nestled the exhausted creature in his palm for Kenzie to see.

"Can he fly?"

"Let's give him a head start." Austin tossed his hand up and the bug shot skyward, its glow merging with others of its kind. "Free," he said.

He took her hand and together they hurried up the slope.

By the time Kenzie and Austin hustled into the banquet room, the receiving line was short and guests were filling plates from the buffet table. The two of them smiled and nodded their way cordially along the string of attendants and family members. When they reached the bride and groom, Lani's eyes lit up. "You look so pretty in that dress! Doesn't she, Dawson?"

Dawson had shed his coat, vest, and tie, and rolled up the sleeves of his black silk shirt. He shook Austin's hand. "I believe we're with the two best-looking women here."

"Can't argue against that."

Lani gave Kenzie air kisses on both cheeks. "I've got some duties to perform right now, but I'd love to chat with you before you leave tonight."

"How 'bout we grab a table on the patio?" Austin asked.

"Perfect, I'll get out there before the cake cutting."

Kenzie nodded and moved out of the way.

Austin pointed to the buffet table. "I'm starving. How about you?"

The line had dwindled, and the caterers had replenished the food supply, so they fixed their plates, grabbed sodas, and made their way to the patio, to the far side of the dance floor, away from the music and noisy chatter. They found a café table sheltered by a short wall with a climbing clematis vine. A floating candle in the table's center flickered in a glass bowl.

She nibbled on a bite-sized meatball, swept the patio with a gaze. "I haven't seen Jon and Ciana, and I know they were coming to the wedding."

Austin washed down an eggroll with a swig of cola. "Yeah, when I was at the bunkhouse getting ready for the wedding, one of the guys said Jon had a mare having a difficult labor. Her foal was breech. Anyway, Doc Perry was on his way. They might have missed the ceremony altogether, depending on how the delivery was playing out."

"When I was growing up, Daddy lost many a night's sleep over mares with problems giving birth." A corner of Austin's mouth quirked. "What?" she asked, seeing his expression.

"I'm trying to remember if I've heard you call him Daddy. It's usually 'my father.'" He deepened his voice as he spoke.

She felt her cheeks grow warm. "All right, *my father*."

"The Cold War still going on between you two?"

Before she could snap out a comeback, the music abruptly stopped and the DJ announced, "Family and friends! I introduce Lani and Dawson Berke." There was a flurry of activity as people crowded around the floor's perimeter.

Austin grabbed Kenzie and joined the well-wishers. After the applause died, the DJ played a slow, sweet song that begged for the closeness of lovers. Dawson took his bride in his arms, and the two of them drifted around the patio. Crystals on Lani's white dress caught the lights, and her hundred-watt smile lit up the night. "If you ever need a measuring stick for 'happy,' remember their faces," Austin told Kenzie.

When the song ended, the two turned to more applause, and Dawson shouted, "Now it's your turn, people!"

Couples poured onto the dance floor. Lani crossed over to Kenzie and Austin. "Where's your table? I'd love to sit for a minute."

As soon as Lani and Kenzie were seated, Austin asked, "Can I get you something to drink?"

"Not right now. I don't have long, but I wanted to thank you for delivering Oro to the Taylor house. Martha texted to say how wonderful you two are and sent along photos of Jamey with her Christmas present. She looked so happy on Oro. I'll forward the photos when we're back from our honeymoon."

"Where are you going?" Kenzie wanted to know.

"Aruba. Ten days at some resort, then home to hang and put away wedding gifts. Just the two of us—no phone, no work, no social media. We have a honeymoon suite at a downtown hotel, and our plane leaves tomorrow afternoon." Lani rotated the glass candleholder with both hands, her smile fading. "I . . . I have a request. Please don't tell me when Jamey passes, if it's during our honeymoon. I'd rather find it out after we return."

"You won't hear it from us," Austin promised.

"Just bring Oro home for me." A shadow passed over Lani's eyes. Kenzie understood the new bride's regrets for a girl she'd cared for deeply, one that medicine couldn't heal. The shadow passed and Lani brightened. "How are your horses?"

"Fine. If Dr. Perry gives them a good report in early August, Sparkle and Blue Bayou go up for adoption. They're fine walking horses and new owners will love them."

Lani snapped her fingers. "Before I forget, Kenzie, I

182

had hoped to begin the Trailblazers program before you returned to college, but I can't start until mid-September. Please promise you'll come over some weekend in the fall for a visit?"

Kenzie didn't question the postponement but saw that Lani was disappointed to have to move her start date. "I will. Besides, you still have a story to tell me about you and Dawson. Oh, and just so you know, I've decided to get a new phone, and I'll send you my first text." A quick smile. "I'd like us to keep in touch."

Lani reached over, squeezed Kenzie's hand. "I'd like that too."

She said goodbye, and while Kenzie watched Lani stroll from table to table, Austin studied Kenzie in profile—the curve of her cheekbone, the hollow beneath, the flutter of eyelashes, the perfect pout of her lips. He itched to put his arms around her. But how? He'd made promises to himself to keep away. And yet, he couldn't let go of her heart-wrenching story. Music in the night intruded. *Mental head slap.* Surely a wedding celebration gave him permission to break the rules. He stood, held out his hand. "Let's dance."

She hesitated. The dance floor was crowded. The dancers moved wildly to fast music. "Oh, I don't know . . ."

"Trust me." He guided her up from the chair as she protested, led her to the DJ's table, and pulled out a five. "Can you play something a little slower?"

The DJ glanced between Austin and Kenzie, flashed a knowing grin, and waved off the money. "I'm here all night, and it's on the house, buddy."

When a tender love song flowed from the speakers, Austin gentled her into an embrace, cupping her chin with his hand. She stiffened at first, but the music, the feel of him, the warmth of his hand holding hers, his arm around her waist, the scent of his skin—pine trees and leather— softened her resolve. *Friends. Just friends.* She closed the distance, melted into the moment.

Too soon, the song ended and he reluctantly stepped away. At the same time, the DJ announced, "Hey, people, time to cut the cake!"

Austin tamped down emotions from the dance floor and reminded himself that his obligation, his job, would soon be over. He simply had to hang on a little while longer.

During the drive home to Bellmeade over empty rural roads bathed in moonlight, Austin berated himself. Tonight he'd lost his balance on the tightrope and hit the ground head- first. Why hadn't he stopped with that single dance with Kenzie? Or after the cake-cutting ceremony, why did he pass on a second chance to leave? Or when Lani and Dawson fled to Nashville in a cascade of birdseed? Instead, he and Kenzie stayed along with a few die-hard party couples and danced to every slow song until the DJ shut down the party and sent everyone home.

On the radio, a weatherman droned on about the coming week of intense summer heat—temps in the low hundreds, heat indexes much higher. Scorchers. And Kenzie was giving Austin a rundown on how they should handle the horses during the coming heat. When he didn't respond, she said, "Hello? Calling my teammate. You okay with the plan?"

He forced a quick smile her way. "Got it," he said, and again turned inward.

He didn't seem inclined to talk shop, so Kenzie's thoughts slipped back to the wedding reception and the good time she'd had tonight. In Austin's arms, she'd felt a sense of belonging. *Silly*, she told herself. Their time together—the hours, days, weeks—were almost over. She imagined not seeing him every day and found it unsettling. She told herself that what she'd felt tonight as they danced was simply a holdover from the afterglow of the wedding, a spell cast by the sultry Southern summer night dappled with stars. Things would return to normal in daylight.

Arriving at Bellmeade, Austin parked beside the old barn. Soldier emerged from inside. "Hey, buddy." Austin reached into the backseat for his dress jacket, fished out a wadded napkin, crouched, and offered the white shepherd a cocktail wiener from the wedding.

"He's going to miss those nighttime snacks," Kenzie said, coming around the back of the car. She stood in the moonlight, the straps of her sandals dangling from two fingers in her left hand.

"I'll miss him too. He's a great dog." Austin stood. "I'll walk you home."

They ambled toward her bungalow, Kenzie barefoot in the dry, scratchy grass. "I had a great time tonight."

"Me too, and if you want to sleep in this morning, I'll let the horses out to graze."

She yawned. "Maybe I will. I've always been a morning person, but sleeping in sounds pretty good right now."

In his mind's eye, he imagined waking up beside her, then shook his head to displace the forbidden picture.

At her doorstep, she found her key in the wristlet purse and unlocked the door, but instead of going inside, turned to him. "I hope what you told me tonight comes true. That somewhere, down the road of life, Dylan will get payback."

"I've seen it happen."

"You . . . you're a good friend, Austin."

Feeling the familiar tingle up his spine, Austin told himself to make a quick getaway. After blurting "Good night," he whipped around and made it halfway to the bunkhouse when he heard her call, "Wait!" He turned as she ran up to him, halting so close to him that he caught her strawberry scent in the breathless night air. She placed both hands against his chest, rose up on her toes, and brushed her lips over his. Pulling away with a saucy smile, she whispered, "Tag, you're it," and ran back to the house.

Austin stood like a statue, watching her sprint, sprite-like hair flowing after her in a moonlit silvery stream, while the lighter-than-air feel of her mouth lingered on his skin.

Twenty-Three

"The weatherman didn't lie. This is one of the hottest weeks in Tennessee history." Doc Perry removed his yellow straw cowboy hat and mopped his forehead. He was in the stable with Kenzie and Austin, finished with his checkup of the three rescue horses. Fans on either end of the pass-through doorways were spinning wide open but had only succeeded in moving around the hot morning air. "But the good news is that you have three healthy horses here, ready to be adopted."

Kenzie and Austin traded high fives. "Mamie's staying," Kenzie reminded him.

"Well, you two have done an amazing job. Especially with Blue. The first time I examined him, we had to blindfold him."

"Austin gets credit for Blue. He worked out Blue's man-phobia."

"Not totally," Austin jumped in. "Blue can get antsy around strange men."

"Aren't all men strange?" Kenzie mused.

"Ow! Right through the heart." Austin clutched his chest and staggered backward.

Perry grinned and started packing up his medical gear.

"Before you go," Kenzie said, "will you take a look at the vetting form I've created? I'd like to get our horses' photos and profiles posted on some horse adoption websites as soon as possible."

"Be glad to," Perry said. She brought paperwork from the tack room on a clipboard. Perry read the form, made a few suggestions, handed it back to her. "When do you head back to college?"

She gave him the end of August start date for upperclassmen, adding, "But I plan to roll out sooner. I owe my mom a long visit."

Perry looked at Austin. "And you?"

"Around the same time."

"And if the horses aren't adopted before you go?" Perry looked again at Kenzie.

"Ciana said she'd handle it." Kenzie scratched Blue's forehead beneath his heat-damp forelock. "He'll be an excellent saddle horse for the right owner."

Perry nodded. "You think you'll do this again next year? You've given these three excellent care, and many horses need help."

"I'd love to, but Jon and Ciana may have other plans for this space." She felt a pang as she said the words. She'd love to do the job again.

Austin shook his head. "Don't count on me."

Kenzie experienced a letdown but gave him a nod of understanding. *No regrets.* She would simply remain a one-summer memory to him.

He didn't meet her eyes. His cell phone chimed from his shirt pocket, and he stepped to one side to take the call. While he talked, Kenzie thanked Perry and waved goodbye. She stood in front of the fan, relishing the cool air. The heat was making her a little light-headed. Where was her tumbler of ice water? She started for the tack room, where she'd left it, then turned to see Austin coming toward her, his expression troubled. "What's up?"

"The call was from Jim Taylor. He . . . um . . . he said we can come pick up Oro this afternoon."

"Jamey died three days ago. Our relatives came for her funeral but didn't clear out until yesterday, so that's why we didn't call sooner." Martha dabbed her eyes while she talked to Kenzie and Austin on the porch. She wore her housecoat, its lone pocket stuffed with tissues.

Kenzie shook her head. "Please, you don't have to explain." A quick calculation told Kenzie that Lani and Dawson would be home from their honeymoon tomorrow and hear the sad news.

Jim put his arm around his wife's shoulders. "I took care of the horse, though, so don't worry that we forgot about him. Oro sure brought our little girl a lot of happiness."

Sweat trickled between Austin's shoulder blades. "We're

really sorry about Jamey. We'll get Oro out of here quickly."
Despite his words, no one moved.

Martha dabbed her cheeks with a tissue. "Toward the
end, when Jamey couldn't sit up, she lay in her bed looking
out at him. She sure loved that horse."

"We'll be sure and let Lani know. That's what she
wanted, for Jamey to love the horse." Kenzie felt the sadness
of the couple in vivid detail as memories of her parents on
the day of Caroline's funeral rushed back. *The pallor of February's light coming through the window above the foyer's grand
staircase, the heavy floral aromas hanging in a silence that announced death had paid a visit.*

Martha stared vacantly at the horse trailer, borrowed
again from Jon and hooked to the hitch mounted on Kenzie's now-repaired SUV. She tapped her forehead. "Where
are my manners? It's hot as blue blazes out here. Come inside where it's cool. I made fresh sweet tea this morning, and
I'll fix you a couple of ice-cold glasses." She stepped aside.

"That's kind of you, but we should load up. We have
other horses at Bellmeade to care for."

Martha looked ready to crumble, and Austin quickly
intervened. "Why don't the two of you go inside where
it's cool? We've got this."

With arms around each other, the couple left the porch.
Kenzie sighed. "I'll get Oro."

"Sounds good. I want to check the trailer connection.
It felt a little loosey-goosey while I was driving. There was
some sway, and we don't need any trouble with a trailer
filled with a horse on a hot day."

"I'll round him up." Kenzie jogged around to the backyard, saw Oro at the far end of the pasture, under the branches of a tree hanging over the fence. Oro was swishing away flies with his tail. She called, whistled, but he ignored her. "Come on, Oro. Don't be stubborn. Time to go home." She unlatched the gate, entered the pasture. "Don't give me a hard time. Come here." The horse refused to move.

Kenzie glanced around for the lead line, saw it hanging in the lean-to. Once the line was attached, Oro would follow. She jogged to the lean-to, stopped to catch a breath, grabbed the line, and walked toward the obstinate horse. She'd left her hat on the car seat, and the sun beat down like a furnace. She began to feel woozy with every step and remembered they'd left before eating lunch.

She crossed the wide field, breathing hard, and snapped the rope onto Oro's halter. "Come on, big boy. Cooler . . . in trailer." She staggered a bit, turned, and started toward the gate that now looked a mile away. The heat felt suffocating, but in spite of it, she began to shiver. Her heart pounded, feeling as if it might jump from her chest. In the center of the pasture, holding the line, she bent, pushed her palms against her thighs, and gasped for air that strangled in her throat. She saw the ground rise up beneath her feet, the bright light of day beginning to blur and fade. She folded sideways and dropped to the grass.

Austin leaned against the side of the trailer, feeling the heat of the metal through the denim of his jeans, his arms crossed, and wondered why it was taking Kenzie so long to round up Oro.

Unless . . .

He straightened and took off running. In the middle of the pasture he saw Oro standing, Kenzie in a heap on the ground. "Kenzie!" Austin cursed his stupidity and rushed to her side. Kneeling, he turned her flat and saw she was unconscious. He felt the side of her neck and found an irregular pulse. Her cheeks looked blotchy, and when he placed his hand on her forehead, her skin felt bone dry. No perspiration. *Hyperthermia!* He scooped her up in his arms and ran to the back door of the Taylors' house, kicked hard with his boot.

Jim opened the door, took one look, and shouted, "What happened?"

"Call 911! Where's your bathroom?"

Jim led the way, stabbing numbers into his cell phone. Martha followed Austin. "What can I do?"

In the bathroom, Austin placed Kenzie in the tub, lowered the stopper, ripped off her boots, and turned the cold water full blast. He snatched a nearby towel and elevated and cushioned Kenzie's head on the back of the tub. Over his shoulder, he barked, "Bring me ice. Lots of ice."

"EMT's on the way," Jim said from the doorway.

Austin willed the water to rise faster and lifted Kenzie's tee, knowing that clothing could act as insulation and that her body needed to cool down quickly. Martha returned with a dishpan full of ice cubes. Austin dumped the pan into the water, swirled the floating ice along Kenzie's torso, tossed the pan to Martha. "Again." When the water was to Kenzie's shoulders, he shut off the tap, rubbed her wrists, poured another pan of ice into the cold water, watched her skin redden. He heard the wail of a siren, and minutes later, a man and woman shoved into the bathroom. "We've got it, buddy," the man said in Austin's ear. "We'll take over."

Reluctantly, Austin stood, backed into the hallway beside Jim and Martha, giving the EMT crew room to work. In no time, Kenzie was hooked to an IV, strapped to a portable gurney, rolled out, and lifted into the emergency vehicle.

Austin wanted to crawl in with her, but the male medic stopped him. "You'll have to come separately, sir. We'll take her to Windemere General's ER, but please calm down before you get on the road." The medic waited a beat, then added, "My name's Cole Langston and I'll take good care of her."

Before the door closed, Austin gripped Cole's arm. "Stop! She . . . Her name is Kenzie Caine and she has a heart problem. Tell the ER doctors."

"I'll radio it in on the way." Cole hesitated a second, looked Austin in the eye. "You did all the right things. Likely saved her life."

Twenty-Four

Sick to his stomach, Austin watched the EMS unit pull away, siren screaming. *My fault.* He should have gone after the horse and then examined the trailer hitch. His legs went rubbery. He was calculating how long it might take him to unhook the horse trailer and race to the hospital, when Jim came up behind him and put his hand on Austin's shoulder.

"You all right?"

"I need to go!" He leaned over the hitch.

Jim's grip tightened. "Martha and I've been talking, and we have an idea about how we can help. Let us load the horse and I'll drive the trailer to Bellmeade. You can take Martha's car to the hospital, and she'll follow me to Bellmeade in my old pickup. Once we get Oro settled, we'll come to the hospital for Martha's car."

Austin's overwrought brain fumbled with Jim's plan. "That . . . that sounds good. Yeah, real good."

"All right, then. Martha's inside changing clothes, and here are her car keys. Car's in the garage."

"I'll call Jon and let him know what's going on," Austin said, clutching the keys in his palm. "He'll meet you up at the front next to the old red barn and take it from there. And thank you. Really, thank you for your help."

"Leave the car door unlocked and the keys under the driver's-side floor mat. And let us know how she's doing whenever you know something," Jim called as Austin ran to the garage.

Austin crammed his big body into the compact car and took off. He floored the accelerator as soon as the Taylor house was in his rearview mirror. He reminded himself that one thing he could do *very* well was drive. A skill finely sharpened in another life. Martha's car was small but surprisingly agile and fast. On the way, he made two calls. He pulled the phone from his shirt pocket and told robo-voice to dial Jon Mercer. When Jon answered, Austin quickly filled him in.

"We'll take care of the horses. You stay with Kenzie."

When he reached town, he was forced to slow. He swung into the hospital parking lot, found an open space, and stopped. *One more call.* He straightened his leg to wiggle the second cell phone from his jeans. With a single touch, he scrolled to Caller 1, and with his heart pounding, he dialed.

Inside the EMS van, a paramedic called Kenzie's name. She struggled to focus, but her eyelids felt gluey, her mind groggy. "Kenzie," the medic said. "My name's Cole. Can you hear me?" She wanted to respond, but couldn't . . . too tired.

Cole adjusted the blanket over her and the oxygen cannula in her nostrils as he spoke in clear, simple sentences. "We're almost at the hospital, and the ER nurses will get those wet clothes off you. The people you were with are coming behind us."

Why were her clothes wet? She fumbled back to the last thing she *did* remember. Oro. Heat. Feeling sick, dizzy. The ground rising to meet her. She closed her eyes, let herself drift on the cushion of the moving vehicle, flying through time and space like a wingless bird.

Austin paced the waiting area in the ER, not a generous space. He kept seeing Kenzie lying in a heap on the ground in the pasture, still holding the lead rope, Oro calmly grazing beside her. When he'd asked whether he could go into triage and stay with Kenzie, a nurse had asked if he was a relative. He'd said no, and she told him, "Not at this time. Maybe once we have her checked over. I'll let you know." Waiting was excruciating.

The double doors of the ER slid open and Jon and Ciana came in with a blast of outside heat. "Any news?" Ciana asked, looking distraught.

"Nothing yet."

"Sorry, man," Jon said. "I called her father, and he's on his way. The Taylors delivered Oro and we left Clyde and Scooter to handle stalling Oro and caring for your and Kenzie's horses."

"What happened?" Ciana asked. Austin recounted the afternoon events, including his own responsibility for letting her retrieve Oro when he should have known better. "How could you have known she'd collapse?"

"I should have considered the heat. And her heart. I knew, just didn't *think*. She seems so strong. I . . . I forgot, she isn't."

"I wouldn't have thought of either one myself. Bringing a horse in from pasture and loading into a trailer isn't strenuous. Especially a horse as tame as Oro. No need to beat yourself up about this. She's safe now and in good hands." Ciana held out a small denim bag. "Martha gave me Kenzie's purse from the SUV."

Austin stared at Kenzie's floppy shoulder bag but didn't reach for it. "Would you . . . could you hold on to it? I . . . I don't think I'm . . ."

"No problem." She patted his arm. "Austin, this isn't your fault. Why don't you sit down?"

"Can't." He started to pace.

"Buy you a cup of coffee?" Jon wanted to know.

"No." The door swished open. Austin glanced over and locked gazes with Avery Caine. Avery charged toward him, the man's expression a mix of fear and fury. Austin rolled his shoulders, shook out his arms, and stood his ground, bracing himself for the coming confrontation.

197

The beeping sound lured Kenzie awake. She lay on her back in a hospital bed, saw thin cable wires, knew they were attached to pads on her chest, followed the lines to machinery to her left, saw a heart monitor, an IV stand. From the right of the bed, she heard the harsh whispers of men's voices, heard one growl, "This should have never happened!"

She turned her head, saw her father and Austin in front of the room's window, each backlit by a red washed sunset sky. "Daddy?"

Both men turned. Her father rushed to her bedside, dropped to his knees, lifted and kissed her hand. "Kenzie, my honey girl! Oh, baby. You scared me! Are you all right, sweetie? How do you feel?"

Tears swelled in her eyes, and instantly she was the same scared little girl in a hospital bed years ago, her daddy at her side. "Is Mama here?"

Avery cleared his throat. "No, no . . . I thought it best to check on you first, before, you know, telling her anything."

Kenzie quickly returned to the present, where she was twenty-one, not four. "Good. Good." He eased onto the mattress, still holding her hand. She nibbled on her lower lip. "I feel . . . spacy, like I can't wake up all the way."

"The doctors in ER sedated you and ran a line up your femoral artery to take a look-see at your heart. And good news, your heart looks fine."

She'd had the procedure done before. A small camera threaded up the artery on the inside of her thigh and into her heart to provide a view of problems or damage to the organ. She was relieved to hear the report. Her gaze shifted to Austin, leaning against the windowsill, arms crossed, expression stony. "What happened to me?"

"You got overheated when you went to get Oro. I found you, called 911." His voice sounded devoid of emotion.

"Heatstroke," Avery snapped. "Shouldn't have happened."

"I . . . I remember an ambulance." Images filtered through the fog in her mind. *The paramedic leaning over her, IVs and oxygen, the ER doctor and nurses, the bustle and chatter between them. She was stripped of her clothing, splayed on a rolling gurney that took her to different rooms for tests.* She zeroed in on Avery. "Don't worry Mama with this. Let's keep it between us."

"Not sure I can make that promise, honey. I'm making arrangements for an ambulance to take you to Vanderbilt."

"What?" She dragged her hand from his. "No. Don't you do that!" The beeping from the heart monitor accelerated, and she forced herself to calm down. "I mean it, Daddy. I'm not going anywhere."

"Your doctors are in Nashville. They know your history. Please, Kenzie, be reasonable. You're my child!"

"No, Daddy. Stop it. I'm not a child. I'm an *adult*, and I make my own choices." With effort, she scooted up in the bed to prove to him she was strong. "Who's my doctor here?" No answer. She reached for the call button on the bed rail.

"Sanchez," Austin said from across the room. "She's the

heart specialist on your case, and I was told one of the best in the Southeast."

"Thank you," Kenzie responded.

Avery glared at him. "Stay out of this."

Austin looked down, softly smiling to himself. He knew that giving her the doctor's name would appease and settle her. This was her fight, and headstrong Kenzie wouldn't do anything she didn't want to do.

"*You* stay out of it," Kenzie snapped at her father, in control of her faculties by now. She'd have climbed out of bed if she thought her legs would hold her and if she weren't hooked to so many medical devices. Besides, her thigh was sore from the procedure.

"Kenzie, honey, please be reasonable. I don't want to argue. I only want the best for you. I want you *safe*." He shot Austin an accusatory glare.

"I don't want a fight either, Dad." She sagged. "But this is my life. Please let me live it." Avery stared down at the floor, his jaw working, grinding his teeth. "I at least want to talk to Dr. Sanchez and get her input. I also want to return to Bellmeade and finish my job with the horses. Two are up for adoption. I want to find new owners for them."

"Honey, slow down. The horses—" Her glare stopped his words. Avery pinched the bridge of his nose, blew out the breath he was holding. "I'll back off the ambulance to Vanderbilt and wait for this local doctor's report."

She knew it wasn't easy for Avery to cede control, so she gave his arm a squeeze. "If the horses aren't adopted out in time, I'll come for a visit before the start of the semester. I . . . I miss home." Tears filled her eyes.

Avery took his time before saying, "Don't leave this hospital until this doctor here gives you a clean bill of health. Understand?" She nodded, childlike. Avery stood. "And I'll hold you to coming home before going off to Vandy. It'll do your mother a world of good to spend time with you. We've both missed you."

A *compromise.* A rare thing for her father to offer, but the look of sorrow on his face tore into her heart. "As soon as Dr. Sanchez releases me, I'll return to Bellmeade." Her gaze sought Austin's. The red sky had been replaced by a sky streaked with pale pink fading into the blue of coming night. "Will you handle the horses until I get there?"

"Yes, we're a team. I have your car keys, and when you're released, I'll pick you up."

"*I'll* pick you up." Avery gave Austin a challenging glare.

Kenzie intervened. "No need for you to make a second trip, Dad. Stay with Mom." Since getting out of bed and leaving the room wasn't an option, Kenzie slid down under the covers and yawned. "If the two of you will excuse me, I'm tired." She rolled onto her side, signaling to both men it was time for them to leave. Austin offered a quick nod and walked out. Avery settled into a chair. "I'm staying until you fall asleep."

She didn't argue, but instead closed her eyes and replayed the night of the wedding in her mind: the sense of joy she'd felt in Austin's arms, the feel of her hand in his, and his chin resting against her forehead. She was going to miss him so. . . .

Twenty-Five

Ciana showed up the next afternoon as Kenzie was signing paperwork in her room to be released. "Your driver is here."

"I thought Austin was coming."

"Our farrier showed up to shoe your horses, so Austin asked me to come. Disappointed?"

Yes. "No, no . . . I don't want to inconvenience you, that's all."

"I consider it a lovely break from my daily grind. And if I were you, I'd be disappointed seeing me instead of him." Ciana held out a gym bag. "I brought you a change of clothes too."

Kenzie dressed in the bathroom and reemerged just as a nurse pushed a wheelchair into the room. Good old hospital policy. "All set?" the orderly asked.

Once they were on the road, Ciana asked, "So, your doctor said it's all right to go back to work? Any restrictions?"

Kenzie had seen Sanchez that morning, and the cardiologist had told her several things, some that didn't need to be shared. "I can work, but she warned me to stay out of the sun in the heat of the day and to hydrate constantly. Basics I already know but forgot to follow. My bad. She said I was fortunate that someone took quick action."

"Austin . . . yes, while we waited in the ER for news about you, he told us. Impressive that he knew how to handle hyperthermia." Ciana flashed a smile. "The important thing is that you're safe. By the way, I think we have a man and his wife seriously interested in Sparkle. He owns a Tennessee walker and wants her to have one so they can ride together. Much more fun than riding bicycles. They're driving in next week to take a trail ride on Sparkle."

The news was surprising. "I *just* posted Sparkle's and Blue's profiles!"

"The Internet isn't the only way news travels, you know."

Summer had flown, and Kenzie was struck with a wave of nostalgia. "Sparkle's a good horse. She needs a good home."

Ciana parked at the front barn, alongside Avery's luxury car. "Why's my dad here?"

"No idea."

Kenzie hurried to the bungalow, tossed her things inside, and took the path to the stable. She neared the pass-through opening and heard Avery growl, "And you didn't think it was *important* to tell me about the car break-in?"

Her stomach grabbed.

She heard Austin reply, "Kenzie asked me not to, so I didn't. I've handled it. She's in no danger."

"You *handled* it? Since when do you handle anything without my knowledge and permission? I *pay* you to keep her safe, not to keep secrets from me!"

Her audible gasp made both men turn to see her standing in the doorway. She marched inside, glaring at her father. "What do you mean *you* pay him? Jon Mercer hired him to help me with the horses."

Like prizefighters at the sound of the bell signaling the end of a round, Austin and Avery stepped away from each other, with Avery coming to Kenzie and Austin stepping into the background. "Jon did hire him." Avery looked uncomfortable. "But . . . but I also pay Boyd to make sure you're safe and secure *on the job*—and he assured me you would be. He's been working with you, honey, but also protecting you."

Her gaze flew to Austin. "Is that true?" Austin gave a firm nod that felt like a slap to her face.

Again, she looked to her father. "Why would you think I needed someone to protect me?"

"Because you did! When I heard about your car—and, by the way, I heard about it from a casual run-in at the country club with our mutual insurance agent"—he shot Austin a scowl—"I knew I'd made the right decision to pay Boyd."

She didn't dare mention her suspicions that the damage

might have been done by Billy Hixson. "It was a crime of opportunity in a parking lot."

"I had to consider your heart problem, too, honey." Again, Avery glanced at Austin. "I was told this guy was trained in CPR, that he could handle a medical emergency if you had one. You did, and he aided you. I'm grateful."

Kenzie flinched. Austin had acted quickly at the Taylors', because he'd been trained. *Austin Boyd, jack of all trades. Helper, protector, medical assistant, trusted friend.* Her anger morphed into bitter resignation. Truth came with a price.

She kept her eyes on Avery, her pulse pounding. "What else aren't you telling me? Because I know there's more. Because there's always more to the story, isn't there?"

Avery's face reddened. He shifted his weight. "You've had security around you for the past two years you've been away from home."

Kenzie's blood ran cold. "Who?"

"I paid a few of the campus security cops to be extra vigilant, to make sure they were close at hand if you left your dorm or library cubicle, especially late at night. I knew if you were being stalked, you'd never see it coming."

"Stalked? That's crazy talk!"

"Think back to how contentious it got between me and Bill when I fired him, and when that soring documentary and undercover video hit TV. Every animal lover on the planet went nuts! Bill was ruined, and we were in the crosshairs, guilty by association."

He *was* guilty for hiring Bill in the first place, but words stuck in her throat, stopped by the look of raw fear in her father's eyes.

"When you stopped talking to me, when you took off to live on campus, I couldn't take a chance that he wouldn't follow through with his threats. I had no choice, Kenzie."

"You had no right—"

"I had *every* right! I'm your father."

"Did Mom know? Did she approve?"

"She was relieved. We both wanted you safe, and hiring extra security reporting to me made us both feel better while you were on campus."

Angry words jammed her throat. Her gaze shifted to Austin, who stood expressionless in front of Blue's stall, her stomach churning over the thought of Austin dutifully "reporting in" to her father. What details might Austin have shared? "They *reported* to you? They were your *spies?*" She turned her fierce anger on her father but meant it for Austin too.

Avery reddened. "It wasn't like that. No one was spying on you. They were ready to protect you if you were in any danger. It wasn't as if you were checking in, you know. You wouldn't even take my phone calls or answer my text messages back then."

"But I talked to Mom." Not exactly the truth—her calls were occasional, not frequent enough. "Why didn't you tell me about having me watched? You should have asked me!"

"Oh, yeah, that would have worked." His tone was derisive. "Please, tell me, what would you have said if I'd asked your permission?" She pressed her lips together. "Exactly,"

206

Avery allowed. "You'd have thrown a fit, said I was 'interfering' in your life. You'd have refused—and I'd have done it anyway." He hit the last few words hard for emphasis.

She toned down her ire. "What about Dr. Kaye, when I went to work for her?"

"You were covered there too. Always discreetly, and she never knew."

"But why *this* summer? All that mess from two years ago is behind us."

"Actually, I was ready to call off security, thinking you'd come home for the summer. But you didn't. You insisted on coming to Bellmeade instead."

"But there's no threat to me here! I'm just rehabilitating hurt horses."

Avery's expression clouded. "Maybe not, but after Caroline . . . we didn't know at first, why she . . ." He paused, started anew. "When you and I got into her computer after her funeral . . ." He trailed off.

Kenzie remembered those dark days before and after her sister's funeral. She remembered the images she and her father had discovered in an innocuous folder marked TERM PAPER—selfies of Caroline unclothed, in provocative poses. The file had provided a window into the secret life of a girl she and her parents had loved, but there was a piece of her that none of them had truly known. Standing in a Bellmeade stable, Kenzie's heart broke all over again.

Avery cleared his throat. "Don't you see, Kenzie? Your mother and I couldn't have survived losing you too. I can't change what happened to Caroline, or what she did, but I'll do whatever's necessary to protect you. Even if I must hire others to do it."

Kenzie's lips trembled. Paying Austin Boyd to keep an eye on her was logical from her father's point of view. Austin's daily proximity made him a natural. What she couldn't sort out was the maelstrom of emotions tumbling through herself about and for him.

Her father intruded into her silence. "I know you're mad at me, but your mother deserves better treatment. Please come home before the semester begins. Just for a few days. It will mean the world to both of us."

Feeling defeated, disillusioned, she said, "I'll come. You have my word."

"I—I've hated being separated from you, Kenzie. You were always my princess."

She stiffened as he awkwardly patted her shoulder. Showing emotion was difficult for them both, and the past lay between them like scorched earth.

Avery looked over at Austin. "You stay on until she leaves for home."

"Yes, sir."

Alone with Austin, Kenzie felt as if the walls were closing in. "Will you please bring in the horses? It's getting pretty hot outside."

"Kenzie, I—"

She held out her hands in a stop motion. "Not now. I'm going back to the house where it's cooler." She walked into the sunlight.

"Sooner or later, we have to talk," he called out.

She ignored him and kept moving.

Austin's insides twisted. He'd hoped to leave Bellmeade without her ever knowing about his and Avery's connection. That hope was gone now, and the landscape of his and Kenzie's relationship lay like fragmented flower petals in the aftermath of a windstorm. The revelations had wounded her, the very last thing he ever wanted to do. He wasn't angry at Avery for telling her. She'd had her father's back to the wall, and the man had nowhere to go except to the truth.

Time to call in the horses. Austin found his hat in the tack room, where he'd been waiting for Kenzie before Avery had unexpectedly shown up. He fingered a vase of flowers on her desk, a bouquet he'd planned on giving her to welcome her back. Now the flowers looked cheesy, misplaced.

For weeks, he'd tried to dissect and deflect his feelings for Kenzie. She could be maddeningly willful and headstrong but also endearingly softhearted and tender for the things she held dear. He had begun to believe that one of those things was him. But today's revelations altered everything. *Betrayal.* Her father, her sister, and now himself.

Austin tried to forget the feel of her in his arms or the brush of her lips across his on the night of the wedding reception. Forgetting was a lost cause. The surface of his skin would never forget. For weeks he'd attempted to stave off his growing feelings for her and had failed miserably. With Kenzie, he'd inadvertently stumbled into a whole different realm.

He'd foolishly fallen in love with her.

Twenty-Six

Doing what she did best, Kenzie turned inside herself and locked Austin out. For the rest of the week, she performed an elaborate dance of avoiding him, which wasn't easy considering they still shared the space and the chores. She arrived later in the mornings, letting him handle early feedings by himself, or groomed and exercised boarders' horses to avoid being alone with him. That weekend, she left him a note to handle *all* the work and spent Saturday morning feverishly cleaning her bungalow.

In the late afternoon, her doorbell rang—persistently. Kenzie wasn't in the mood to see anyone, determined not to open the door if it was Austin. She peered through the peephole and saw Lani standing on the porch. Kenzie hoped she could be cordial, forced a smile, and pulled open the door. "Come in, welcome home! How was Aruba?"

Lani stepped inside, looking relived. "How are *you*? I stopped by the hospital this morning to catch up before I start work again on Monday. I was told that you'd been a patient. Went to the stable first, and Austin said you were resting."

"He exaggerates. I'm taking a break from stable work to catch up on work here in the house." Kenzie walked them into the living room, where they nestled on opposite ends of the sofa. "And I'm fine, or they wouldn't have kicked me out of the hospital. Just got a little overheated, that's all."

"*Overheated*? Is that what you're calling hyperthermia? It's serious. Don't make light of it. I was also told it happened at the Taylors when you went to retrieve Oro."

"It was my own fault. I wasn't paying attention to the heat index. I wanted to get Oro home and out of the Taylors' way. They were grieving and didn't need extra baggage of caring for a horse."

Lani's solemn gaze met Kenzie's. "Jamey's death is sad, but it was expected. Your collapse wasn't. I saw your chart, the list of tests that were run." A furrow creased the space between her eyes. "Some tests were atypical for heatstroke, and the physician on your case was unexpected too." Lani's medical experience gave her a clear edge on reading charts.

"I was well treated at the hospital. And I've been released." Kenzie skirted Lani's concerns and closed the door on a discussion of her health. She flashed a bright smile. "How about some fresh lemonade? It's Ciana's grandmother's recipe, and it's really tasty."

Taking the hint to back off, Lani trailed Kenzie into the kitchen. Ice clinked into glasses. "Nurses told me Austin's quick thinking of using cold-water immersion to lower your body temp was genius."

Kenzie took a pitcher from the refrigerator, poured the pale-colored liquid into the glasses. "Yes, he saved the day." The comment was clipped. She headed again for the sofa. "Now tell me about Aruba."

Lani settled, offered a sigh soft with reminiscence. "The place is paradise, and the resort was gorgeous. Just the two of us together without a care in the world . . . heavenly." Lani took a sip from her glass. "And speaking of twos, you and Austin looked pretty cozy at the reception. You make a lovely couple, you know."

Kenzie's smile faded when she realized Lani wasn't giving up her hunt for information. She eased her glass onto a coffee table coaster. "Get that idea out of your head, please. We are not a couple and never will be."

Her voice held more snap than she'd meant, and Lani's eyes widened. "What happened? You both looked so happy that night."

Feeling tears edge into her eyes, Kenzie told Lani how she had overheard her father and Austin and of her confrontation with Avery. "As soon as Dad left the stable, so did I. It was humiliating, you know, learning that I was just part of Austin's job description. 'Watch the girl. Feed the horses. Paycheck in the mail.'" Tears again pooled in her eyes, a few sliding down her cheeks. She swatted them away like bothersome flies.

Lani had sat patiently throughout Kenzie's story and set her glass aside. "Look at me." Ashamed, Kenzie refused. "Okay, then listen to me. I've seen the way that man looks at you, Kenzie Caine. You are far more than a 'job' to Austin, so let that idea go. I noticed it on Memorial Day, I suspected it when I brought the kids here that Saturday, and I *clearly* saw it at the reception. He's crazy about you."

Kenzie shook her head, sighing. "I've made plans for my life, Lani, and they don't include Austin Boyd." She'd come to terms with truth and reality. She already had one path into the future with an ending beyond her control.

Lani tried one more time. "I almost walked out of Dawson's life once because I was afraid to let him know how I felt about him. Don't make that mistake. Don't look back on this summer and have regrets about things left unsaid, and undone." Kenzie leaned into the sofa cushion, shut her eyes, let her silence be her response. After a long silence, Lani said, "Okay, none of my business." She touched Kenzie's shoulder, understanding. "But since I'm already at Bellmeade today, I'm going on a nice long ride on Oro."

"He'll be glad to see you. I exercised him yesterday, and he's truly a fine horse." Kenzie walked with Lani to the front door. "And thanks for checking on me."

Lani took hold of Kenzie's hands. "Don't forget your promise to visit in the fall when I get Trailblazers going."

"I won't."

They hugged and said goodbye. As soon as the door closed, Kenzie braced her back against its solid frame and did the one thing she'd put off since her return from the hospital. She let tears flow freely, weeping over what lay be-hind her, over what couldn't be.

"She's beautiful!" The words came from Elaine, a middle-aged woman stroking Sparkle, the bay horse saddled with reins tied to the hitching post.

"Glad you like her." Kenzie untied the reins.

"She's a beauty, all right." Elaine's husband stood be-hind his wife, hands on her shoulders.

Elaine took the reins. "Charlie's had a walking horse for years, and he's always wanted me to ride with him. But I was so busy with the kids and the house. Now our last one's headed off to college and it's *our* time to do the things we talked about doing after the kids grew up." The woman stroked Sparkle's neck. "She's a rescue, right? We live on a farm in northern Alabama, and we take care of several adopted dogs, cats, goats, even a calf rejected by its mother."

"A menagerie," Charlie said. "But we love all of them."

"She's a rescue," Kenzie confirmed.

"We got a phone call from a friend about her, and read your online posting. I called, and Mrs. Mercer invited us to take a test ride. We hoped to be first in line."

"And you are." In the week between the call and arrival, Kenzie had vetted the couple's paperwork online and all looked good. "Take her for a spin on our riding trail. Her gaits are smooth as silk."

Just then, Austin came along, leading another saddled

horse, one of Jon and Ciana's trusted trail mounts. "In case you'd like to ride along," he told Charlie.

"That would be terrific!"

Kenzie directed the couple to the riding trail and watched them head out.

"I think they're serious buyers," Austin said in Kenzie's ear. Her aloofness had continued since she'd learned the truth about him and her father. He told himself it was just as well. Soon they'd be going their separate ways. He had accepted that ending, but he wouldn't allow them to part without settling this rift.

She edged away. He touched her elbow. "Please, stop. You've shut me out long enough. It's time we talked. You owe me that much after three months of working together. Please, Kenzie."

His tone was soft but firm, and his touch, his breath on her skin, brought memories she couldn't block. He was right, of course. Ignoring him wasn't working, nor was it fair. She nodded. "Where?"

"How about I drag out the lawn chairs from July Fourth and we sit in the pasture?" The intense heat spell had broken, and temps had fallen. Today was breezy, with the sun ducking behind sullen-looking clouds. In another month, autumn would arrive.

Austin set up the chairs by the pasture fence where Blue grazed alone on one side and Mamie on the other. *Apart . . . like us,* Kenzie thought.

"You first," he said, believing it was better to listen, hear her out, instead of trying to defend himself.

She'd had days to think about what she'd heard in the stable, and although her emotions weren't as raw and fiery, she still wrestled with the situation's complexity—Austin's motives and actions. "When I heard you and my father arguing, the first words that registered were about what happened to my car. At first I was just upset because I thought we'd agreed to keep it between us. But then the rest of the words sank in—that you were working *for* him. That all summer long you've been a glorified babysitter for me." She struggled to keep herself together, never wanting him to know how hurt she'd been over that realization. *Angry, yes. Wounded, no.*

"Ouch, that's harsh. A *babysitter*? Is that how you think of me?" He groaned and took a few minutes to align his thoughts. "Okay, let's backtrack. Here are the facts. Jon hired me to work *for* you and *with* you. When your dad learned from Jon about me being your exclusive hire, he called and insisted we meet. I came into town a few days early, met with him in a coffee shop in Murfreesboro. He told me about Hixson's threats and about hiring special security men to make sure you were safe away from home. He offered to pay me to be an 'extra layer of protection' this summer, and I agreed."

He offered no apology, not that she would have accepted one from him. "Go on."

"I also scoped out Bellmeade before my official arrival. And frankly, the size of the place was off-putting, full of areas where you could have been accosted—the stable and pasture where we'd be working alone, the barn up front, the wooded trail you freely walked." He thought back to how Kenzie and Ciana passed him in the bushes on that day of surveillance, both easy targets for anyone looking to do harm.

"I walk that path by myself all the time."

"Not usually. I follow you, to make certain you arrive home safely. And I wait inside the tree line before you head to the stable every morning."

Another confession. Another illusion shattered. She bit hard on her lip, fought for composure. "My father over-reacted by hiring you, and you should have told him so. But I get it—I was your second source of income while you were working the same job for Jon. And you're planning on law school. How convenient for you. Getting paid double for the same work. Makes good business sense."

Her conclusion and sarcasm as she said the words struck him like a stone. She'd heard the facts, but not the truth. Being with her every day far outweighed anything he'd been hired to do, either for her father or Jon Mercer. He saw her eyes go gemstone hard and knew there was no way she'd believe anything he said about his feelings for her. He moved forward with his explanation of what she'd overheard— more facts. "As your dad said, the car news came from someone else. Avery showed up and nailed me with it. He was angry, Kenzie, but I'd made a promise to you not to tell him, and I didn't. We were in the middle of a shouting match when you walked in."

If he was trying to score points by telling her he'd kept his word about the car, she wasn't willing to let him off. Another memory rose—another possible deception. "So when you showed up at my birthday party, Dad's surprise over seeing you was . . . ? Please, fill in the blank for me."

A short silence. "If you remember, I'd asked you to tell him I was coming with you."

"Oh, my bad," she shot back. "*You* should have called and told him you were coming, since I'm certain you have his number."

No need to mention the burner cell where Avery's number was stored. "Well, I didn't. His surprise was genuine, but he covered it well."

She thought of the stories she'd told Austin of her childhood, of how she'd leaned on him, trusted him with her deepest source of pain. "So when the two of you met at the coffee shop, did my father also tell you about Caroline? Or did you just listen when I talked about her to be polite?"

Austin understood her deeper concern. An act of betrayal contained levels and degrees, all the way from little white lies to no-way-back. He twisted his chair in the grass to face her, rested his forearms along his thighs, and without flinching, zeroed in on her gaze. "No, Kenzie. He never said a word to me about the daughter he lost. He only wanted me to be fiercely vigilant over the daughter he still had. And loved. Everything I know about your sister, I've heard from you. And I hold your confidences close, all of them. A sacred trust, Kenzie. My word of honor."

Her heartbeat, rapid with dread, slowed. If Austin was telling the truth, then that part of herself—those often-raw and bleeding feelings—were still between the two of them. His expression looked sincere, and with everything inside her, she wanted to believe him.

"You should also know that you were right about Billy being the person who vandalized your SUV." He subtly shifted the conversation's direction and leaned back in the chair.

His words gave her whiplash. "He . . . he was? How do you know for sure? Do you have proof?"

"Hold on. There's no physical evidence, but I know it's true because I went to see him that night you were in the hospital, and he told me he'd done it and he wasn't sorry."

"What did you say to him?"

"We discussed boundaries and how he'd stepped over the line."

Images of flying fists. Billy wouldn't have had much of a chance against the larger, more muscled Austin. "What did you *do* to him?"

"Unimportant. Let's just say we came to an understanding. Nothing's going to stop him from soring his horses, but he won't bother you anymore."

The certainty in Austin's voice gave her pause, yet she didn't press him for more details. "All right, so how did he find my car in that parking lot? That shopping trip was impromptu, spur of the moment."

"The attack on your car wasn't premeditated. It really was a crime of opportunity. Billy saw us leaving the hospital that day we talked to Lani about Jamey Taylor. He followed us to the mall, gave us enough time to walk to the main boulevard. He popped your window, and even though your car alarm was going full blast, he slashed the seats and took off. Probably took him less than two minutes. Maximum damage in minimum time."

The news was sobering. She'd never liked Billy, knew the kind of person he was, but hadn't meant to start a war with him. She shouldered some of the responsibility for damage to her SUV. "Why was Billy at the hospital?"

"He'd been visiting his grandfather in the Alzheimer's unit."

"*What?* Bill Hixson has Alzheimer's? I didn't know."

"According to Billy boy, his grandfather has dementia, and his family moved him from Nashville to a Windemere care facility to keep the media out of it for as long as possible. He's been there for several months." Austin rolled his shoulders. "Dementia is a harsh sentence, but *he* won't be hurting horses again."

Kenzie thought back to summer days from when Bill showed up at their stables wearing a grin and asking Kenzie and Caroline, "How are the two prettiest little girls in the county today?" How friendly and nice she'd thought him in those days. She wondered if her father knew what had happened to his former trainer.

She had other questions but heard Mamie neigh and looked over to see the Appaloosa trot to the side of the pasture fence nearest the trailhead. Moments later, Sparkle came into view with her rider, Elaine, and Charlie on the other horse close behind. Kenzie and Austin met them at the hitching post.

"Oh wow," Elaine said after dismounting. "What a wonderful ride. She responded to every command. I love her!"

Charlie dismounted, wrapped his reins around the post. "Nothing finer than a ride on a Tennessee walking horse."

He stroked the neck of the quarter horse he'd ridden. "This boy's a beaut, but his gaits can't match Miss Sparkle's."

Kenzie wiped Sparkle's lathered neck, beaming. "We'll cool her down."

"Let me do that," Elaine said, glancing at her husband. "We want to take her home with us."

"Just happen to have my horse trailer parked up by the front barn. Brought it just in case." Charlie added a sly wink.

Austin took the reins of Charlie's mount. "I'll take care of this one while you three handle the details for Sparkle."

Kenzie watched him lead the horse away, feeling disjointed over their talk and the emotions it had stirred up. She returned to the task at hand, stripping Sparkle of her tack. Elaine started the cool-down walk around the open space, and Charlie grabbed a brush from the bucket in the stable for grooming.

Kenzie stored the tack, then went to her desk to look for paperwork, her mind still on Austin. She had more-complex questions for him, but perhaps it was better to leave it this way. Time was growing short. She'd go home for the promised visit with her parents. Classes would begin. Another semester. Another season. Another loss. This time, her connection with Austin Boyd. The night of the wedding was long gone, too, and the memory of being in his arms, one she must bury.

"We're finished," Elaine announced from the doorway.

Kenzie folded her memories, put them away.

"You ready to let us adopt a horse?" Charles asked.

"Certainly! Let's seal the deal."

Later that night, under a canopy of stars, Austin walked the grounds of Bellmeade with Soldier at his side. Reaching down, he scratched the top of the big dog's white head. "Gonna miss you, boy." The burner cell vibrated, and he dug it out of his jeans, saw Caller 2 on the readout. It had been a while since they'd talked.

"I'm here."

"Something's come up." The words sounded ominous. "Did you know you made the local papers?"

"What are you talking about?"

"Some local reporter did an interview with a couple who lost a daughter to cancer. The newspaper gave the feel-good story a full-page spread."

Austin's heart sank. "I didn't know. Who reads the local paper?"

"The reporter wrote glowingly about the generosity of some nurse who loaned the parents a horse to fulfill their girl's dying wish. They had photos in the story too—you and Kenzie unloading the horse, their daughter on the horse, their house decorated for Christmas for the girl. It made for a fine teary-eyed read." His tone was caustic.

Austin groaned. Beside him, Soldier alerted. "We were just being Good Samaritans."

"Not finished," the man snapped. "And they also told the reporter about how, when you came to retrieve the horse, Kenzie collapsed and Austin Boyd kept her safe until EMTs showed up."

Austin gritted his teeth, worked his jaw. "I did what had to be done. She was in serious medical trouble."

"Of course." The man sighed, resigned. "Has she recovered?"

"Completely."

"That's good, because I know how you feel about her. But let me be clear, I want you out of there as soon as possible."

"I can't just walk out right now."

"You can't stay either."

"Look, I'll leave when she does. Another couple of weeks."

"Are you *defying* me?"

"Nonnegotiable. I made a promise. I won't break it." Austin broke the connection and shoved the phone into his jeans.

Twenty-Seven

Kenzie watched the teenage girl and her mother coming toward the stable, the girl with a pronounced limp and leaning on a cane, her mother keeping a slow pace alongside her. Their call to come and check out Blue Bayou for adoption had come last night. Kenzie was nervous, because if any horse needed just the right owner, it was Blue.

"Hello. I'm Marilyn Williams, and this my daughter, Sarah." The woman offered her hand when she reached the hitching post.

"And I'm Kenzie."

"Is this the horse? He's lovely."

"The one and only." Kenzie backed away from the big gelding, unsaddled but bridled and tied to the post. She was nervous about how Blue might react to a cane. Bill had used canes to threaten and strike horses, and Blue's former owner might have also. Kenzie watched Blue's ears. They twitched but didn't flatten. A good sign. Sarah came closer, keeping her cane close to the side of her leg.

"Can I offer him a treat?" Sarah asked.

"He loves treats."

Sarah reached into her shirt pocket, removed a carrot stub, and held it out on a flattened palm for Blue to sniff. His lips closed over the offering. As the horse chewed, Sarah smoothed her hand along his neck and down his withers. "He's very handsome." Her long hair was as dark as Blue's bay coat.

Kenzie hadn't saddled Blue for the girl to ride because of what her mother, Marilyn, had told her on the phone. *Sarah's picky, and if she decides she'd rather not ride, we'll be on our way. The decision is entirely hers.*

Sarah's hand swept over Blue's side, his wide back and hindquarters, down his powerful hind leg, assessing the horse with knowledgeable eyes. Kenzie realized Sarah was no novice. "I've never owned a walking horse, but I've ridden a few. I'd like to ride Blue."

"I'll saddle him."

"Do you have English tack?"

Marilyn added, "Sarah's wearing an inflexible knee brace." Sarah's left leg, the traditional mounting leg, was her affected limb.

"I have a mounting block and English tack," Kenzie said. "Bellmeade has an exercise track. And a riding trail. Your choice."

"The track is preferable."

Kenzie scurried off to grab the saddle, knowing that this would have been something Austin would be doing, but since their talk yesterday he'd made a habit of keeping away from the stable after finishing chores. Still, she missed him. *Foolish sentiment*, she thought. Parting had been on their schedules since day one.

Minutes later, Sarah was seated on Blue, stirrups adjusted for Sarah's bad leg. They walked to the track, Kenzie beside the horse and rider, Marilyn's hand on Blue's neck. At the track, Blue walked onto the loamy turf, and Sarah gave Blue a nudge with her good leg. Kenzie stood with an anxious Marilyn at the rail, watching Blue and Sarah move down the track in the flat walk indigenous to the breed. "I can see Sarah's a pro," Kenzie ventured.

"A champion, actually. Her trophies are for steeplechase racing."

"Don't know much about that sport."

Midway around the mile-long track, Sarah urged Blue into his running walk, a loping long stride and a Tennessee walker's most mastered gait. Marilyn tensed. "Almost two years ago, her horse, Ballyhoo, missed a fence on a course and fell with Sarah. He landed on his side, crushed her leg. He was hurt so badly he had to be put down."

Kenzie grimaced. "I'm so sorry."

"Sarah was only sixteen. She's been through several operations, has a leg full of pins and screws, and has spent eight months in physical therapy. She grieved for Ballyhoo every minute. Her dad and I promised her that as soon as her doctors allowed, we'd get another horse for her. No more jumpers, though. Her surgeon owns a walking horse and suggested Sarah try one." Marilyn smiled wistfully. "When the time came, Sarah only wanted to look at rescue horses because most have been broken and put back together. Kinship. A fellow traveler," she explained. "We've looked at several horses already, but she's still undecided."

"Hard to replace a horse you loved." *Hard to replace anything you love,* Kenzie thought, sharing a knowing look with Marilyn. "Humans and horses are a lot more similar than people realize. The way you treat someone, no matter if it's a person or a creature, can have a lifelong impact."

Sarah and Blue rounded the turn, and coming into the stretch, she heeled him into a full canter. Blue switched into the distinctive rocking chair motion inherit in his DNA. Marilyn remained white-knuckled at the rail.

"Your daughter's an excellent rider, and Blue was once a champion himself in the show ring. From where I'm standing, they look like a single unit moving together." *A team.* She shook away the implications that came with the thought.

Moments later, Sarah reined in Blue and met Kenzie and Marilyn at the gate. "He's not even breathing hard." A smile lit Sarah's eyes. "Well trained."

"Yes, he is," Kenzie said, seeing in her mind's eye the days and weeks Austin had spent working with Blue and teaching him to overcome his fears and trust people again. She glanced toward the stable, half hoping to see Austin standing in the stable's doorway. He wasn't, and in that moment, she was struck by finality. Once he left, he would never stand there again.

Five straight days of rain broke the heat spell. With the rain came boredom. The horses were cooped up, restless. And so was Kenzie. She and Austin did what work they could, and although Austin remained helpful, he wasn't nearly as talkative or attentive as he'd been in the past. He arrived, did his job, left early. Neither spoke of their earlier rift, no more questions were asked or answered, and they never recaptured the playfulness of previous summer days.

Kenzie was shutting down for the evening when Ciana, on foot, swung into the stable. "How's it going?"

"Good, now that the sun's reappeared. I'm heading to the house. Walk with me."

Ciana fell into step beside her. "Any news about Blue's adoption?" Kenzie shook her head. "The poor horse was a mess when he arrived. You've done a fine job of rehabbing him. If you're gone before he's adopted, I'll handle the transaction." Another nod. "When are you leaving?"

"Saturday morning."

"And Austin?"

She didn't want Ciana to know about problems between her and Austin. It was enough that Lani knew and might say something after Kenzie was gone. "He hasn't told me, but I'm guessing soon. Every good thing must end."

"And speaking of ending, I have a question for you. Do you think you'd like take this job again next summer?"

Kenzie stopped in the middle of the path. "Are you serious?"

"Dr. Perry is impressed, and said so. Jon said you'd be

most welcome to take on more rescues next summer. I told him I'd ask you. We know Austin won't return, but Jon will hire another helper for you."

Another helper. Kenzie found it hard to get her head around the idea. "Certainly I'll come back. I love this job!" She paused, contemplating how best to frame her concerns. Vet visits, required inoculations, extra feed, and grain and nutrition didn't come cheap for three horses, especially abandoned and abused ones. "Ciana, I know you've had extra expenses this summer. The sales of Sparkle and Blue will help offset costs, but I'm sure we've used up Dr. Kay's donation by now. Next summer, I'll work for free."

Ciana laughed. "No way! You'll be paid, and no worries, the program is in good financial shape." They emerged onto the lawn where sunlight cast their shadows across the clipped grass. "All summer, Austin's had us deposit his paycheck in a special savings account. He told Jon to donate the money to next year's rescue program, especially if you were coming back. Jon said he'd send the money to him if you didn't return. And now you've said you will!"

Kenzie's chest tightened, and moisture crept into her eyes. "I didn't know."

Ciana scrunched her face. "Maybe he was saving it as a surprise? *Really* sorry if I stole his thunder. Please act surprised if he tells you."

Kenzie ate a microwave dinner on Friday night and packed up her belongings. She would buzz clean the bungalow in the morning and head home, fulfilling her promise to her parents. Ciana would care for Mamie and Blue until Sarah made up her mind. With her checklist complete and feeling restless, Kenzie stepped out onto her patio to watch the moon rise over the tree line. With the night, the day's warmth was gone, the air felt cooler, softer. Tree frogs were now silent, and fireflies few. Nature was slowly rotating toward another season. From behind her, Austin's voice cut through the quiet. "Incoming."

A warm glow spread through her, head to toe. She spun, offered a smile. "I used to think summers between school years went fast, but this one set a speed record."

He came alongside her. "I agree."

Austin had purposely busied himself all week working in the big barn, mostly to avoid alone time with Kenzie. Now, seeing her in the moonlight was unsettling. Leaving her should be done quickly, like cauterizing a wound. Pain came with the burn, but also sealed the gash.

She told him about the prospect for Blue's adoption. "I'll be shocked if Sarah doesn't take him."

"I know you wanted it done before you left." He rolled his shoulders. "I'll be heading out tomorrow."

"So . . . this is goodbye?"

"Seems so. Before I forget—" He reached into his shirt pocket, pulled out a gold hair clasp. "I found it when I was packing. Forgot I had it."

"The firefly rescue. Yes, I remember." *Every. Minute.* She took the barrette, still warm from his hand. A lump wedged in her throat. "I think we made a good team, and . . . and, I'm very sorry for the way I acted at the end. I was mad at my father, and I took it out on you."

230

"I think this is where I came into the picture in May—you mad at your father."

She offered a wry smile. "I get it that you couldn't tell me he asked you to 'protect' me. Knowing my father, you likely didn't have a choice."

A grin. "Being with you all summer was a pleasure."

The lump threatened to dissolve into tears. "For me too."

He stepped away. Standing too close to her had become hazardous to his heart. "I should just keep moving. I want to tell Blue goodbye."

Kenzie wanted to draw out their parting. And to figure a way to thank him for giving his salary to her project, without revealing Ciana's slip. "Did you hear that the Mercers have asked me to come again next summer and do rescue work? I agreed."

"I'm not surprised. You're a natural." His grin was fast, his eyes dark pools, and she quickly realized he wasn't going to say anything about his donation.

"Take care."

"Let me know when you get that law degree."

He closed his eyes, started to say something, decided against it, turned, and jogged across the grass. In the moonlight, the world had turned an ethereal shade of white.

Kenzie watched him disappear into the woods, reminding herself that building walls around herself was a well-practiced habit. Casual dating, yes. Serious entanglements, no. Austin had almost broken through. She lifted her face skyward, let the moon wash over her. "Goodbye, Austin." *My love.*

Blue and Mamie were bedded down for the night in their stalls on fresh straw. The horses' heads popped over the tops of the half doors. "Hi there." He obliged each with a treat, scratched Blue's broad forehead. "You be good for a new owner, you hear?" Blue chewed, eyes half closed. All at once, his head came up, ears forward, on alert. The big horse whinnied deep in his throat, edged backward in his stall, ears flattened. "Hey, what's wrong, Blue?"

A boot's scrape. Austin turned, his brain registering in slow motion a man in a ski mask, arm raised, a long knife on a downward thrust plunging into his chest. He gagged, heard a *whoosh*—his lung blown, deflating. He staggered, twisted away from the stall, fell backward, his head slamming against the hard floor. Flashes of light. Searing, burning pain.

Malevolent dark eyes stared down from the mask. Bending with hand outstretched, the man said, "I want my knife back."

Struggling for air, Austin saw a streak of white from the corner of his eye, and the assailant was hurled to one side, then hauled backward amid growls and snarls. The man screamed. Human bone crunched. Austin fought to stay conscious, lost the battle, and darkness swallowed him whole.

Twenty-Eight

The journey into consciousness was like swimming through gelatin. Austin drifted, forced his way upward, and drifted again, until finally he broke the surface and opened his eyes. He was in a dark space. A cup covering his mouth and nose was held in place with a stretchy band. He blinked, attempting to focus. He was in a room, on a bed, machines humming in one ear. He turned his head and was swamped by pain from inside his skull. He gulped deep breaths, clearing away the gelatin remnants.

Gingerly, he cut his eyes to his left, made out machine shapes beside the bed—monitors with squiggly lines and blurry numbers, tubes leading from a stand attached to his immobilized right arm, another tube protruding from his chest. His whole body felt strange, fuzzy. He sorted through dense, murky images. *A man, a knife. Panic. Pounding heart.*

He cut his eyes to the right, saw Kenzie, curled up and asleep, covered with a blanket in a nearby chair. She became his visual anchor, his connection to reality. If she was with him, he was alive and grounded. Austin settled, closed his eyes, and slept.

The next time Austin awoke, midmorning sunlight flowed through the window. Kenzie sat upright in the chair, awake and reading a book.

"Kenzie."

At the sound of his voice, Kenzie leaped forward, sending the book crashing to the floor, and rushed to his bedside. He held up his untethered hand and she cradled his palm to her cheek. Tears swam in her eyes. "Welcome back."

Her whispered, trembling words and the look on her face caused him to lift his head, sending a mini-explosion through his skull. "Water?" he asked, his throat burning with thirst.

She grabbed a cup from a bedside table and raised the oxygen cup covering his mouth and nose and rested it on his forehead. She scooped out an ice chip and laid it on his lips. He sucked it into his mouth, and for the next few minutes, she fed him chips until he felt revived enough to ask, "What's happened?"

"A man stabbed you. You've had surgery. You have a concussion and you're hurt, very hurt." She reached behind and hooked her foot around the leg of the heavy chair, dragging it closer and sitting. "Do you remember anything?"

He closed his eyes, an attempt to shut out the throbbing inside his head. "Blue . . . I was talking to him. His ears went flat. Heard a noise behind me." Images flowed, ebbed. Menacing images of a man in a ski mask, arm raised, hand gripping a knife. "No, not too much." He shut out the pictures.

"I was still standing on my patio when I heard the horses whinnying. They sounded panicked. And then Soldier shot past me like a freight train and a man started screaming. I took off through the woods—"

"You shouldn't have done that. The guy, he could have attacked you."

Her sprint from the patio, the blind run in the dark along the path, bushes and tree leaves slapping, stinging against her arms and face. Fear had coursed through her, driving her. Coming into the stable, Austin had been on the floor, a knife protruding from his chest, while Soldier was attacking a screaming man, blood on the dog's white fur. Reliving the minutes spiked her heart rate. She touched Austin, managed a smile. "Not a problem. Soldier had the guy pinned and bleeding. The ruckus was heard all the way up to the bunkhouse and everybody came running. Jon got there first with his shotgun, called off the dog, called 911. I . . . I went to you . . . and saw a knife." She rocked in the chair, bereft. "Why, Austin? Why did he stab you?"

"Hey, no tears. I'm all right." Deep breaths were difficult. His chest felt compressed, as if bearing weights he couldn't lift.

Kenzie didn't believe his claim. His color was chalky,

and his voice sounded strained. Seeing him fight for breath scared her. She knew firsthand the smothery sensation of oxygen deprivation. She quickly lowered the oxygen mask from his forehead to his nose and mouth. "This will help."

He sucked in the pure air, and it chased away the light-headedness. "What else?"

"You were unconscious. You didn't even wake up when the EMTs came, and when they got you to the hospital, you went right into surgery. We all came and waited. It . . . it took a long time."

"How long have you been here?"

"Since they brought you down from the recovery room, about two this morning. The others left after the surgeon came out and said—" Her voice snagged. Her lips trembled. "He said you would make it."

"You should have gone home with the others. I've slept in those chairs; it's no way to spend a night."

"I wanted to be here when you woke up." *Needed to be.*

"Well, now I'm awake. Please go, get some rest." He saw the strain of the night on her face, the paleness of her skin. "Come back later. I'll be better company, promise." Pain was coming in waves.

She saw he was hurting, put his hand on a remote attached to his bed rail. "You have a morphine infusion pump. Push the call button, and a nurse will come, tell you what you need to know about using the pump. I'm not leaving until she comes."

He pushed the button on the remote. "There, it's done." Kenzie rose, pushed the chair into its previous position, and went to stand at his bedside. He itched to smooth her hand over his forehead but didn't. He remembered how he'd sat at *her* bedside all night, how scared he'd been. "We've got to stop meeting like this . . . in hospital rooms."

She laced her fingers through his, rewarded him with a watery smile. "I agree."

A nurse bustled into the room, and Kenzie stepped aside while the woman offered kind words and instructions about the morphine pump's red button. The nurse fiddled with the IV lines, smoothed the sheets, and left. "Kenzie, this is going to knock me out. I'll sleep."

She didn't want to leave but was afraid he wouldn't push the button if she didn't go. At the door, she turned, remembering something. "Before I forget, a man came to see you early this morning. He wasn't familiar to me, and he didn't tell me his name. He just stood staring at you, looking sad. He was older, with white hair in a buzz cut. Finally, I asked if I could help him. He shook his head, said, 'I'll stop by later.'" She waited. Austin kept his silence. She prodded. "Do you know the guy? Because he seemed to know you."

Austin played dumb. "I'm sure he'll return; now please go on. And tell Jon to give Soldier a steak, on me."

"See you later. Count on it."

Once she was gone, Austin put his thumb on the morphine pump's button, torn between taking a dose of the drug and knocking himself out and waiting for his earlier visitor to return. The guy would likely be somewhere nearby, watching and waiting for Austin to be alone in the room. But Austin wasn't in any condition to talk to him. Not yet. He pushed the red button.

Kenzie drove to Bellmeade in a quandary. She'd been at his bedside, catnapping off and on, terrified. She had almost lost him. Hearing his voice had jump-started memories and emotions she'd worked to banish. Now she was in limbo all over again. It was one thing to say goodbye at summer's end, quite another to lose him forever. Like Caro. No coming back. It had been hard enough letting go of the idea that she'd never see him again after this summer, and of knowing that their lives had touched, then diverged into separate paths, but to lose him completely was unthinkable.

Kenzie shivered, parked at the barn, and hurried to the back pasture, anxious to see the familiar. Mamie and Blue were grazing, and when she stepped inside on the grass, the horses came to her. Mamie nuzzled and Blue gently lipped her arm, as if both sensed Kenzie's turmoil. She put her arms around the Appaloosa's neck, buried her face in the horse's dark mane, and wept.

Austin awoke groggily to find a man in a white lab coat redressing his chest bandage. "I'm Dr. Shepherd, your surgeon."

Austin fought to clear cobwebs from his brain. "Will I live?"

"Absolutely." Shepherd grinned. "The knife went deep, through muscle wall and into your right lung. It collapsed. Good thing we're given two, because your left lung kept you alive long enough for the EMTs to arrive. Now you're all patched and your lung's inflated. That chest tube is for drainage but will come out in a couple of days. You cracked two ribs when you fell, and banged your head hard enough to concuss your brain. But believe it or not, you were lucky. If you'd turned to your left instead of your right, the knife might have hit your heart."

"When can I get out of here?"

"Slow down. Don't be so eager. You've got a lot of sutures inside and out, and a good bit of healing to do. Your IV contains a broad-spectrum antibiotic to ward off infections. In short, we need to keep an eye on you, so your stay is a day-by-day thing." The doctor finished dressing the wound and then scribbled some notes on the electronic tablet he carried. "You were in my OR before the knife was removed. It acted like a plug. If it had been removed prematurely, you would have bled to death. A nasty weapon, too—serrated on one side, razor sharp on the other. The police have taken charge of it. Roll on your left side, please."

Austin grabbed the bedrail, and groaning, he turned. "Hurts."

"No doubt. Your ribs will take time to knit together. You'll have to take it easy even after you leave the hospital." The doctor placed his stethoscope against Austin's upper and lower back, listening. "Your lung's clear, a good sign. It's also good that you're in top physical condition. It will help toward your recovery." The physician poked the end of his scope into the front top pocket of his white coat as Austin gingerly eased onto his back to again lie flat on the bed. "We'll take you off the pump and switch you to oral pain meds tomorrow. You'll also be getting out of bed and walking the halls. I'll check you again in the morning."

The surgeon tucked the tablet under his arm, offered a nod, and left. Austin rubbed his eyes with his free hand, saw that sunlight no longer stretched across the floor, and guessed it was late afternoon. He wondered if his visitor had come while he was knocked out, but also knew the man would keep coming until the two of them spoke face to face. He only hoped he could get the visit over with before Kenzie showed up again. He was also feeling hungry and was about to call for a nurse to ask about getting a food tray when another visitor stalked into the room. Avery Caine.

Avery crossed to the bed, his face a mask of cold fury. "Kenzie called and told me what happened last night."

Austin shuddered a breath. He was in no shape to spar with Kenzie's father. "I was the target, not her."

"What if she'd been with you?"

"She wasn't."

"You were attacked! *Stabbed!* Why? You told me Bellmeade was safe. You told me you could protect her. You couldn't even protect *yourself.*"

Austin's whole body ached from the ordeal, but the force of Avery's anger hurt more, a hurt that not even morphine could ease. The man was right—Austin had been taken by surprise. If Soldier hadn't interceded, he would be dead. And Kenzie had run toward the evil that could have killed her.

"Stay away from my daughter! You understand? When

you get out of this place, don't come anywhere near Kenzie. You got that?"

Austin gritted his teeth, feeling as if his head would explode from pain. "Once I'm out of the hospital, I'll be gone for good. No worries."

"Make sure you keep that promise." Avery stabbed the air with his forefinger, his eyes diamond hard. "No contact at all. I mean it."

Austin kept silent, staring up at the ceiling.

Avery went to the door, spun, and with ice in his voice, said, "Who are you, Boyd? Who the *hell* are you?"

Twenty-Nine

Austin kept his finger off the red button, using sheer determination to ward off his physical pain and waiting for his early-morning visitor to reappear. Austin had asked the nurse to put a privacy sign on his door, wanting to discourage any other unexpected guests. He knew Avery was correct; he needed to be gone. If he was out of the picture, perhaps the breach between Avery and his daughter would have a better chance of healing.

The hospital's dinner food trays had come and gone before Caller 2 on his throwaway cell arrived, shutting the door behind him. The man was middle-aged and barrel-chested, with short hair, eagle-sharp brown eyes, and a broad nose. Bags under his eyes attested that he needed a good night's sleep. He rested big, beefy hands on Austin's bedrail, gazed at the medical equipment on the other side of the bed, and shook his head wearily.

"It's not as bad as it looks," Austin said.

"Well, from where I'm standing, it looks bad enough. Give me a medical update. No holding back either." Austin reported what Dr. Shepherd had told him, and the visitor scowled. "You know I would have been here sooner, but I had to face off with local police about what happened. The crime and the perpetrator is in their jurisdiction, so there's a whole lot of paperwork involved."

"Where is the guy? I heard the dog tore him up."

"Ironically, he's two floors below you, being treated, and is cuffed to a bed. It's possible he'll lose his arm, or at least part of it."

Soldier was a formidable force. The white shepherd weighed over eighty pounds, and his jaws could exert two hundred and forty pounds of bite pressure. The attacker hadn't stood a chance when the dog had come after him in defense of Austin. "Do you know who he is? Are there others?"

"Unlikely."

By now, Austin's mask had been replaced with a cannula to facilitate talking and eating, and deep breaths were painful, but Austin took one anyway. "I want out of here. Can you get me moved to another hospital?"

"More paperwork? What's wrong with this hospital?"

"Am I interrupting?" Kenzie peeked around the edge of the door, which she'd quietly pushed open. She recognized the man at Austin bedside from his predawn visit. The man turned, gave her a nod.

Austin's heart did a flip-flop. Either Avery hadn't yet talked to her about keeping her distance, or she'd ignored

243

what he'd said and come anyway. Austin remembered how he'd poured out his feelings about Kenzie to his visitor and felt embarrassed.

Kenzie stepped into the room, shutting the door behind her. Coming bedside, she gave Austin's visitor a tentative smile. "I see you two finally connected. I'm Kenzie Caine. Austin and I work together. Or we did this past summer."

"Rescue horse work. Yes, Austin's spoken of you."

Kenzie laid her hand on Austin's, asked, "How are you?"

"Doing good."

The air was thick with tension. She glanced between the two men. "What's going on?"

The older man caught Austin's eye, took a step back, and offered a nod and a look that said, *You have my permission to tell her.*

Still Austin hesitated, knowing that he was about to break her trust one final time. Kenzie hated lies. And liars. His head pounded. He longed to push the red button on the overdue respite from his pain, but instead looked up into Kenzie's questioning blue eyes. "This is Dale Stinson, my boss."

Her eyebrows shot up. "Just how many bosses do you have?"

"Detective Dale Stinson." The man fingered a business card from a pocket. She took it. Black type. Official crest. "Go on," Stinson said to Austin. "Give her the big picture and I'll fill in the blanks."

Resigned, Austin said, "My name isn't Austin Boyd. It's Tyler Austin Buchanan. I never graduated from the University of Virginia." He gritted his teeth, pain swamping him. He pushed the red button and felt the drowsiness start to set in.

"So going to law school—that's not true either?" Her stomach knotted.

"No," he said, grimacing, eyelids heavy. "I'm a cop with the Knoxville police force. Six years in." And with that, Austin gave Stinson a pleading look, closed his eyes, and let the morphine take him.

Kenzie watched Austin's face go slack as he fell into the oblivion granted by the narcotic. Numbly, she tried to get her head around what he'd just told her. All that she'd known about him, all she'd believed—no, all she'd been told—had been untrue.

"Miss?"

She startled, having forgotten the man still standing next to her. A man with tired eyes and meaty jowls.

"He's going to be out for quite a while." Stinson shoved his hands into the pockets of rumpled khaki slacks. "I know this is a shock, and you must have questions. There's a consultation room down the hall, where doctors meet with patients' family members. If you'll walk down there with me, I'll tell you everything I can about what's going on."

She shouldered her purse, threw Austin a lingering look, and followed Stinson down the corridor. Her vision tunneled along the stretch of pale blue walls, red flooring, and patient room doors until they entered a cubbyhole of a space across from the nurses' station. Modern furniture, including a two-person settee, two armchairs, and a side table with a lamp, filled the area, and a larger table divided the seating. Boxes of tissues sat on both surfaces. A room ready for tears. Kenzie squared her chin. No way would she break down and cry. She wanted the truth; she could handle it.

She took the sofa, and Stinson grabbed a chair across from her. He steepled his fingers, caught her gaze, held on. "Kids were dying. Opioids. Five area high schools had lost seven teens in four months. The whole county was in an uproar, not to mention parents, grandparents, friends, neighbors, law enforcement. The deaths touched and broke a lot of families."

Kenzie was no stranger to the weight of grief. She'd fought it, wallowed in it, cursed it. The anguish clung like an unwelcome parasite, its tentacles sneaking up and snaking around her head and heart without warning. Working with wounded horses had certainly assuaged her pain and helped her focus on the things she could change, the things she could heal. And this summer, with Austin at her side, she'd felt a lessening, a distancing from Caroline's suicide.

Austin, who'd lied to her.

Stinson blew out a breath. "At the time, we couldn't understand how so many got hooked so fast. National addiction studies stated that it could take five doses to hook a person on heroin, but we were seeing junk that could hook in one hit. And worse, one hit that could kill." He held up a finger for emphasis. "One. An epidemic—that's what we called it." Stinson ran a hand over his hair stubble. "I recognized a kid we booked one night for possession, also an addict. I asked him, 'Why? You're a champion wrestler who can write your own ticket to college!' He told me, 'The first time I used, I felt like I'd been kissed by an angel. Every time after, I was chasing that feeling. Never got it again.' That kid's life is ruined, Kenzie. May I call you Kenzie?"

She bobbed her head, seeing a line of faceless teens, like the ones she'd known in high school. *February. Cold. Headstones in a cemetery.* She kept silent.

Stinson eased back into the chair. "We didn't know where the stuff was coming from, but we had to do something about it. We worked out an undercover scenario, to put somebody into those schools and find the sources. Tyler—Austin," Stinson corrected himself, "he volunteered."

"Austin returned to high school?"

Stinson shook his head. "The guy's good, but he couldn't pass for a high schooler." For the first time since meeting him, Kenzie saw a half smile lift the corner of Stinson's mouth. "Instead, we gave him a fast car. We used his middle name, made up his last name, gave him a legend—that's a background story kids could believe—and we sent him to the rural back roads of our county, where serious illegal drag racing was happening every weekend. He took on all comers and consistently beat them. He became the guy the kids wanted to challenge. As cops, we backed off interfering with the racing. Oh, we made a few busts, just to make it look like we were still policing, but mostly we kept away and let Austin do his job."

Kenzie didn't doubt it; she, too, had been one of the jobs he'd done well.

"Those meets were also where so many of the drug deals

were going down. An elaborate scheme where the producer distributed product to a few key sellers, who took it back to schools and resold it to others who resold it—you get the picture. It took a couple of months for Austin to work his way into their group, but the more races he won, the more he was respected. And trusted."

Kenzie recalled how she'd lectured Austin about gaining the trust of an abused horse. Only now did she understand how much of a pro he truly was. Her lips trembled, but she said nothing.

"We were after the producer, of course, and that person was elusive. It took Austin five months undercover, but he found the source. Turned out to be locals, a family clan up in the mountains, brothers and cousins who used to cook and sell meth. But meth is volatile and dangerous, so they turned to opioids and mixed it with some chemistry of their own to enhance a high. Thing is, it was also lethal." Stinson shifted in his seat wearily. "We raided their makeshift factory in April, jailed the whole lot of them, and charged them with every crime on the books.

"We wanted to keep Austin's part in the takedown secret, for his protection. We looked for a place to stash him for a few months, until things cooled off and we could bring him back to work in Knoxville again. We needed an out-of-the-way place, where he could hide in plain sight."

"Bellmeade," she said. From the police's perspective, living in rural farm country and working with a girl to rehabilitate neglected horses was a safe, ideal location. A perfect cover.

"Exactly. He had a background with horses, and word

248

came through channels that Jon Mercer was looking for someone to help with a summer horse rescue program."

"So did Jon know about Austin? Who he was hiring, and why?"

"No. But the police chief in Windemere knew what we were trying to do and called Jon, talked up Austin." *A friend of a friend . . . word of mouth. A helper for Kenzie Caine, and safety for their man.*

Stinson's big hands scrubbed his face, and he sank lower in the chair. "Then your father got involved. He insisted on meeting Austin, laid out his reasons why he wanted Austin to watch over you."

"That's been explained to me. Please, go on."

"Austin and I talked it over. I couldn't see any reason why he shouldn't agree, so he told your father he would. A win-win."

Simple. Cut and dried. Her mind flashed to the night of the stabbing. "But Austin wasn't safe, was he?"

"We hadn't counted on a cousin not caught in the raid, a lone wolf, who made it his life's mission to destroy the snitch who'd taken down his family *and* its lucrative business. Guy got his name from conversations with the kids, other drag racers."

She curled her legs on the sofa. "So how did he find Austin?"

"Your act of kindness. The story in the paper."

Thirty

"What story?"

Stinson pinched the bridge of his nose and sighed. "Don't people read newspapers anymore?" Her shrug was his answer. "The story your local paper printed about the little girl with cancer and the horse you and Austin gave her."

His words felt like a physical blow. That "act of kindness" had almost gotten Austin killed? Her stomach went queasy. "I never knew about the article."

Stinson shook his head. "After it was printed, it got spread around Facebook as a story to warm the heart."

He waited a beat. Finally, she said, "I don't have a Facebook page."

"Our bad guy does. You two got a ton of likes and shares. He eventually read it and knew right where to look for Boyd. According to the perp's confession, he came to

Windemere on a Harley, rented a motel room, surveilled Bellmeade from across the road for days, waiting for the opportunity to get Austin alone. The perpetrator is a hunter. He's patient and very careful. On Friday night, Austin went to the stable alone. The guy saw his opportunity and took it."

The horror of that night returned in vivid color. Kenzie buried her face in her hands. When she looked up again, she couldn't hide the dampness in her eyes and reached for a tissue.

"The guy snuck into the stable, aiming to stab Austin in the back. Austin turned just in time, so that makes the perp a bad dude *and* a coward. Face to face, one on one, Austin had a chance of taking the guy down because he's been trained in hand-to-hand combat. The man's been charged with attempted murder. He'll go away for a long time."

Justice. Austin deserved it. "Thank you for talking to me."

"Do you have any other questions?"

She had a thousand questions but couldn't begin to put into words what was going through her head. The world from outside the consultation room intruded. Nurses' soft chatter. Dings from elevators. Footfalls whisking along the hallway. *Life goes on.* "Not now."

"Then if you don't mind, I'd like to sit with my man for a while. I know you came to be with him, but—"

"I don't mind. I'll sit here for a bit, peek in on him before I leave." She needed to process what Stinson had told her.

The detective rose from the chair stiffly, stretched his

back. At the open doorway, he paused. "I know you've heard a lot information tonight. You have my card, so if you want to talk again, call. Truth is, our world—a cop's world—has a dark underbelly. It's a tough job filled with people you'd rather not ever meet and a job that can go side- ways in the blink of an eye." He fisted his hand on the door- jamb. "If there's any consolation for you in all this, trust me when I tell you that working with you and those horses this summer brought Austin a lot of happiness." Kenzie quickly looked down, her cheeks flushed with embarrassment. "Just for the record, Austin 'Boyd' Buchanan is one of the finest young cops I've ever worked with."

Much later, Kenzie checked on Austin, still sleeping soundly. She ran the back of her hand over his scratchy dark stubble of beard, bent over the bed, and kissed his forehead, torn between what she desired and the risks that she faced over having it.

She left the hospital. Night had fallen, and mercury lights lit the dark. She climbed into her SUV and rested her forehead on the steering wheel, her mind warring with her heart about all she'd heard, remembered, known, felt, and experienced over the past several months. *Too much!* Loss was loss, no matter the circumstances. A sister. A summer. A man she desired. Mended horses. Broken dreams. What was left for her?

Grabbing her phone, Kenzie did something unusual for her and shot a text to Lani.

Will you let me know when the hospital releases him?

Of course I will, Lani replied.

Just remember, I'm fifty miles away. I'll need time to drive over.

Not a problem. Our staff knows how to slow-walk paperwork. I'll put out the word.

Satisfied, Kenzie dropped the phone into her bag, started the engine, exited the parking lot, and drove west, determined to fulfill a promise she'd made on the day her summer illusions had begun to unravel. Kenzie Caine went home.

Days later, Kenzie leaned against the doorway of Austin's room, watching as he sat on the side of his bed in jeans, barefoot and struggling to pull a shirt over his head. An Ace bandage circled his torso, and a clean new dressing covered the wound in his chest. Lifting his arms was proving painful. "Want some help?"

Startled, he eased the tee onto his lap. He hadn't seen her since the evening Stinson had talked to her. When Austin had been alert enough to ask his boss how she'd received the information, the man had said, "She listened, asked a few questions, but that's about it." The fact that Austin hadn't heard from Kenzie for days told him she'd washed her hands of him. During his five-day stay, he'd had several visitors, but not Kenzie. Yet now, here she was in front of him, her unbound hair, spilling in a silver-gold tumble over her shoulders.

He'd showered and shaved earlier, and smelled of antiseptic hospital soap. "The broken ribs are the worst part, because I can't bend in the middle." He was feeling helpless and sounded apologetic.

"Let me. Please." Taking the T-shirt, she stretched the neck hole, pulled it over his head, and gently worked both his arms through the sleeves and brought the shirt down his body.

"Thanks." He raked a hand through his tousled shaggy hair, darker now, less sun-streaked. "Um, why are you here?"

"I heard you were escaping today."

"How?"

"Friends in high places."

Lani. She'd stopped by his room a couple of times, full of cheer. "Kenzie, you're not supposed—" He stopped, knowing he'd said too much.

"To be near you?" she finished. "Are you talking about my father's rant when you were lying in this hospital bed, barely conscious and in pain?" She rolled her eyes. "I know all about it. Detective Stinson came to the house, and the three of us had a talk. My dad's sorry for what he said and how he said it. He'll get around to telling you himself at some point."

"He was concerned for you. A father's prerogative." Austin realized he was staring at her like a hungry vagrant.

He cleared his throat, fumbled around on the bed for his hospital "goodie bag" of pills and pamphlets and written instructions. He needed to keep the conversation informative, devoid of his feelings for her. "Jon's scheduled to pick me up today. He brought these clothes yesterday and said I could stay at the bunkhouse as long as necessary. I have a checkup in ten days, but after that, I expect to be cleared for duty. I'm supposed to call Jon when I'm ready to leave, but the paperwork is moving at the speed of a glacier." He glanced up to see the corner of Kenzie's mouth lift. "Can't figure out what's taking so long. Stinson gave them all department insurance info days ago, and I signed the release forms."

"Shoes and socks?" she asked, ignoring his grumbling.

"On the chair."

Kenzie grabbed the clean socks, saw his familiar work boots on the floor beneath the chair, felt a hitch in her breath. "Let me do this."

He cupped his hands over hers, holding the socks. "Kenzie, please . . . stop it."

"You're hurt, Austin. I want to help."

His eyes, green as the sea in the room's light, bore into hers. "I appreciate that, but I'm not one of your rescue horses."

Her face flushed. "Of course not. But you're about as stubborn." She regained possession of the socks, bent her knee, and thrust her jeans-clad thigh forward. "Put your foot here, and let me work the end over your toes. If it will make you feel manly, you can pull it up."

255

"You sure are bossy." He grinned, placed his foot flat against the length of her upper leg.

While she worked, first with one foot, then the other, she told him, "Sarah adopted Blue. Ciana said Sarah picked him up three days ago. I think the two of them are a fine fit. They need one another, you know." Kenzie's heartbeat raced as she said the words.

Austin lowered his foot, reached out, lifted her chin. Her gaze, so clear and deep blue, held his. Had she sent him a message? He didn't want to assume anything. Instead, he changed the subject. "Why aren't you in classes?"

"Change of plans. I'm waiting out this semester and living at home through the Christmas holidays. I'll return to Vanderbilt full-time in January. Meanwhile, I'm taking a few courses online."

"What changed your mind?"

"Mom. She asked me and Dad to go with her to her therapist. She insists we'll all benefit from family counseling. So we're going. These last months have been hard for all of us."

Austin tried to imagine a man like Avery agreeing to attend therapy sessions. A man could do a lot of things for someone he loves. "It's a smart move. Healing takes work. And time."

"Ready to roll?" A hefty male nurse pushed a wheelchair into the room.

Austin tapped his forehead. "Ah! I haven't called Jon yet."

"I asked Jon if I could come in his place," Kenzie confessed. "Do you mind if I take you?"

His grin was her answer.

Austin was buckled into the passenger seat, and Kenzie had inched the car to the parking lot exit, where she stopped and let the engine idle. "What's wrong?" he asked.

"I . . . I want to ask you something." Her hands were white knuckled on the wheel, and her heart raced. She turned, looked in his eyes. "I want you to come someplace with me while you recover."

"Where?"

"Our family cabin, up in the mountains. The woods are beautiful, and . . . and I want to see them again. With you. While you get stronger. But only if you want to go."

The unexpected request left him lost for words. Seconds ticked past. Finally, he came up with "I haven't got a thing to wear."

She burst out laughing, and so did he. "We'll go to the bunkhouse long enough for you to pack a duffel bag. How's that?"

"You're on."

With that, she popped the SUV in gear and headed to Bellmeade.

Thirty-One

The drive to the Caine mountain retreat took four and a half hours with a stop for gas and a burger. At some point, Austin reclined his seat from its upright position, easing the ache in his midsection. He slept for a while, with Kenzie slipping him sidelong glances, in part to make sure he was all right, and in part to be certain he was really with her and not a figment of her imagination.

He awoke when the car began a steep ascent and winced when the road became a bumpy crawl of curves and bends over steep, stony terrain. The view out her windshield was of darkness lit by headlights skirting trees and rocks. He raised the seat. "Where are we?"

"Almost there. Did I mention that the cabin's isolated?" Minutes later, she raised a garage door with a remote and parked.

He grimaced, exiting the car. "I'll grab my bag. Where's your stuff?"

"It's already here. I was coming whether you came with me or not, because this cabin is one of my favorite places on earth."

They climbed a short flight of garage stairs and entered a side door where she flipped on light switches. "The place isn't huge, just one story and a basement, but the views are amazing. We used to come every summer, and most school fall breaks."

Austin thought the cabin unpretentious—a large single room with a kitchen at one end with a freestanding island, synthetic log walls, a wood-beamed ceiling, and wide-plank pine floors smelling of lemon oil and dotted with colorful area rugs. It was the epitome of homey, and totally different from the Caine house in Nashville.

The living area was arranged into two activity areas - one with a pool table, a game table, a dartboard, and two old-fashioned pinball machines. The other section held two L-shaped sofas, an oversized leather recliner, and side tables, all facing an enormous rock fireplace with generous windows on either side, now curtained. "Nice place. Looks brand-new."

"Mom and Dad remodeled the place years ago to suit our family. I hired a cleaning crew to spiff it up and stock the refrigerator. There's a small town at the foot of the mountain because the area has year-round residents. If we need anything, it's only twenty minutes away in the valley."

"When was the last time you were here as a family?"

"I was sixteen. Caro was twelve, and put out and pouty because she'd had to leave friends and ballet classes for the summer." Reminiscences warmed Kenzie face. "Of course, I was in heaven."

"Without your horse?"

"There's a stable in town, and Dad boarded Princess Ronan and a horse for himself while we were here. He and I rode together every day."

"He trailered two horses all this way? Amazing."

"It was our thing. Before his fall from grace." She chased away the cloud. "Come, see your room." He followed her to a door that opened from a small foyer. The room held two twin beds, stacked with pillows, on matelassé coverlets of forest green. "There're only two bedrooms in the cabin. The other is the master, behind the kitchen. This was mine and Caroline's. There's a bathroom behind that door." She pointed.

"Which bed was yours?"

"The one beside the window. I loved lying there at night staring at the moon and stars."

He dropped his duffel bag on it. "Now it's mine."

His closeness sent goose bumps up her arms. She backed out of the room, and he followed. She walked to the fridge, opened the door. "Want a snack? A drink?"

"A soda."

She brought it to him. "I'll show you the deck and the view tomorrow when it's daylight." He could see that Kenzie was nervous, fidgety, and wondered if she was having second thoughts about bringing him here.

"I don't need television. What are you going to do now?"

"I think I'll sit in the recliner and read. Feel free to pass out."

"I slept in the car." His smile was quick. "And if you're staying out here, so am I." He went to a sofa, stretched out so that he had eyes on the recliner.

"You don't have to—"

He pulled out his cell. "Just happen to have a book downloaded to my phone. I want to be where you are, Kenzie. It'll go a long way to help with my recovery."

Austin woke to the smell of frying bacon. He eased out of bed, his ribs protesting, washed up, and walked to the island where Kenzie was turning strips of bacon in a frying pan. "You sure know how to get a guy moving in the morning."

Her smile was mischievous. "Bacon, better than an alarm clock. Eggs and toast?" He nodded. "Don't fear—we won't starve. I have a wide range of cooking skills. Peanut butter and jelly, frozen pizza, mac 'n' cheese, hot dogs, and sub sandwiches. Balanced."

"No ramen noodles?" He feigned shock.

"Please, every cook has standards."

He chuckled. "Well, count on me for spaghetti, tacos, grilled cheese, and tomato soup."

"And cleanup?"

"We'll work side by side. Teamwork."

She dazzled him with a smile.

They ate a leisurely breakfast, and afterward she walked

261

him outside to an expansive deck, chandeliered over the side of the mountain. He saw an uninterrupted view of far-off mountain peaks and treetops tinged with autumn, in air crisp enough for him to see his breath. "Wow!"

"Beautiful, isn't it?"

He turned to look at her. "Amazing view."

Her pulse ticked up. She stepped back from the railing. "Later this morning, we'll take a walk."

They went inside, and she opened the curtains, letting the morning light fill the room. "The deck faces west, so sunsets are spectacular."

He caught her hand. "I'm glad you brought me here."

She got lost in the look in his eyes, gave a slight nod. "Glad you came with me."

He let go of her hand. "Before we walk, I'll need help wrapping my rib cage. The extra support helps."

When it was time, he sat on the island's countertop because it was easier for her to reach around him from an angle. With his chest and midsection bare, she easily saw the bruising, large areas of black and blue fading to a greenish tinge at the edges. Seeing her look of dismay, he rested his hands on her shoulders. "It'll go away. Bodies heal." He patted the patch on his chest. "Stitches come out next time I see the doc. I'll be good as new."

Kenzie's throat had closed with emotion. All she could do was reach around him and grab the rolled bandage, her cheek grazing his skin. He took the roll from her at his side and pulled it tight across his middle. "Just like wrapping a horse's forelegs," he said to lighten her mood.

"Except very different," she countered, taking the roll

around his back again. *Life and death hinging on a single twist of his body.*

Their walks in the woods became a daily habit, sometimes twice daily. The cool air of morning warmed, then cooled again with the shadows of late afternoon. Austin wore a sweatshirt, the only heavy layer of clothing he'd brought with him to Bellmeade. Kenzie had her pick of several she'd brought from home. They threaded their way through leaves that had already fallen on makeshift trails. In the valley, trees would likely still be green since autumn rolled down mountains, and springtime marched up them. Winter would arrive here first too. Laws of nature.

On one of their walks, she gathered the courage to ask a question she'd wanted to pose since the night she talked to Stinson. "Was anything that you told me about growing up true? Your family? Braveheart?"

"Absolutely. Always tell the truth. Boy Scout code." He winked when she looked at him, and she smiled because it made her feel better about so many of their talks, when she'd been so heartrendingly truthful to him. "I left out a highlight, though. My father was a cop, a detective. He's retired now, but from the time I was twelve, I wanted to be a cop just like him."

That gave her pause. "Still?"

"It's who I am, Kenzie. Can't change that." Of course, she understood because she knew what she wanted, how important her plans were to her.

A leaf fell, caught in her hair. She'd worn it down the

past few days, only tied it in a ponytail when she was cooking. They had stopped in the middle of the wooded trail and were facing each other. He plucked out the errant leaf. "Does your family know what happened to you? The attack?"

"Not yet. It would just make Mom anxious, and I don't want that. I'll tell them eventually. Maybe if I go home for Christmas." He tucked a hank of her hair behind her ear. *Any excuse to touch her.*

Christmas. Her family's first without Caroline. Austin realized where her thoughts had gone. He draped his arm over her shoulder. "Come on, let's keep moving."

He stopped wrapping his torso after several days. His flexibility had improved, but having her so close to him each morning was difficult. His self-control was eroding, and physical distance was necessary. At least outdoors, on their walks, he could distract himself. Inside, he kept to the sofa, she to the recliner. He went into his room at night before she went to hers. He lay in the dark, and with his blood running hot, sleep came slowly. Through the window he'd watch the moon arc across the sky while lying in bed, just as she must have done years ago. The empty bed across from his held the ghost of a girl he'd never known, a sister who'd broken Kenzie's heart. Instinct told him Kenzie was wrapped in a fragile shell, wanting to get out and not knowing how. He had to be patient. She was worth the wait.

Midweek, they made a trip into town for groceries, because Austin insisted. "I can't make spaghetti sauce without tomato paste and pasta." It was after Labor Day, and the small town was tourist-free, with several storefront signs reading SEE YOU NEXT SUMMER. Sunshine edged with an autumn chill reminded him of Virginia.

While shopping, Kenzie bought two bags of marshmallows. "We'll roast them in the fireplace for dessert. Caro and I used to do that."

That night, Austin straightened two wire coat hangers, got a fire going. Kenzie turned off all other lights so that only the fire logs lit the room. They sat on the floor side by side, the bag of marshmallows between them. She was roasting her third when she whispered, "Thank you for the donations to my rescue program."

Left field. She'd tossed him another live one. "You weren't supposed to know—"

"But I *do* know, and I'm saying thank you. Listen, I don't mind if you keep your salary for the work you did. It's only fair. You worked hard and deserve to be paid. I'll get some extra money from Dad now that things are better between us."

"What makes you think you haven't already?" Austin stared into the flames, turned the wire so that the marshmallow didn't char.

She pondered his comment until she caught the meaning. "You gave the money my father paid you to the rescue program too?"

Austin kept his eye on the marshmallow, pulled it out

of the fire, saw that it was toasted perfectly brown. "The department was still paying me while I was sequestered. I didn't need the extra money. Your rescue program did." He blew on the sugary puff to cool it, pulled it off the wire. He faced her, saw her moist eyes shimmering in the fire's light. "Open," he said. She did, and he popped the confectionary into her mouth. "It's no big deal."

Kenzie felt tears rising inside her like a tide. "Having you with me this summer . . ." She stopped. "I'll miss you." She rose and eased onto the sofa behind them.

He came to sit beside her. "If it matters, I'm seriously considering looking for a job with the Windemere police department. I think I can make detective sooner there than in Knoxville." A half-truth. Windemere was a pleasant and expanding small town, but in truth, he wanted to be nearer to Kenzie while she attended Vanderbilt. "I told my boss and he promised he'd do what he could to facilitate my transfer."

"Seriously?"

"Boy Scouts don't lie." The look in his eyes dove into her heart.

She was momentarily overcome by the idea he might remain. The miles between them would be scant as compared to the distance between Nashville and Knoxville. But what then?

"Now I have a question for you, Kenzie." He locked his fingers behind his head, leaned back. This was an opening he'd been waiting for, and he took it. "Will you tell me about your heart problem? The whole story?"

She startled. "I . . . I have told you. You've seen my heart do a number on me. I don't count the hyperthermia. That can happen to anyone."

"No, you told me about the past, your diagnosis when you were a kid. You've told me about the present, your meds, tests, and annual visits. What you haven't told me, Kenzie, is about your future. What's coming?"

Thirty-Two

Austin had walked her into the only place she hadn't wanted to go with him. Her heart issues. "Why talk about that now? It's marshmallow time."

"Because it's important. And because I want to know."

She felt deflated. Leveling with him would likely alter everything between them—whatever *it* was. Yet he had been with her twice when she'd encountered serious medical problems, and both times he'd run into the situation, not away from it. "You've seen me work. You know I don't hold back. You've seen how I heft saddles, pitch hay, wash and groom the horses. I'm strong."

"All true. You're strong and brave. I've watched you fight and overcome, but I still want the clear, unvarnished truth."

She saw there was no squirming out of the discussion tonight. If he insisted on hearing the truth, she'd give it to him. "So, after my tests in April, my doctor took me into his office for a consultation, just like he always does. He enjoys giving me a good report. You know, statistics, facts, numbers, graphs, comparisons to past reports and time-lines. But my parents weren't there this year. It was just me and the doctor." She plucked at a button embedded in the cushion.

"He had my folder on his desk in front of him with my latest test results. He gave me a big smile and flipped it open, but I reached across his desk, flattened my hand on the paperwork, and said, 'Please, no numbers. Keep it simple.'" Her hand movements reinforced her words.

She stopped speaking, her expression far away, seeing another room, another face. Austin sat absolutely still and, feeling his own heart speed up, tasted fear. Kenzie returned to the present, gentled him with a look. "My doctor looked me full in the face, his eyes very serious, and he said, 'Kenzie, you will never grow old.'"

Austin felt as if he'd been stabbed all over again. He struggled to absorb her brutal words, but couldn't. "Can it be fixed?"

"Eventually I'll need a valve replacement. You know, out with the old, in with the new. Such a surgery will slow deterioration, but it won't fix the underlying problem: stenosis. My childhood illness is hardening my arteries and constricting blood flow throughout my body. It worsens over time."

"What about a heart transplant?"

"I'm not a good candidate. Currently, I have 'youth on my side,' but the Windemere cardiologist did tests and warned me that there was scarring of my heart and blood vessels. She sent her report to my medical team in Vanderbilt." Kenzie remained dry-eyed as she talked. "In some people, the problems move more quickly."

Austin's face told the story of everything he was feeling. She wished she could walk back the truth. Wanting to sound more upbeat, she said, "I have plans, Austin, just as you do. I'm already behind schedule with college because of taking this semester off. I have my dream job ready to go next summer. And honestly, if valve replacement were a permanent solution, I'd go through open-heart surgery tomorrow. But it isn't. All I want is a chance to live my life on my terms. Why change my plans simply because I had a lousy hand dealt to me?"

"I love you."

His unexpected statement stopped her cold. "You love me? I . . . I don't know what to say."

He looked bemused. "Typically, the other person says 'I love you too.' Unless, of course, you *don't* love me." He was taking a gamble. In or out. Win or lose. Winner take all.

Tears filled her eyes. "I didn't think you . . . thought of me that way. All summer, you held back, walked away, if I got close." She pulled out every word as if it were a thorn, remembering the times he'd left her wanting, longing for more of him. He touched her only when necessary, retreated if she came too near. *She'd* been the one to kiss him the summer night after the wedding. And he'd never asked her for another.

He moved forward, so close she could see the fire's reflection in his eyes, cradled her face in his hands, wiped tears off her cheeks with his thumbs. All summer, they'd been like trains passing in the night. Lighted windows flying past each other, glimpses of light and movement, but not shapes or images. He needed to explain his reasons to her and could only hope she'd understand where he'd been coming from during those summer months. "I thought you were beautiful from the first time I saw you—through binoculars, I might add." A shake of her head as she recalled what had divided them. "And all summer long, all I wanted was to be with you, Kenzie. First as a friend, and later . . . well, later, a whole lot more.

"But I'd made commitments. First, I had to lie low for safety's sake, because that's why Stinson put me at Bellmeade." A sympathetic nod from Kenzie. "And second, I'd told your father I would protect you. In short, what I wanted to do when we were together slammed head-on into what I'd promised to do. He *trusted* me, Kenzie. How could I violate that?"

Cop code. Preserve and protect. She leaned into him. "News flash—I'd never have told him." He roared out a laugh. She eased away, holding his gaze. "Just so you know, I don't want to be someone's duty."

His eyes flickered with an inner fire. "Trust me, you will never again be my duty. And just so *you* know—I don't care about your health problems. I want all the days you have left. One at a time. That's all anybody gets, Kenzie. That perp's knife taught me that much."

A shadow crossed her face when she remembered the

terror of the night he'd almost died. One breath, then another. One minute, then the next. *Life uninterrupted.* "Yes, Tyler Austin Boyd Buchanan, and whatever other names you might have that I don't know—I love you."

His grin stoked fires deep inside her. He took her hand, stood, guided her upward. "Dance with me."

"But there's no music."

He pulled her against his body, with a hairbreadth between them, nestled their joined hands beneath his chin, and laid his cheek against her hair. "You're wrong about that, Kenzie, my love. Listen."

The logs in the fireplace, mostly embers, cast pale yellow light. Beyond, the room was in shadows. Trusting him, she closed her eyes, rested her cheek against his chest, let him lead her in slow, lazy circles. She felt her pulse kick up and her breathing fall whisper-soft. And that was when she heard the music. The only music in the room. The mystical, lyrical music of their two beating hearts.

Acknowledgments

My thanks in gathering a knowledge base for this book go to Dale Lee and Adam Presley of the Saddle Pals riding group in Soddy Daisy, Tennessee. They are anti-soring, and regular rescuers of the Tennessee walking horse.

And a special thank you to Dr. Michael Shepherd for his valuable medical input.

About the Author

Meghan Green and Jon Lancaster

LURLENE McDANIEL began writing inspirational novels about teenagers facing life-altering situations when her son was diagnosed with juvenile diabetes. "I saw firsthand how chronic illness affects every aspect of a person's life," she has said. "I want kids to know that while people don't get to choose what life gives to them, they do get to choose how they respond."

Lurlene McDaniel's novels are hard-hitting and realistic, but also leave readers with inspiration and hope. Her bestselling books have received acclaim from readers, teachers, parents, and reviewers; they include *The Year of Luminous Love* and its companion *The Year of Chasing Dreams*; *Don't Die, My Love*; *Till Death Do Us Part*; *Hit and Run*; *Telling Christina Goodbye*; *True Love: Three Novels*; and *The End of Forever*.

Lurlene McDaniel lives in Chattanooga, Tennessee. Visit her online at LurleneMcDaniel.com and on Facebook and follow her on Twitter at @Lurlene_McD.